Rude Awakenings of a Jane Austen Addict

**Center Point
Large Print**

Also by Laurie Viera Rigler
and available from Center Point Large Print:

Confessions of a Jane Austen Addict

**This Large Print Book carries the
Seal of Approval of N.A.V.H.**

Rude Awakenings of a Jane Austen Addict

LAURIE VIERA RIGLER

CENTER POINT PUBLISHING
THORNDIKE, MAINE

This Center Point Large Print edition
is published in the year 2010 by arrangement with
Dutton, a member of Penguin Group (USA) Inc.

The text of this Large Print edition is unabridged.
In other aspects, this book may vary
from the original edition.
Printed in the United States of America.
Set in 16-point Times New Roman type.

ISBN: 978-1-60285-626-4

Library of Congress Cataloging-in-Publication Data

Rigler, Laurie Viera.
  Rude awakenings of a Jane Austen addict / Laurie Viera Rigler.
     p. cm.
  ISBN 978-1-60285-626-4 (lib. bdg. : alk. paper)
  1. Single women--England--Fiction. 2. Time travel--Fiction.
    3. Austen, Jane, 1775-1817--Influence--Fiction.
    4. Los Angeles (Calif.)--Social life and customs--21st century--Fiction.
    5. Large type books. I. Title.
  PS3618.I427R83 2009b
   813'.6--dc22
  2009027801

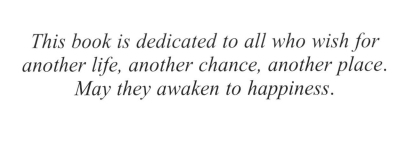

This book is dedicated to all who wish for another life, another chance, another place. May they awaken to happiness.

One

A piercing sound, like a ship's horn but higher, shriller, shakes my frame. I open one eye, then the other; the lids seem stuck together. From a gap in the curtains a tiny, knife-thin strip of light slices the darkness.

I clap my hands over my ears, but the sound is relentless. As is the pain. It feels as if an entire regiment of soldiers marches behind my eyes.

"Barnes?" My voice is a faint croak, too weak for Barnes to hear. No matter; she will of course be roused by the high-pitched horn. Only a corpse could sleep through such a cacophony.

Why hasn't Barnes put a stop to that blasted noise? I fumble for the bell pull behind me, but my hand feels only bare wall. Odd. I shall have to get out of bed and find Barnes myself.

I swing my legs over the side of the bed; they hit the floor instead of dangling a few inches above it. Could a headache make one's bed seem lower than it is? The worst of my headaches have been heralded by broken rainbows of light before my eyes, but never have I experienced such a lowering sensation. Lowering indeed. I can almost laugh at my facility with words this morning, despite the sorry state of my head. And my ears. How harsh and insistent is that sound.

My feet touch bare wood floor instead of the

woven rug in its customary place. And my bed shoes? Not there. I fumble in the dark and crash my right hip into a great lump of wood; blast it all to—I clench my teeth in an effort not to scream. This is enough punishment to put even the punster in me to rest. Barnes must be rearranging furniture again. Except—

There are numbers, glowing red, on top of the offending lump of wood. 8 0 8. What is this wondrous thing? The numbers are in some sort of a box, the front of it smooth and cold beneath my fingertips, the top of it scored and bumpy. I run my fingers over the bumps, and the shrill sound stops. Oh, thank heaven.

Blessed silence. I move towards the thin strip of light to open the curtains wide; surely the sun's rays shall reveal the source of this odd geographic puzzle which has become my room. But instead of the thick velvet nap of the curtains which have hung on my windows these five years at least, my hands grasp what feels like coarse burlap. Perhaps Barnes slipped in early and exchanged them so that she could beat the dust from the velvet ones. First the rearrangement of furniture, then this. I have never known her to engage in such haphazard housekeeping.

I grasp the edges of the burlap curtains—why are my hands shaking? I pull them open.

There are iron bars on my window.

I hear myself gasp. This is not, cannot, be my

window. Indeed, as I wheel around to take in the space behind me, I see that this is not my room. Head pounding, I survey the tall, unornamented chest of drawers; the wide, low bed devoid of hangings; the box with the glowing numbers atop the chest. There is no pink marble fireplace, no armoire, no dressing table. There is, however, a low table bearing a large, rectangular box whose front is made mostly of glass; the rest is of a shiny-smooth, gray material that I have never seen before.

My knees shake, almost buckling under me. I must move to the bed; just a minute of sitting down will be a restorative.

I sink down atop a tangle of bedclothes, and the glass box roars to life.

I jump back, clutching the covers. There are small figures talking and dancing inside the glass box. Who are they? Is this some sort of window? The figures are small, so they must be some distance away. Yet I can distinguish their words and their features as clearly as if they were right in the room with me. How can this be?

"I remember hearing you once say," says the beautiful lady in the window to the gentleman dancing with her, "that you hardly ever forgave. That your resentment, once created, was implacable. You are very careful, are you not, in allowing your resentment to be created?"

The gentleman dancing with her says, "I am."

"And never allow yourself to be blinded by prejudice?" asks the lady.

"I hope not," says the gentleman. "May I ask to what these questions tend?"

"Merely to the illustration of your character," says she. "I'm trying to make it out."

I know these words—I have read them! It is the Netherfield Ball from my favorite book, *Pride and Prejudice*, and the gentleman and lady are Mr. Darcy and Miss Elizabeth Bennet. To think that Elizabeth and Darcy are real people, and that I am watching them, right now, through a window! This is something I cannot explain, nor can I make sense of the fact that they are apparently far away yet completely distinguishable.

I shall call out to the lady and see if she can solve the mystery. "I beg your pardon, Miss Bennet. We have not been introduced, but I seem to be your neighbor, and I am lost. Can you hear me?"

But the brightly lit figures in the window make no sign of having heard me, though I continue to hear their conversation as clearly as if they were right here in the room with me.

I reach out my hand to the glass box and touch its hard, shiny surface. I tap on the glass to see if I can get the attention of the figures inside; no luck. I move my face closer to the glass to see if I can get a better look, but indeed the figures look flatter and less real, somehow, the closer I am to the window. How very curious.

But that is not the worst of it. Odder still is the sound of my own voice, which is, as a matter of fact, not my voice at all.

"Miss Bennet?" I say, marveling at the tone and accent of what issues from my own mouth, and not at this point expecting Miss Bennet to hear me. The voice is not my own, the accent having hints of something almost of Bristol and perhaps a bit like Captain Stevens sounded when he was imitating people who lived in the Americas. How incensed my mother would be if she could hear me speak like a barbaric American. Delightful thought.

I glance around the strange room again, and at the glass window with the people from *Pride and Prejudice* conversing with one another as if I were not here trying to get their attention, and all at once I understand: Of course. I am having a dream. Nothing like the other dreams I have had in which I also knew I was dreaming, but a dream nevertheless. What a relief to know that I do not have to ascertain where I am or find my way back to my own room; all I have to do is wake up.

In the meantime, I shall divert myself by finding out if Barnes is here, and, if so, where; surely she would delight as much as I in the wondrous sight and sound of Lizzy and Darcy dancing in the glass rectangle.

I shall put on my dressing gown and explore. Where might the gowns be kept? I open a door, revealing at least two yards of hanging garments, none of which look like my own clothes. I pull out a long, filmy, sashed thing; it might do. If only there were a looking-glass.

Ah, there it is, on the other side of the door to this vast repository of garments. I pull open the door and see a petite, pale-haired young woman in the glass. She and I gasp in unison. I wheel around, for the woman must be behind me, but there is only the empty room. Except for Miss Bennet and Mr. Darcy, that is.

I turn back to the mirror, and the truth literally stares me in the face: I am looking at my own reflection.

Two

The woman in the glass is no one whom I recognize. I watch the reflection in the glass as I reach up to touch the pale yellow hair striped with light brown that falls to my shoulders, feel the silky texture of it as the woman in the mirror does the same. I touch the round thighs of the short but shapely legs which are completely bare, and the reflection mirrors my movements. I regard my chest and torso, which are covered by a thinly woven, short-sleeved shift whose hem touches the tops of my thighs—I have never slept in such a garment before. Quite immodest; I smile at the thought of what my mother would say if she saw me in it. Fingering the hem, I catch sight of small, shapely feet tipped with azure-blue nails— and my knees nearly give way again.

Don't be such a frightened little creepmouse. I take a deep breath, look at the feet again, and giggle. In a dream my toenails may be any color of the rainbow, and why should they not be? Have I not always longed to be small and round with fuller limbs, instead of the thin, long-legged creature who never fills out my gowns the way I wish to do? Have I not always wished for my sister Clara's golden tresses in vain? Now she is not the only Mansfield daughter with fair hair.

Still, I am not sure I would like to remain in this dream much longer. It is, after all, one thing to imagine being someone else. And quite another actually to *be* someone else. I know this cannot be real, but it feels as if it were.

A couple of quick knocks that sound as if they are coming from the next room, a key turning in a lock, and then a male voice. "Courtney?"

I snatch up the dressing gown, which I must have dropped on the floor, and belt it tightly around my waist.

"Are you awake?" That voice again.

I can feel myself trembling, but I shall be mistress of myself. "Who, might I ask, sir, are you?"

Whoever it is pops his head round the doorway, a sweet smile on his bespectacled countenance. Despite my state of deshabille, I perceive not the least bit of danger from this stranger with a head of tousled curls like an angel. His coarse trousers, short-sleeved, collarless shirt, thick boots, and coatless state declare him to be a servant or a laborer rather than a gentleman, but still I cannot summon any alarm at his presence.

He smiles and makes a clumsy little bow. "Your humble servant, madam. With coffee and eggs, as promised." He gestures for me to join him in the next room.

"I shall be there directly," I say, and shut the door. My stomach rumbles at the mention of food, but I am not about to converse with an ill-clad manservant while wearing a shift and dressing gown.

His laughter floats in from the other room. "All you need is an English accent, and you'll sound just like the actors in *Pride and Prejudice*. Which obviously you've been watching. Again."

I turn back to the glass box; the figures are still moving about and talking, completely oblivious to my presence. Actors indeed. That would explain their not acknowledging me when I called out to them. Of course. It takes a great deal of focus to be a good actor. But how very odd that *Pride and Prejudice* should be a play and I not hear of it till now. Of course I would not have heard of it; this is a dream, silly goose. And of course I would dream of seeing on-stage the story I love so well.

What shall I wear? The row of hanging garments

is far longer than that in my own armoire; however, there seems to be an abundance of trousers—could this be the servant's room? My face grows hot at the very thought of awakening in a man's room. Nonsense. I am being missish. I shan't think about such nonsense; I must get dressed.

Ah, yes. Here are gauzy garments that might be dresses. When I hold them against my body, however, they are not gowns at all, falling to just below my knees at best and high above them at worst.

What an immodest chit I am in this dream. Wait; there does seem to be something in the farthest recess that looks a proper length—I pull it out and remove a clear, shiny film that encases it. A white gown of the finest silk, with a pearl-encrusted bodice. Overly fine for my taste, let alone for morning and in such a place as this. The length is unexceptionable, but there are no sleeves at all, merely two thin bands of fabric to go over the shoulders. It will have to do. I pull off the sleeping shift and step into the white gown. The back is all tiny pearl buttons and loops; I most certainly will need help with those.

I call out to the curly-haired man through the closed door. "Hallo there! Would you be so kind as to send in a servant to help me dress?" Again that strange voice coming from my mouth. It is curious indeed.

"At your service, milady," says the curly-haired

man, who has the audacity to open the door and walk towards me.

I back away from him so that the unfastened part of the gown is against the wall. Hugging my bare arms to myself, I say with as much authority as I can, "Entering a lady's room without her leave is not at all the thing."

He just stands there, gaping at me.

I feel my face flush. "Have you been struck dumb, sir?"

"I . . . what are you doing in that dress?" His voice is soft, his eyes kind and gentle behind his spectacles.

"I am merely trying to find something appropriate to wear. No easy task, I might add. Now do leave me and send in a woman."

He stretches out a hand and touches my forehead. I flinch from the pain in my head. "You don't feel feverish. The pain's not worse, is it?" His eyes are full of concern.

"It is merely the headache. If I had my aromatic vinegar I should be well in a trice."

"Hitting your head on the bottom of a pool is not what I'd call a headache. Are you sure you're okay, Courtney?"

"It is tiresome enough that I do not even sound like myself. But might I have at least the comfort of being addressed by my own name?"

He motions to the bed. "Here, sit for a minute. You're scaring me."

I reach for the dressing gown and, throwing it around my shoulders, allow the curly-haired young man to lead me back to the bed. He really does look harmless, and after all, what harm could come to me? Thankfully, he makes no motion to join me; instead, he rushes out of the room. I recline against the wall, which feels delightfully cool; my head really does ache most dreadfully. I do not wish to remain here much longer, although the figures in the box are still acting out *Pride and Prejudice*, which eases the pain in my head more than any aromatic vinegar could do.

The young man hurries back into the chamber, bearing a glass of water, which he sets on the low table at the side of the bed, and a white opaque glass that he thrusts into my hands. No, it is not glass at all; it is heavy paper, I believe—and hot, too. How very strange. I inhale the scent of the steaming coffee within and venture a taste. Strong and rich with foamy milk on top.

"Why don't you tell me your name, then," he says.

"So it is a game now, is it? Very well, then. I am Miss Mansfield. And who are you, aside from the most impertinent young man I have ever met?"

He smiles broadly, revealing unusually bright white teeth. "I should have known you were playing with me—just couldn't resist making a fool out of Mr. Gullibility here, could you?

Though you might have had a little mercy after what you put me through last night."

He even has a lovely cleft in his chin like Edgeworth. No, I pray he is nothing like Edgeworth. I sip the delightfully hot coffee; how bracing it is. The throb in my head is almost gone.

"And what, may I ask, occurred last night, Mr. . . . ? Or do you intend to remain incognito?"

His smile loses its confidence. Indeed, he looks quite as stern as a judge.

"If you are going to be cross, then do be so good as to take your leave and send in a maid."

"You're frightening me, Courtney. Tell me what you remember about last night."

"Dear me. You are becoming most tiresome."

"You went swimming, remember? Wait—" He runs out of the room and returns with a bit of what looks like soft blue fabric in his hands. He holds it up to me; it looks like short stays with a bottom attached. "Remember? You were wearing this bathing suit."

The laughter explodes out of me; it is impossible to be irked by such a character. "Indeed! As if any respectable woman would go around clothed in such a costume, if I may use such a word for this diminutive article."

He thrusts the bit of fabric at me again, and I wonder at its oddly silky texture.

"Courtney, listen to me. You went swimming

and hit your head on the bottom of the pool. They called an ambulance, and you asked the nurse at the hospital to call me." His eyes are pleading with me. "Don't you remember anything?"

I sigh; I have had quite enough of this drama. "If you will not take your leave, sir, then I shall. Good day to you. I command all of this"—and I wave my hand to indicate the room and the young man "to end now." I close my eyes tightly.

I open them.

The curly-haired man is still standing at the foot of the bed. "You do not exist," I say with as much command as I can summon, but there is a hollow in my stomach now. "I awaken!"

Yet in the strange bedchamber I remain. How can this be? Sometimes I awaken from my dreams, the pleasanter ones, that is, long before I wish to do so. But when the dream is disagreeable, I simply command myself to awaken, and I do. Instantly.

How can I still be here? The only possible explanation is—

"Courtney," he says. "You are not asleep."

It is as if I am sinking into the floor, and I grip the bedclothes. This cannot be possible. I must have a quiet moment to think this through.

Here is what I know to be true: I dream of what is most delightful; I almost always awaken before I wish. I dream of what is unpleasant, and I need only command myself awake to leave it all behind. Yet I have not awakened; here I stay. How can this be? There is only one possibility, but it cannot be—

"Courtney?"

"What is it you said?"

"You are not asleep."

Three

I ndeed I am not. But how can I be awake yet not have my own name, my own body, my own voice?

When I am able to form words my voice croaks. "Where am I?"

"Don't worry. You're going to be fine," he says.

"What is this place?"

His eyes widen. "Your apartment."

"And where, might I ask, is this apartment?"

He sits down next to me on the bed and takes my hand. "L.A."

"I do not understand."

"Los Angeles. California. United States of America. Oh dear God, please be okay."

I snatch my hand away. "What? Has my mother had me drugged and transported to the Americas? Lord knows she told me a dozen times that a girl who committed the sin of filial disobedience as many times as I, deserved transportation to the Americas. But that was when I was a child, and even then my mother was teasing me with what could not be, for it was my history master who relieved my fears and . . . No! Impossible."

"Courtney, I have no idea what you're talking about."

The young man starts to pace back and forth and pulls a smooth squarish object from his pocket. "Should I call your mother? Maybe Anna or Paula? Tell me what to do, Courtney."

Laughter bubbles out of me, unbidden; I seem to have lost control of that particular faculty. "Blast your infernal names!" Dear me. Now my voice is croaking so that I sound like a frog. I cannot stop laughing. "I am Jane. Jane Mansfield."

"Of course you are." He blanches. "Jane Mansfield, screen legend. Hang on; I'm calling Anna."

Finally, there is no more laughter. Only a cold hard lump in my stomach.

The young man is now talking into the strange little object, which he holds to his ear. How absurd he looks. I cannot treat my situation with any degree of seriousness if I am to watch a grown man speak into an I-don't-know-what and act as if he were actually conversing with another person in the room. Especially when there is no other person in the room. How droll he looks. Hand gestures, dramatic delivery. Perhaps he is an actor, not a servant.

". . . no, Anna. If I bring her back to the emergency room they might want to keep her there. . . . No, I won't agree to that. . . ."

Ah. The imaginary person in the room has a name.

Well, then. Here are the facts. I am not asleep. I have a body and a voice that bear no resemblance to my own. And I am not the person the man named me to be. Courtney. I shiver, though the room is warm. I will not surrender to fear. I shall be mistress of myself. I still have my rational mind, though nothing about this situation is rational. I may not look like myself, but I know who I am.

The man continues to pace and talk to an imaginary woman named Anna. Perhaps I am in —dear God, no—an asylum? No. Impossible. Too clean and tidy by half.

"No, Anna . . ." His eyes flick over to me, then down. "Yeah, bring her. And no, I'm not leaving. If Paula can't deal with me, that's her problem. . . ."

How did I get here? And where exactly is "here"?

What is the last thing I remember about last night? Nothing. It is a blank. But in the morning . . . Riding Belle. Jumping her over a fallen tree, that leap in my stomach as we cleared it; good girl. Galloping into the woods, sending up clods of earth and clouds of dust. Into a clearing dotted with bright blue flowers, back into the woods, the sweep and crunch of branches, my bonnet lifted off my head by a low-hanging branch, turning round to look, then back again, Belle's muscles bunching against my legs as she shied, the sensation of flying through air.

And then blackness.

"Courtney?"

Four

*H*e's staring at me. The curly-headed angel. Perhaps I died when I fell off Belle, and this is heaven.

"Anna and Paula are on their way. Sure you don't want to talk to your mother?"

My stomach lurches. "She is here?"

"Of course not. But I can get her for you." He shows me the little object into which he was speaking, as if for emphasis.

This most assuredly cannot be heaven, for no angel would ever offer to summon my mother. Although perhaps he means to put her inside that little object in his hand? That would be most convenient. I am giggling again; this is most unladylike. "I thank you, no. That will not be necessary."

He looks relieved and gives me a little smile. "Yeah, probably not a good idea."

"And the woman I asked you for? To help me?" I indicate the white dress I am still almost wearing, the dressing gown still over my shoulders.

He regards me gravely and thrusts his hands in his pockets. "Anna and Paula will be here in a few minutes. In the meantime I'll just—I need some water. Would you like your breakfast?" He heads out towards the other room.

The thought of food makes me shudder. "I thank you, no. And do be so kind as to close the door behind you." The situation may be extraordinary, but it won't do to have this strange man traipsing in and out of my—whomsoever's bedchamber this is—whenever he pleases.

I turn my attention back to the *Pride and Prejudice* play in the little window. Perhaps I am dead; that seems far more rational than the thought that I am indeed awake in another country, let alone that I am awake in another body. Is this how it is when you die?

Of course my heaven would be a place where *Pride and Prejudice* is a play performed right in my own bedroom, a place where I see the figures perform my favorite story over and over and see them so close that I feel as if they are my friends and I can practically touch them. And then there is the curly-headed angel who is here to take care of me after my accident and is so gentle and sweet that I could not summon the least bit of alarm at his presence.

To be sure, this is not Mr. Grant's sort of heaven with its choirs of angels, nor is it the hell he preaches every Sunday till the village children quake in their pews. What would he know of heaven indeed? With all his prosing about virtue, the way he would look at me of a Sunday made me feel as if I needed a good scrubbing.

"Courtney?"

There are now two ladies, the aforementioned Paula and Anna, I presume, standing before the bed. Though which is which . . .

One of them has long, light brown hair streaked with pink and blue in vibrant shades that I never imagined existed, let alone in the color of one's hair. More shocking than even the color of my toenails. More shocking still is the immodest mode of their dress: Both are in tight bodices without sleeves, skirts which reach mid-thigh, and shoes which are mere strings of leather attached to heels, exposing almost the entire foot. Their toenails are also colored.

The one with the pink-and-blue-striped hair speaks. "You okay, darling? And what's with the dress?" Despite the vulgar familiarity, her manner is sweet, and the throatiness of her voice reminds me of Mary.

I smile at her. "Are we acquainted?" She is really quite pretty, despite the varicolored tresses. She peers at me with her large, up-tilted brown eyes. Her full lips, which shimmer with a sort of sandy color, look as if they would like to smile but are not quite sure about moving in that direction.

"You're kidding, right? Because Benedict Arnold here isn't so sure you are." She inclines her chin towards the curly-haired man, who has reentered the room. "And I hate to admit it, but he may have a point, unless . . ."

She whispers something into the ear of the other woman, who has a cap of shiny brown hair that reaches her chin and which is cut straight just above her brows. The brown-haired woman gives the woman with the peacock hair a worried look and a shrug.

The peacock turns her attention back to me. "Did you, and God help you if you did, decide to see a certain ex who shall remain unnamed, or more important, take something he gave you? Something that might inspire you to lie on your bed channeling Miss Havisham? Because if you took anything, let alone saw that philandering piece of dirt, Courtney, I swear . . ."

The young man cuts in. "No way she saw him. No way." His eyes search my face. "You didn't, right?"

They are all mad. "Who?"

"Frank," the three of them say almost in unison. The brown-haired one gives me an encouraging smile. "You didn't honey, did you?"

"Who's Frank?"

"You see, Paula?" curly-hair says to the peacock. "I told you she wouldn't."

"That's my girl," says Paula to me.

26

"All right then," says the one with the brown hair, who must be Anna. "One: We know that this is a psychotropic-free situation. Two: We know you hit your head."

She tilts her chin towards the curly-haired gentleman. "Though if your friend Wes here"—and she sneers at the word "friend"—"had seen fit to let us know right away you had an accident instead of waiting till half an hour ago to call Paula and me, we would have been here for you last night. Though none of that explains why you're wearing that, that . . ."

Paula cuts in. "Go ahead. Say it. Wedding dress. Which, I might add, should be in your Dumpster by now or run over by your car or burned to ashes instead of hanging in your closet, let alone on your body."

Anna says, "She could give it to charity, you know. Then at least it's not wasteful."

Paula rolls her eyes. "Give me a break, Anna."

Wedding dress? I look down at the frothy skirt, the pearl-encrusted bodice. "It is overly trimmed, to be sure, and I am most certainly not marrying, but that is a trifle compared to all—this. This voice. This body. This place. Why should my gown be of any consequence to you?"

Paula sputters, hands on hips. "Excuse me. We're only your best friends. And you're acting like a lunatic."

"Just because I tried to cover myself with a

garment of a respectable length does not mean I have lost my mind. My identity, yes. My body, yes. My voice, yes. But not my mind."

Paula turns to Wes. "I told you she should see a doctor. Didn't I, Anna?"

Anna regards me kindly. "Sweetie, maybe we should take you to see someone."

Paula turns her attention back to me. "You said you lost your identity. So who are you, exactly?"

"My name is Miss Mansfield. Jane Mansfield. My father's estate is in Somerset."

Paula turns to Anna. "This is worse than I thought. Come on," she says, grabbing my hand and pulling me off the bed, "I'm taking you to a doctor. Anna, get her into some clothes."

Wes—I do like this name somehow—puts his hand up and scowls at the two ladies. "No shrinks, okay? They'll just pump her full of drugs till she really doesn't know who she is."

Paula flicks back a strand of bright pink hair. "Since when are you so concerned with her welfare? Where was all that concern when you knew Frank was sneaking around?"

"You don't know what you're talking about, Paula."

But she merely turns her back on Wes and pulls out a shiny little flat object, which she taps several times, then starts talking into it in the same odd manner that Wes did. "Suzanne," she says, "it's Paula. I've got a little emergency here."

And with that she leaves the room and I cannot make out anything else.

Anna rummages through drawers and the hanging garments and presents me with a miniature dress and a pair of ridiculous, strappy shoe-like things.

"You must be joking," I say. "I most certainly will not appear in public with my legs and arms completely exposed."

Anna sighs, rummages a little longer, and produces a pair of long, dove-gray trousers and a white, short-sleeved bodice with buttons down the front.

I hold up the trousers in front of me. "What a novel idea—I've always wished to wear trousers and ride Belle astride. It always struck me as the most practical and comfortable way to ride." And then the thought darts through me: Could Belle have been lamed in the fall? Would they have had to—dear God, please let that sweet creature be well.

Anna's lower lip trembles. "Courtney, you're frightening me."

I feel a tear rolling down my cheek, and I brush it away with the back of my hand. I realize I have dropped the trousers on the floor. "Do calm yourself," I say, retrieving them from the floor. "I am merely commenting on the advantages of masculine attire."

Anna looks at Wes, who shrugs. Paula strides

back into the room, flinging a stray strand of pink-and-blue hair out of her face. "My cousin Suzanne, a respected psychopharmacologist, has agreed to squeeze us in."

Wes glares at her. "Fancy name for a high-priced drug pusher."

Paula ignores him. "We have to leave right now. It's just over by Huntington Hospital."

I do not see how I am going to step into these lovely soft trousers if they keep arguing. "Do be kind enough to take your disagreements outside so I might dress." I hold up the trousers for emphasis. "Besides, your shouting is making my head throb."

"Sorry," says Wes, moving towards the door. He turns back to Paula. "All I'm saying is, there's a lot of overprescribing going on. And not everyone who's grief-stricken or heartbroken or—"

"Or lying around wearing a wedding dress and saying she's someone else? Even you must admit we're out of our depth. And why are you still here anyway?"

"She asked me to be here." Wes regards me. "But if you want me to leave . . ."

If you want me to leave. The heat rushes to my face as those words take me back to the library of Mansfield House, where I stood before the glass doors opening onto the garden. "If you want me to leave," said Edgeworth, "I will of course do as you choose. But I beg you to tell me what I have done."

30

How dare he act the innocent? "Sir, I see no need to tell you what you already know. Now leave me in peace."

Face bleached of color, he closed his eyes and let his head fall down, as if all the life had gone out of him.

"Courtney? What are you talking about?"

It is Wes who is looking at me, not Edgeworth. His eyes are soft behind his spectacles.

"You will leave my room at once. I am not in the habit of explaining myself, particularly to a man who is nothing to me."

He blinks, as if flinching from the force of my words, and for an instant I want to take them back.

But he turns and walks slowly out of the room. "That's my girl," Paula says, jabbing a thumb in the air for emphasis, and sails out the door after Wes.

While the quarrel continues unabated in the next room, Anna helps me out of the white dress, puts it away, and produces two tiny garments from a drawer.

"I don't get it," says Anna. "You said weeks ago that you wanted nothing to do with Wes."

"I never set eyes on him till this morning."

"What?" Her eyes widen in alarm.

"Whatever you are talking of has nothing to do with me."

"You poor thing," she says. "Don't worry, Paula's cousin will know what to do." She indicates the two odd-looking garments on the bed. "Why don't you get dressed, okay?"

One of the garments is bright pink with three large openings; the other consists of two bowl-shaped pieces of fabric in a pale yellow, connected with strips of fabric and decorated with lace and embroidery of the same color. Anna hands me the yellow article; I turn it this way and that. Ah. I could fit one of the bowls inside the other and— yes, that must be it. I place the bowl-like sections upon my head and attempt to tie the strips of fabric under my chin.

Anna's mouth is agape, then she starts to giggle, snatching the bonnet off my head. "At this rate we'll never get out of here." She unfolds the bonnet and places it against my chest, and I realize that it is no bonnet at all. Apparently, it is meant to serve as fitted stays to go under the bodice. I have not the slightest notion of how one dons such a garment, and I suppose Anna can deduce that fact from my posture and countenance, as she tugs my crossed arms, puts my arms through the semi-circular straps, fits the bowls over my breasts, and fastens the back of the garment. Astonishing how the garment lifts the bosom and how com-fortable it is compared to the busk in my stays that forces my torso upright.

"At least you didn't call Frank," she says. "That's something to be thankful for." She picks up the bright pink garment. "You're really not going to dress yourself, are you." She sits me down on the bed, pulls off the sheet in which I've wrapped the lower part of my body, and has me step into two of the openings in the garment, then pulls it up to cover my bottom. Some of the faster women of the ton may wear drawers under their petticoats, but such garments are most certainly a good deal longer than this tiny bit of fabric.

The rest I can manage myself, and I don the trousers—they have the most curious front closures, no buttons, but a device that closes when pulled up and opens when tugged down—and button the bodice.

The quarrel in the next room, which had descended from shouting to hissing, now erupts every several seconds to outbursts such as "What gives you the right" or "You have no idea what you're talking about" and then a final "Then I'm going with you" from Wes, followed by more hissing.

I tuck the bodice into the waistband of the trousers—a comfortable garment indeed—and roll my eyes at Anna. "Do you think they will cease anytime soon?"

Anna, who has been watching me with a tight line to her mouth and a little line between her brows, relaxes into a broad smile. She's actually quite pretty, she, too, with very white teeth and a little dimple in her left cheek. "Paula's not the forgiving type, in case you haven't noticed."

"Whatever did he do to her?"

Anna's brow furrows again, all the amusement gone from her countenance. She opens her mouth as if to speak, then closes it. The door opens and Paula flounces in, varicolored tresses bouncing.

"Good," she says, with a sweeping glance that assesses me from head to toe. "Come. We'll miss Suzanne."

I touch my bonnet-less head and note that in addition to their other oddities of dress, the two women are also bareheaded. "Bonnet?" I say, looking to each for an answer. Anna's eyes widen, as if in fright, while Paula simply strides over and takes my arm.

"Come on, you," she says, propelling me out of the room. As if comfortable trousers for women were not agreeable enough, the thought of not having to wear a hot, close bonnet in summer is felicity itself. Paula leads me into a room even smaller than the bedchamber. It appears to be the servants' dining parlor. And at the perimeter of this room is a folding screen that is not completely extended, and beyond it is a bright orange sofa with a long, low table before it and a large arm-chair piled high with a colorful mass of unfolded garments beside it. Where is the rest of the house? This cannot be the extent of it. Wait, there is another door ajar, near a tall upright rectangular object. I move towards it and—

"Courtney? We'll be late."

"For God's sake, Paula. Let the girl go to the bathroom," Anna says.

"Bath room"? Ignoring Wes's stare, I brush past him, put a hand on the door and push it all the way open, slip in, and close the door behind me. I have had enough of all this staring. Except that now I am staring, too. At the reflection in the mirror, the blond-haired woman who is supposed to be me but who is an absolute stranger to me.

I regard the woman in the mirror; she does fill out the white bodice rather well, and the waistband of the trousers rests against the form in a way that shows off the smallness of her waist in comparison to the roundness of her hips. I can only imagine what my mother would say if she saw me in a pair of trousers. The O her little mouth would make at the scandal of it, followed by the cold blue glare of her eyes and an imperious "You will change clothes at once," the same tone she took when I dared to wear my yellow gown when Edgeworth was once expected for dinner, instead of the pale blue she had chosen.

The woman in the mirror is smiling.

A drip-drip sound captures my attention—under the mirror there is a curved, glossy metal pipe from which water steadily drips. I fumble around the curved surfaces of the pipe, which protrudes from a thicker pipe, atop which is—a pump-handle? Could it be possible that this meager dwelling has piped water? Sure enough, it yields to my touch, and a trickle, then a powerful stream, of water issues from the curved pipe. And neither a creak nor a shudder, neither a dead insect nor a hint of sulfurous stench nor a brown tinge. Just clear, cold—and dear heaven, when I move the handle to the left, the water is warm, then hot! How can such a miracle exist? I move the handle until the water is the perfect temperature and hold my hands under the luxurious stream, splashing water on my face. I glance up at the mirror, and the face looking back at me reflects delight in the refreshing sensation of the water. I'll wager there isn't a house in London that has such clear water pouring out of its pipes. And none of them has hot water unless it is heated under a fire.

If only there were soap. Ah, yes. A clear bottle which looks to be glass but has not the heft of glass, and which gives under the pressure of my fingers, has a label which proclaims it "geranium liquid soap." The pumplike top produces a thin stream of pearly liquid, which foams easily in my wet hands, and I use the sweet-smelling mixture on my face. Heaven indeed to be clean and smell lovely.

A quick rap at the door—"It's me," says a female voice, and in walks Paula. I see there is little respect for closed doors in this house.

"Thought I might as well in case we hit traffic," she says, and lifts the lid of a white cylindrical object, which reveals a white, horseshoe-shaped thing atop a bowl of water. She hitches up her tiny skirt, pulls down a light blue undergarment like the one I am wearing, sits upon the horseshoe, and relieves herself. I am about to protest her vulgar behavior, but I am so fascinated by what she does next that I can only stare with as little manners as she possesses. She grabs some soft-looking, thin white paper from a roll which is fastened to the wall and uses it to clean herself, readjusts her clothing, and depresses a lever on the bowl which flushes everything away with a mighty gush of water.

"Almost forgot," she says, opening a cupboard and removing a blue box. "I'd better steal one of these." She holds up a thin white cylindrical object with a paper wrapper. "I'm going to start bleeding any moment. I can feel it." And down comes the undergarment again, up goes the skirt, and ripping off the paper wrapping, she actually pushes the white tube inside her body!

"Are you okay?" she says, her brow creased with worry. "Stupid question. Of course you're not okay. But you're done, right? Can we go?"

"I, well—if you would be so kind—" I indicate the porcelain bowl. "I will just be a moment."

"Hurry up, then," she says, and, thankfully, leaves me to try out the device myself. It is a thousand times more impressive than the flushing water closet in Miss Allens's London town house, and far more comfortable, too. Miss

Allens's barely has an edge to perch upon, let alone a bona fide seat. And this soft, delicate paper is far more agreeable than waste paper.

They are all staring at me when I emerge from the bath room. Paula grabs my arm and steers me towards another door, and I get a glimpse of an astonishingly lifelike picture of the two actors from *Pride and Prejudice*, under which are the numbers 2009 and a calendar of all the months and days of the year.

"Two thousand nine?" I hear myself say, in that strange voice, before I am aware of having spoken. "Two thousand nine?" I disengage my arm from Paula's grasp and search the faces of the three strangers. "Is this a joke?"

If it is, they are not laughing, and I am suddenly so dizzy that I grip the top of one of the chairs.

Five

"Courtney, we'll be late." Paula reaches for my hand.

"Late? As in later than 2009? How much later can one possibly be?"

"Sweetie," Anna says, stroking my arm, "we'll talk about it on the way to the doctor."

A sudden blast of noise—music, I believe, but unlike any music I have ever heard. A male voice singing and yelping almost, something about "loving you," accompanied by soaring, wailing instruments. There must be musicians outside, but how they achieve such loudness is beyond imagining.

Paula stomps her foot on the floor. "That idiot again," she shouts, or at least I think that is what she says, for the roar of the voice and instruments practically drowns her voice.

"Let's get out of here," yells Wes.

Anna opens the door and holds it open for us. Paula tugs on my arm, and I let her lead me outside.

Paula steers me down a flight of steps. The noise is still strong, but slightly muffled.

"Damn," says Paula. "If it's not Shostakovich down there conducting the best of the eighties, it's the soothing sounds of LAPD helicopters circling the skies."

"Not to mention the occasional gunshot," Anna adds.

"When are you gonna move out of here?" says Paula.

"I'll talk to him later," says Wes.

I lock eyes with Wes. "Is this truly 2009?"

His eyes widen, and his face turns pale.

"I must be dead, then, for no one can live that long. Oh, dear God. And Belle, is she dead, too?"

Suddenly I no longer care about piped hot water and cleverly fashioned water closets and being a pretty blonde. I want to be alive, in my life, not in this strange place—this heaven or hell or whatever it is.

"Courtney, you are not dead," says Wes. "Thank God. You just hurt your head, that's all."

"Which is why you're confused," Paula says.

I hear myself gasp as she propels me down the street. "What sort of place is this?" The outside of the house is defaced with indecipherable black-and-red scrawls of paint. The pavement we walk upon is hard and tan-colored and cracked with sprouts of grass protruding from the cracks here and there.

Tall wooden poles tower over the street, each connected to the other with black cord. Most astonishing of all are the hulking, shiny wheeled things in various shapes and colors—black, white, silver, red, a multitude of shades—which line each side of the street. One of them begins to belch smoke and moves. It makes a loud humming noise. What sort of equipage moves without horses pulling it, and without anyone to hold the reins, if there are indeed horses to rein?

"Ouch, you're hurting me," Paula says, and I realize I am gripping her arm with considerable force.

I loosen my grip and point my free hand at the now rapidly moving equipage. "What is that thing?"

"I know; do you believe it? Another hybrid SUV. What a joke. Unlike my baby here, nearly as fuel-efficient as a Prius." She stops at a shorter, more rounded machine than the so-called SUV;

this one is of a light blue color with a black roof. Paula reaches into her bag and retrieves a small object, which she points at the machine and then opens what is apparently a door. She motions for me to enter.

"You are not serious."

"Sit in the front then."

"I do not know if I wish to sit in this—thing—at all."

"Since when do you not like my car?"

"Car." I am, in truth, curious. And so I settle into the forward-facing seat, which is far more comfortable than a carriage; Wes sits beside me. Paula and Anna sit in the front, entering by a different set of doors. Instead of their seat facing ours, as in a carriage, they, too, face forward. Paula inserts the object she used to open the door into a slot next to a wheel-like thing that is level with her chest, and the car makes a fast whirring noise. She turns the wheel, and the car begins to move!

It is as fast as a fast-moving carriage, and without horses! But then it is much faster than a carriage, and the street is full of other cars in a variety of shapes, sizes, and colors, all moving faster and faster until ours speeds onto a vast stretch of road divided by painted lines into equally spaced sections full of these strange machines, all racing as if the devil were in pursuit, and I realize that I have grabbed on to Wes's arm with one hand and am gripping a handle protruding from my door with another.

"Wait—no—too fast, I—"

"Are you all right?" Wes says.

"Please—do slow down." I can barely get the words out. I am beginning to gasp for breath—all these cars speeding down this endless road, racing one another, emitting blasts like a ship's horn; a large black squarish monster of a machine roars past Paula's car and slips in front of her, and we nearly crash into its rear—this is hell, this is hell, I know this is hell, how did I end up in hell; cannot get enough air, cannot breathe.

"She's hyperventilating," says Wes.

Paula meets my eyes via a mirror that is above the inside wheel. "You want me to pull over, darling? Are you going to be sick?"

"Courtney?" Wes says.

I cannot answer just yet; I force myself to slow my breathing until I am able to take in a long, deep breath. "Of course I am not going to be sick. I may be frightened out of my senses, but I am not one of those fainting misses who needs to be physicked every minute."

Anna turns round and leans over the back of her seat. "You're perfectly safe, sweetheart. I promise you." She looks sharply at Paula. "Would you stop with the Indy 500 lane changes? And a little less pressure on the gas pedal, okay?"

Paula bridles. "For God's sake, I'm only doing

forty-five. I couldn't do more in this traffic if I wanted to."

Wes simply pats my hand and gives me a reassuring nod. Behind him I get a glimpse of a white car that is next to ours; inside it is a party of young children. They see me watching them and wave and smile. One of them, a boy of about six, pulls his mouth into a grotesque grin with both hands while a younger boy of perhaps four years jostles him and giggles.

I feel my own mouth lift in a smile, and I realize that I have relaxed my grip on both Wes's arm and the door handle. The sensation in my stomach is no longer a sickening lurch—the cars on either side of us and the trees and houses become a blur—and I surrender to the speed, the colors, the refreshing wind on my face, for somehow the glass next to me has lowered partway. If this is heaven, then I am traveling with the angels, and what indeed is there to fear?

"Car"—what an apt name for such a mythical equipage! "Car," a word which summons Shakespeare and Spenser and verses on Phoebus's "fiery carre."

We race past shops, houses, and buildings which are as varied in color and shape as the human beings who stream in and out of their doorways. Some of the buildings are so tall and have so much glazing that the window tax alone must be beyond reckoning. The many structures we pass are in various states of dilapidation or elegance: some smoke-scarred and ragged, others sleek and shining. No uniformity of style at all.

Here and there the brickwork and lintels are reminiscent of a London town house, but most of the facades are either devoid of ornamentation or else adorned in a manner that I have never even imagined: green and red panels in rectangular shapes; whimsical paintings of flowers and animals; enormous, looping letters that are sculpted of what appears to be glass; and giant mosaic tiles. It is as if a child had reign over this city and, laughing all the time, created whatever it wished for its inhabitants, willy-nilly, and without any regard for artistic harmony.

And the trees! Immensely tall, stalklike things with bark marked by geometric zigzags and topped by a mop of giant spiky leaves.

I can hardly begin to marvel over these trees when we pass colossal structures, rectangular metal armatures on four legs which are connected to one another with giant cords. I cannot imagine the purpose of such behemoths.

Is this what the world looks like in 2009?

I feel eyes upon me and realize that I have spoken the words aloud. Paula glances at me through the mirror, her brow furrowed. Anna glances at Wes; they both look at me and nod.

I cannot bear the pity on their countenances. I close my eyes and let the wind wash over me.

Either I am dead—or mad—or somehow I am in a future time, as someone else.

Could this be what the Society of Asiatic Studies meant in their essay on the Hindu belief in the transmigration of souls? But that, if I understood rightly, was a transfer of the soul of the deceased into a newly born babe. Yet here I am, another adult person.

If my soul has transmigrated, then everyone I know must be long dead—dear sweet Papa, shall I never see you again? If it is indeed 2009, then my dearest Mary, I shall never look upon your sweet countenance again, nor that of your brother—at this moment I cannot feel the slightest bit of resentment towards Charles Edgeworth, for he must be at least a century and a half in his grave. Dear Mama, I was never to you what my sister and brother were, yet you were the only mother I knew. And you, too, are dead. Hot tears gather behind my eyelids. And Barnes—dear sweet faithful Barnes—who will mourn you now but I?

Wes's hand patting my arm rouses me; his gray-blue eyes are gentle. Anna leans over her seat to wipe away my tears with something softer than the finest linen.

"We're almost there," Paula says.

I may be insane, I may be dead, I may have a transmigrated soul, but I shall be mistress of myself. I force a smile to prove it to my traveling companions, and their countenances show what appears to be relief.

Paula's car turns off the endless, inconceivably wide expanse of road onto a smaller, slower road, and then we are before an astonishingly tall and massive building with hundreds of windows.

We come to a stop and disembark onto a vast coach-yard filled with stationary cars. "I feel better already," says Paula, and points in the direction we are to walk.

Suddenly I am seized with laughter, which simply bubbles out of me and shakes my frame until I am nearly bent over with it.

Wes, Paula, and Anna's countenances are anything but mirthful. "Oh, no," says Anna, a fretful tone in her voice.

"Are you all right?" Wes says.

The laughter subsides into unladylike snorts and giggles, and finally I manage, "Oh, yes. Like Paula, I feel better already. Who would not feel better after racing a thousand cars to a destination where a thousand cars stand still? Who would not feel better after learning that everyone she knows has been dead for at least a hundred and fifty years?"

I look around me at the field of cars, the building looming with its glittering windows. "If they are dead, then so must I be."

"Do you really feel dead?" says Anna, her eyes full of concern. "Because you're not. You've got your whole life ahead of you. I know it doesn't feel that way right now, but it will. I promise you."

"I—" But I cannot finish the thought, for a pair of white butterflies are suddenly dancing in the air between Anna and me. And, as suddenly, they flutter away and are replaced by a lone orange-and-black-spotted butterfly, which promptly lands on my arm and appears to be looking up at me. I want to laugh with delight, but I dare not frighten it. I move my hand as if to touch it, but Wes gently stops my hand with his.

"Its wings are too fragile to be touched."

I know those words—I remember this moment, this very moment. But how?

And all at once the butterfly takes flight and the sun comes from behind a cloud and the tingling of my skin where the butterfly just stood and the glow of the sun on my face and the wisp of citron scent from Wes and the touch of his skin on mine are more vivid, more present, than any sensations I have ever known.

And all at once I know that I am alive; indeed I am more alive than I have ever been before. Impossibly and undeniably alive. In this body which is not mine, with these people I do not know, in this far distant time, in this faraway place. Impossible, inexplicable, yet it is so. One moment I was riding Belle through the woods. The next moment I was here.

I should be frightened. I should question my sanity. But I cannot.

I smile. At Wes. At Paula. At Anna.

Anna takes my arm and squeezes it affectionately. "I believe that each of us has the power to create heaven or hell, right here, right now."

Paula disengages Anna from my arm and steers me towards the building. "Anna, the last thing this girl needs is a steaming pile of your new-age crap."

I look round at Anna, whose cheeks are flaming, and say, "I believe I like your thought."

She glances at me, then glares at Paula's back. "I happen to have read that in a book, Paula. A reputable book. Twenty weeks on the *New York Times* bestseller list."

"Let's get you inside," Paula says to me, pointedly ignoring Anna.

Anna is apparently undaunted. *"There are more things in heaven and earth, Horatio, than are dreamt of in your philosophy."*

Paula rolls her eyes. "If she's not spouting the received wisdom of some creepy guy channeling an 'ascended master,' then she's showing off her MFA in theatre."

I give Anna an encouraging smile. "I happen to be quite fond of Shakespeare myself."

We reach the building, and Wes holds open an enormous door that is all glass—such a huge pane of glass I have not seen before—and I am whisked into a box of a room with doors which open and close of their own accord, but not as normal doors do; it is as if they disappear into the walls when they open.

Paula presses one of the many numbered circles on the wall next to the strange doors, which are now closed, and the room gives a little shudder. A few moments pass, and the doors disappear into the wall again, and outside the room is a scene entirely different from the one which had previously been there.

And in that moment I realize that the tiny room we are standing in has actually moved! We have actually ascended from the ground to an upper floor. Has the room literally flown upstairs? Laughter begins to bubble inside me, and I force myself to keep my countenance. How can the people around me maintain such solemn expressions when they stand inside such a conveyance? I can only assume that such wonders are daily occurrences in 2009.

A quick walk down a checkered tile passageway, and Paula motions for us to seat ourselves in curiously shaped chairs which are orange and seem to be molded of some kind of hard substance. Paula speaks to an attendant who sits behind a windowed wall, then rejoins our party. A disheveled man of about thirty years, his complexion nearly as gray as the drab garments he wears, takes one of the chairs in the row in front of us and immediately twists round in his seat, fixing his bespectacled eyes upon me. "Are you here for the facts? Are you here for the facts? Here for the facts? Here for the facts? Are you here for the facts? Are you here for the facts?"

He continues spewing this nonsense at me, getting more agitated with each repetition until the gray in his face turns pink, then red, and Paula is shouting at the woman behind the windowed wall to do something about him, and Wes is urging him, in gentle tones, to desist, and Anna grips my arm, her face in an attitude of fear, and the man continues to fix me with his gaze, the light winking off his black-framed spectacles.

The light—yes, the light—another wonder. There are no candles anywhere, yet there is glowing light behind glass in the high ceiling, emanating from a lamp beside the bank of chairs, shining upon the woman behind the windowed wall.

"Are you here for the facts? Here for the facts?"

I stand up and gaze into the upturned face of the suffering man. "Indeed. I cannot imagine any-one more eager than I to know the facts."

Six

7he man halts in mid-rant, his mouth open, his eyes wide behind the spectacles. And slowly, the O of his mouth shapes itself into a broad grin. "God bless you," he whispers. "God bless you."

"Miss Stone?" A lovely Chinese woman in a rose-pink bodice and matching trousers is speaking to me. Is my name supposed to be Miss Stone?

I turn towards Anna, who is nodding her head at the Chinese woman and pointing at me.

"Miss Stone, Dr. Menziger will see you now." The Chinese woman's English is perfect, though also not in the accent of my country.

Wes rises from his seat and lightly touches my arm. "Are you sure you want to do this?"

Paula fixes him with a baleful eye and takes my arm. "She needs help, you idiot."

An older man and a woman, he in a gray coat and trousers and a crisp white shirt, she in a relatively modest dress of dark blue that falls to her calves, make their way down the passageway in front of us. They are supporting between them a young man of no more than sixteen years, long black-brown hair falling into his face, the rest of it sticking up as if he were a child roused from slumber, his eyes half closed, stumbling between these two more capable-looking adults, their faces lined with anxious care for their charge, the young man saying, over and over, "I won't do it again. I promise. I won't do it again."

Wes sweeps his arm in a gesture that takes in the unfortunate threesome and the man who has seated himself in front of us. "You call this help?"

Paula ignores him. "Come on, Courtney." She and I follow the Chinese woman through a door, down a checkered corridor, past white tables and chattering females, brown-and black-and white-skinned females, all uniformly clad in the same rose-pink trousers and short-sleeved bodices, and atop the tables are glowing boxes that remind me of the one in the room where I awoke but which appear to have lines of printed text on them instead of actors, and before I can make any sense of what I am seeing—as if there is sense to be made—I am inside a room without Paula and facing a large, lightly colored wooden table, behind which is a person rising out of a chair and offering a hand for me to shake.

"Welcome, Courtney. I'm Dr. Menziger, Paula's cousin. Call me Suzanne."

This sweet, feminine voice is most unexpected, for she has a bristly head of closely cropped, dark-blond hair, broad shoulders, and squarish white teeth smiling in a square face. The hand held out to me is blunt and square as well, with closely trimmed, squarish nails. Her one beauty, her eyes, are azure-blue and sparkle with dia-monds, like the sun shimmering on the sea.

Her eyes are those of an angel. I smile my approbation as I shake her hand, though it is an intimate gesture for one I have just met.

I take one of two chairs which face her, and I find my attention seized by a most astonishing picture which sits in a frame atop a light-colored wooden cabinet behind Dr. Menziger. The render-ing of a brown-haired woman with a confident smile is as lifelike as the picture in the calendar on the wall of the rooms in which I awakened. I have never seen any artist's efforts create such likenesses; they are so true they could be mistaken for the original.

Dr. Menziger's voice recalls my attention from the picture. "Is there anything in particular that interests you about that photo?"

"Photo . . . I have never seen anything so life-like. It is as if she were in the room with us."

"That's my partner, and I'm sure she would be pleased to hear that. She took the picture herself."

"Indeed." I cannot begin to imagine why Dr. Menziger would choose to display a portrait of her business partner, let alone why a fellow physician would also be such an accomplished artist. And a lady. But they are both ladies. Lady physicians. What a novel idea.

"Is something amusing you?" Dr. Menziger asks, her expression kind.

"Not at all," I say, hoping my face does not betray my thoughts. After all, why should women not be physicians? Is it not they who nurse the sick, who nurture babies, who attend to the unwell and unfortunate of the parish?

"Tell me why your friends brought you to see me," she says, folding her square hands before her and gazing at me, her blue eyes twinkling with the hint of a smile on her lips. "And please understand that whatever you say to me in this room is strictly confidential."

"All well and good, but will it land me in an asylum?"

"Interesting choice of words, 'asylum.'" She scribbles into a book of ruled paper with what appears to be a pen, though it has no quill. "We are not so antiquated as all that, though if you mean asylum in terms of a safe place, a sanctuary that keeps away harm, then yes, we offer asylum."

I think of the poor creature outside ranting about "the facts" and that young man practically carried through the corridor by, presumably, his parents, who paid no heed to his pleadings. "Pretty words, but I have no wish to be locked away."

"It would not be in my interest, or in yours, to keep you anywhere against your will. I'd like to help you."

"If that means draining me of offensive humors, as my mother's favorite medical man likes to say, then I respectfully decline your offer."

"I am not so dogmatic about comedy as all that."

A hint of a smile plays about Dr. Menziger's mouth. It takes me a moment to understand her witticism, and I laugh.

She scribbles into her book. Odd; there is no inkpot anywhere to be seen, yet ink continues to issue from her pen.

"So," she says. "Why do you think your friends brought you here?"

"They think I am Courtney—Stone, is it? But I am not."

Dr. Menziger says not a word, just gazes at me with her sparkling blue eyes and nods slightly.

"I am Miss Mansfield. Jane is my Christian name. I neither look nor sound like this. When last I went to sleep I was in my own bed, on my father's estate, in Somerset, and it was the year thirteen. 1813. Not"—and there it is, on her desk, a leather-bound book open to the frontispiece, a calendar topped by the numbers 2009. "It was not 2009. I am not ill, Dr. Menziger. I am simply lost."

She nods. "How does that make you feel?"

"How would it make anyone feel? Confused. Frightened sometimes. Curious . . . how, for example, does that lamp on your table emit light without candles?"

She nods kindly. "I understand you were treated last night for an injury to your head." She indicates some papers on her desk. "Your thoughts and feelings could be simply the result of your concussion, and in that case will likely pass soon enough. Memory loss is another not uncommon result, usually temporary. And Paula did mention that you recently broke off an engagement, which would certainly contribute to your emotional state."

She poises her writing instrument atop her paper. "Do you have any history of mental illness? How about in your family?"

What an impertinent question. As if any family would reveal such information. "Indeed not."

"Have you any thoughts of hurting yourself? Any suicidal thoughts?"

"Of course not. Are you a magistrate as well?"

"I would like to keep you here for a few days, give you some medication, observe your progress, although—"

My stomach drops. "I am perfectly well, I assure you."

"There is an alternative, of course. . . ."

"Yes, yes, whatever it is."

She reaches into a drawer and pulls out a thin, rectangular object which is flat and shiny silver on one side; its reverse side is topped by evenly spaced, elliptical bumps. "If you take this pill," she says, jabbing a thumbnail into the flat side and extracting a pink oval from one of the bumps, "and faithfully take one every day, I will see you in a week and we'll see how you're doing." She scribbles on two pieces of paper and hands both to me, then fills a cup from a white, rectangular object topped by a transparent tank full of water.

She hands me the pill and the cup, which is made of paper. "I believe this will make you feel like yourself again. Isn't that what you want?"

I cannot argue with that point, and so I swallow the pill.

"Have my receptionist make an appointment for you for next week, okay?" She stands up and offers me her hand again to shake. "And have one of your friends spend the night with you, just in case you need looking after. You should not be alone with a concussion anyway."

"I am much obliged to you," I say, and slip out the door. As I make my way past the rose-pink-clad women to where I assume my escorts await me, I say a silent prayer of thanks for my escape. If this pill is anything like the physic that Mr. Jones peddles, then it will do no more than make me sleepy—and, fortunately, this one went down without the usual offensive flavor—or do nothing at all.

As for making an appointment to see Dr. Menziger again, well, that is something I shall forget. She may have the eyes of an angel, but she was as crafty as an I-don't-know-what in nearly turning me into an inmate of this place.

As I near the bank of orange chairs—the ranting man is, thankfully, gone—Paula, Anna, and Wes rise to meet me. Paula reaches me first and snatches the papers from my hand.

She examines them, mumbling something about stopping to "fill this right away"; Wes peers over her shoulder and groans.

Anna takes me by the hand; Wes grabs the other paper away from Paula and addresses me. "It says here you're not to stay alone; I'll watch over you tonight."

"Give it a rest, Sir Galahad," Paula says. "Your kind of protection she doesn't need."

"Then why did she have them call me from the emergency room, huh?"

"She had a blow to the head, remember?"

"Could you two stop fighting already?" Anna says. "It's not exactly helpful."

"Fine," says Paula, "but he's not going home with her."

"Why don't we ask Courtney what she wants," Wes says.

"Indeed," I say, wondering why my tongue is so thick and unwieldy that I can barely form an intelligible word, "why don't we ask Courtney, whosoever she may be." How have we progressed from the room with the orange chairs to the sea of cars without my noting any of my surroundings until this moment?

"Are you okay?" Paula says, gripping my arm tighter. "Help me, she's starting to fall . . . fall . . . fall." Paula's words echo in a most diverting manner. Even more amusing is the fact that I am now looking up at the faces of Paula, Anna, and

Wes, who are looking down at me. Pink and blue strands of hair dangle towards me, like thick strands of yarn. Their gay colors are so unlike the stern expression on Paula's face. My giggles echo.

"Don't just stand there. Help me get her off the ground . . . ground . . . ground. . . ."

Leaning against side-glass in car. Blur of clouds, buildings, machines, trees. Wes's shoulder serves as my pillow; his arm round my shoulder; what a forward little baggage I am. She is. Not my body. Not my conduct. Silly goose. I should sit up. Anna's white face frowning. So very tired. Paula's eyes in the mirror. Need water. Sleep first.

*S*omehow back in the bedchamber; Paula and Anna tugging silky garment over my head, trousers to match. What happened to other clothes? Wes not in the room, thankfully. What am I thinking? "Water . . ." My voice is a croak. Throat terribly dry.

Paula holds a glass to my lips. Oh blessed water so parched so parched I can barely swallow. Oh dear it has wet the front of this garment oh why am I so awkward as if I have drunk a bottle of Constantia wine, except that the wine gladdened my heart before it sent me to my slumbers but this is dull, dull, everything is so dull. I am gray inside. Gray. My heart is gray my throat is dry gray dust there are ashes in my mouth so thirsty I cannot swallow cannot stay awake but cannot sleep I do not want to fall into this gray abyss I will not I will not oh how heavy my eyes are and behind them only gray. . . .

*W*es is slumped on a chair beside the bed; it is night. A single lamp illuminates half of his face. He is sleeping, snoring softly, like a child worn out from its holidays. A few of his curls are tumbled on his forehead; he is not wearing his spectacles, and he looks very young indeed. And handsome. A frown contracts his brow, and he opens his eyes. The corners of his mouth lift. "Courtney." His voice is thick with sleep. "I was worried."

"As was I," I say, but my voice is an unintelligible croak. I am so relieved to see the golden light falling on his face instead of the dreadful gray hue and to feel the bedclothes against my arms that the dryness in my throat is but a trifle. I can feel again. I do not even care that what I feel is in a body not my own. How delightful, how delicious to feel something, anything.

"Water. Please."

He grabs his spectacles from the top of the bookcase and scrambles out of the room, returning posthaste with a glass of cool water, which I consume in one unladylike gulp.

"Feel better?" he asks.

I nod. He points to the glass. "Would you like some more?"

"Thank you, no."

Wes perches upon the chair beside the bed and takes my hand in both of his. How strong and gentle his hands are. And his eyes, so soft and kind behind his spectacles.

"Can I get you anything?"

In truth, I want nothing more at this moment than to lie here with Wes sitting beside the bed, holding my hand. He stretches his neck from side to side, and it makes an audible crack.

"Sorry," says he, "I must have put my neck out of whack from sleeping in the chair."

In that moment I am sensible of the impropriety of his having slept in my bedchamber. With me. I can feel my face grow hot. I wonder how he managed to get past the ladies, especially because they so clearly disapprove of him. Though their disapprobation seemed to have nothing to do with Wes's unchaperoned presence in my rooms.

My face grows hotter. "Perhaps if you could get me another glass of water?"

Wes leaps up to fill my glass. "Listen," he says as he hands me the glass. "I did some research online while you were sleeping"—he indicates a glowing box on a table across the room, thinner and flatter than the ones which the rose-clad ladies at Dr. Menziger's establishment had—"and the bottom line is that no one can make you take those pills. Or go to a hospital. You don't have to do anything you don't want to do."

I sit up in bed. "That has a lovely sound to it."

I don't have to do anything I don't want to do. When has anyone ever said that to me? Honor, duty, obedience. My entire life. Honor thy mother and father, even if thy mother wishes you were never born, considers you an embarrassment to the family name, compares you to a host of other, more dutiful females ad infinitum. Do your duty. To your family, your neighbors, your friends, even if you care for none of them, even if you are tired to death of the endless prattle and polite nothings and left-handed chatter that passes for "respectable" discourse. Obey your parents, your elders, your aunts and uncles, your vicar, even if he who preaches charity on Sunday says the maintenance of fatherless children should be another parish's burden.

And all at once, I hear Anna's words: *Each of us has the power to create heaven or hell, right here, right now.*

"There is one thing, though," Wes says, putting his hands in his trouser pockets and biting his lip. "Do you think you might consider not saying that you don't know your friends or that you're someone else? Not that I think you're putting on an act or anything; I mean, you did hit your head pretty hard—but you're making your friends really nervous. Uncomfortable. Scared, even. And when people are scared for their friends, they start putting pressure on them. They can't make you go back to Dr. Menziger. Or anyone else for that matter. But they'll be on your case to do it night and day. All I'm saying is, it would go easier for you if you could just agree that you're you."

"But I know nothing about this woman. I would be seen as the impostor I am."

He stands stock-still, his eyes wide. " 'This woman'? Now you're scaring me. You actually don't remember me, do you? Or Anna. Or Paula. You really truly think you're—" He shakes his head, as if to clear it.

"That is correct."

"Jane Mansfield."

I nod.

"And I take it you don't mean the screen goddess of the 1950s. I suppose that should be a relief."

"Whatever are you talking of?"

"Where does this Jane Mansfield come from?"

"I wish you would do me the honor of attending me when I speak to you. I told you all this already. Or is there another method to your questions?"

"I know, I know. Your father's estate is in Somerset. You play that stupid DVD till it's worn out. You hit your head on the bottom of a pool, and all of a sudden you've stepped right out of the pages of *Pride and Prejudice*."

"Indeed, those pleasing little theatricals resemble my life more than anything else in this place."

"Would you please just consider telling people you've got temporary memory loss from the concussion? Which is, after all, the truth. At least a dozen reliable sources online mention amnesia as a possible symptom. And confusion. I'm sure Paula's cousin mentioned that to you."

"She also mentioned that those infernal pills would make me feel like myself again."

"Do what you want. It's your life."

"It does not feel like my life."

"It'll pass. I promise. I'm going to sleep, okay? On the couch this time. I don't think you should be alone tonight."

I smile at him. *Do what you want. It's your life.* It may not be my life, but his words may very well be the sweetest music I have ever heard.

Seven

A rooster is crowing, the same sound to which I awaken every morning, and for one delicious moment I am back in my very own bed in Mansfield House. But then I open my eyes and I am in Courtney's bedchamber; it was the sound that deceived me.

A quick rap on the door and Wes pops his head in, and in that same moment the most gorgeous pianoforte concerto envelops me. And somehow I am not displeased to be here still.

Wes approaches the bed, bearing a tray with

two tall white cups of fragrant coffee, which he places atop the bookcase.

"I thought you might like to wake up to Beethoven instead of that nightmare of an alarm clock," he says, indicating the box with the glowing numbers that I encountered yesterday morning.

"But where are the musicians?" I cannot make out whence the music comes; it sounds as if the pianoforte, oboes, flute, and bassoons are in the room. Every note is so clear and crisp it resonates in my chest.

He looks at me quizzically, then fiddles with a small white rectangular object which is standing on the bookcase and a larger, grayish rectangle with letters and symbols all over it. The music lowers to a whisper.

"That better?" he asks.

"How did you do that?"

He hands me one of the cups. "Very funny." He brings over the grayish object. "Apparently, your amnesia entails the simple things as well. Don't worry; it will all come back. Here's volume, on and off, CD, DVD, auxiliary, and so on. And— wait a sec." He presses a button and the music stops mid-phrase, and he removes the white rectangle from its stand and brings that over, too. "Here's how to find your music by artist, genre, album, song."

Then he retrieves a third object, also flat and

rectangular. "You do remember how to use a phone, don't you?" He regards me skeptically. "You're kidding, right? This should be surgically implanted in your ear. Here, this is how you can call me." He clears his throat. "Or anyone you want to talk to."

I can hardly follow the rapid movement of his fingers on these odd contrivances; I am so caught up in the citron freshness of this man's scent as he perches on the bed next to me, so enchanted by the damp curls of hair on his neck as he bends his head to focus on what he is doing, that I am only vaguely aware of the sound of a key in a lock. In fact, I would hardly blink an eye if a host of musicians, in the flesh, were to suddenly appear in my room.

Instead, it is Paula who sails in, steaming containers of coffee in hand, resplendent in a scarlet dress, longer than yesterday's, pink and blue tresses wild about her face, and Anna trailing behind her in an unornamented, short-sleeved gray bodice and snug white trousers.

"Good morning, darling, I've got your pills," she says, waving a paper bag in my direction. "Did you sleep well?" Her toothy smile vanishes as she regards Wes and me on the bed. I pull the bed-clothes up around my neck and am instantly vexed with myself. Who is Paula, with her bare arms and legs and scarlet lips that match her dress, to pass judgment upon me? Or is Wes indeed a member of the serving class, as I had first suspected, and is this the source of her disapprobation?

Impossible. Despite his coarse clothing, from what I have observed, he has most certainly comported himself as an equal with the ladies in every possible way, even attempting to assert his dominance whenever he could.

"Wes," Paula says, "don't you have a website to optimize or something?"

"Like you even know what you're talking about."

"What are you doing here?"

"Give me a break, Paula. You know Courtney asked me to stay."

I asked Wes to stay here? Heaven only knows what else I might have said under the sway of that evil pill. My face is burning.

Paula flashes me a conciliatory smile, then turns to Wes with a softened tone. "Would you mind terribly if Anna and I took over for a while?" And turning to me, "If you think you're up to it, it's a typical L.A. blue sky and not too hot yet, so Anna and I would like to take you to breakfast."

I glance over at Wes, who is watching me with what looks like a feeble attempt to affect unconcern at my answer.

Paula turns to Wes. "There are some things we need to discuss—just us girls." The tightness returns to her tone. "Do I need to spell it out?"

Wes is looking at me instead of Paula. "If that's what Courtney wants, I'll leave you to it."

"Yes," I say, "I suppose I had better. . . ."

"Call me later if you need anything," Wes says, placing a card on top of the bookcase. He gives me a wry grin. "Just in case you've wiped out all traces of my contact info." Paula gives him an icy look and Anna raises an eyebrow. "Oh, yeah, I folded your laundry; it's still in the living room." A quick wave and he is gone.

Within fifteen minutes I am washed—oh heavenly water and soap and thick downy towels—and dressed, with the help of Paula and Anna, who assist me in choosing my ensemble and fastening myself into the various garments. Today this lovely, shapely body is clad in loose white trousers and a long chemise of sheer white with little opaque spots, and underneath a surprisingly comfortable yet form-molded sleeveless bodice in a pale pink.

"One thing that knock on the head did for you is make you appreciate your beauty," Anna says. "I don't think I have ever seen you get dressed without rattling off a laundry list of complaints."

"A pity, that." It seems the owner of this body has little appreciation for it. Curiously I have not, until this moment, thought of who Courtney Stone actually might be. Or where she might be, if she has vacated this body and left it for me. If my soul has transmigrated to her body, then has her soul transmigrated to mine? Or—

"Dear Lord." I cannot believe what I am seeing

in the bookcase in front of me: a book lying on its side, *Pride and Prejudice* by Jane Austen. And shelved neatly behind it, *Sense and Sensibility* by Jane Austen. *Emma* by Jane Austen . . .

"Sweetie?"

"Are you okay?"

"I—yes, I am perfectly well. Would you be so kind as to allow me a few minutes? I assure you I am well."

Paula and Anna exchange glances, Anna shrugs. "Sure, darling," Paula says. "We'll be right out here."

I close the door behind them and remove *Pride and Prejudice* from the bookcase, which is packed with books, so much so that they are piled every which way and are two deep in places. This must be—is it—there cannot be two books with that title—yet I have never known the name of the author, who is simply referred to on the title page of my copy as "the author of 'Sense and Sensibility.'" I turn to the first page: *It is a truth universally acknowledged* . . . yes, it is indeed the same book. And in this bookcase are not only *Pride and Prejudice* and *Sense and Sensibility*, the only two novels I have ever known to have been written by this author, this Miss Austen, but there is a third, *Emma*. And—could it be—a fourth, and a fifth, and a sixth novel, *Mansfield Park, Northanger Abbey, Persuasion*. All by Jane Austen. Six novels in all! What an embarrassment of riches!

I turn to the title pages of the other four novels —they were published after 1813, which is why I do not know of them. . . .

"Courtney?"

"A moment, please." I cannot wait to return here and read every one of these books—these curious, future-world things that are complete in a single volume and bound in paper instead of boards or leather, but nonetheless precious treasures.

Each of us has the power to create heaven or hell, right here, right now. I do not know how I have come to be in this time, in this place, in this body. But I do know that any place where there are six novels by the author of *Pride and Prejudice* must be a very special sort of heaven.

Eight

*N*ow that I am able to keep my seat in Paula's car without having to grip anyone's arm, I am at leisure to observe the world passing by at an astonishing pace. There are men, women, and children of a variety of complexions going about their business, a few walking in and out of shops, most riding in cars, laughing, frowning, talking, silent— they are brown and white and black, they are Asian and European and even African, all apparently in a state of perfect freedom and equanimity. I thought this must be so when I saw a couple of African ladies at Dr. Menziger's establishment, but now I know that slavery itself, and not just the trade, is finally at an end. This is a most delightful aspect to the world in which I find myself.

Whenever I manage to tear my eyes from the wonders of the streets, I observe Paula closely, for I would like to understand how she drives. All I can glean from her movements is that driving involves depressing something on the floor with her foot as well as maneuvering a wheel with her hands.

"Why can't they synchronize these stupid lights?" she says as she brings the car to a sudden stop at a crossroads, and it is then that I notice a bank of circular lights suspended over the road and alternating red, green, and yellow. As with the other lights of this world, I cannot make out the source of the illumination.

Another curiosity are the signs. They are everywhere. Big signs. Enormous signs. One promising relief for aching feet. Another the size of a workingman's cottage and featuring a scantily clad woman, twenty feet tall, looking inside a large white illuminated box. Some of the printed messages are taller than a person. And mostly unintelligible. "Senior Living." "Hotter Than Hot." "More Minutes." "Half the Carbs."

Paula brings her car to a final stop, and we alight before a bustling establishment crowded with people dining alfresco and many more at tables inside.

It appears to be a public breakfast, for ladies as well as gentlemen are being served, yet there is no shrubbery or promenade or anything resembling a pleasure garden. Curious indeed—a public breakfast taking place in an establishment which appears to exist expressly for the purpose of providing its guests with food and drink. The platters of food being carried from the kitchen by a battalion of white-aproned waiters, male and female, tell me that this is no mere tea shop.

Nor does it appear to be a chophouse, for it has not the filth of the places my brother frequents, the horrors of which he delights in retailing to his fastidious sister. No gravy stains or blotches of grease on the spotless white tablecloths, no litter of bones on the floor. It is most certainly not an inn or a hotel, for the single story seems wholly occupied by tables and chairs. And it is far grander than I imagine any tavern would be.

Most remarkable is that there are as many ladies dining as there are gentlemen, and no chop-house, let alone a tavern, would serve a lady.

A waiter appears at our table. "Ready to order?" he says, and I realize I have not even looked at the bill of fare, which Anna and Paula are perusing, and which is the length of an epic poem. The cover refers to the establishment as a "restaurant," in the manner of the French.

"Ooh, that looks good," says Anna as another waiter rushes by carrying an armload of enormous, steaming platters to a neighboring table.

She and Paula choose their meals, and when Paula suggests I have what she's having, I agree, as the sheer number of choices is overwhelming. Indeed, the variety of dishes listed within these pages exceeds what I imagine even the prince regent's cooks, let alone a mere genteel eating-house, would be capable of producing for the most festive occasion.

"So," says Anna, the waiter having been dispatched, "what's the deal with you and Wes?"

"I couldn't believe you asked him to stay with you instead of us, that you called him from the hospital instead of us," says Paula. "Who watched over you, took you out, wiped your tears, held your head while you puked up your guts, listened to you no matter how late it was and whether or not I was in the middle of production or whether or not Anna had to be at a meeting at some ungodly hour?"

She points at her chest. "We did. And who lied to cover for Frank when he was sneaking around with Miss Arsenic-in-your-wedding-cake? Wes, that's who. Wes, who's all I'm-so-sorry-Courtney and I-didn't-mean-to-hurt-anyone and all that bullshit."

I look from Paula to Anna and back, quite at a loss. "Forgive me, ladies, but I have not the honor of understanding you."

"The only thing I could get out of Suzanne about

your case," says Paula, "is that memory loss and confusion are not uncommon with concussion. She also said it would likely pass. But you really don't remember what happened with Wes?"

"Or Frank?" adds Anna.

"I must confess I do not," I say, noting the shocked looks they exchange with one another and seeing the wisdom of Wes's admonition that I refrain from insisting I am not, in fact, who they believe me to be.

Paula reaches for one of the three basins of coffee with foamy milk which the waiter has just deposited before us. "But you remember who they are, right?"

"Indeed I do not."

"And what about me? Do you really not remember me?" says Paula, enormous coffee cup poised at her scarlet lips.

"Or me?" Anna's eyes are eager, hopeful.

I muster what I hope looks like an encouraging smile. "I am sure it will all come back very soon."

"Jesus," says Paula, and, calling out to a waiter, "Could I have a mimosa over here?

"Luckily," she adds, reaching into a large, square black bag with shiny white flowers and pulling out a flat rectangular object like the one Wes tried to show me how to use, "I came armed with visual aids."

She lays the rectangle on the table and taps its flat, hard surface, sometimes moving her pointing and middle finger across it as if smoothing it out. Small pictures, as colorful and lifelike as the one atop the cabinet in Dr. Menziger's room, appear on the surface for a fleeting moment, instantly replaced by another, and another, and yet another.

"Here it is." She slides the rectangle before me.

I am looking at a picture of the blond woman I have become, standing beside a man who is two heads taller than she and has his arm round her, quite an unseemly display of affection for a portrait. He has a playful grin and dark hair, nearly black, which falls over his forehead and tumbles over the open collar of his shirt. Does no gentleman wear a coat or neckcloth in this world? As a matter of fact, not a single gentleman in this establishment is wearing a coat. Unless—

Unless they are none of them gentlemen. Could it be that I have taken on not only a new body, but also a new rank, one lower than that of a gentleman's daughter? That could account for the unladylike dress and painted lips of the two ladies, unless they are—no, unthinkable—though I must venture to gain some intelligence of their families, their pursuits, their situation in life. And what of Wes? What could account for the air and manner and dress of Wes and Paula and Anna, for their ill-bred familiarity towards me and one another, for the brazen manners of the ladies and gentlemen all around me—if ladies and gentlemen they be?

Good lord. What have I become?

A hypocrite. Nothing less. I, who proclaimed to James that "rank and fortune don't signify," and here I am lamenting my fall from the polite world. Although Paula must be a woman of substance in order to keep her own carriage—or car. And while there is no evidence of a servant in the blond woman's rooms, no one expected her/me to have anything to do with the laundry —Wes did say he folded it, did he not? And the ladies did help me dress.

There it is. They must be my servants after all. And Paula is some sort of coachman—coachwoman. No. Impossible. There is not the smallest degree of deference in their manner towards me. Dictating to me, addressing me by my/her Christian name. In fact—

"Courtney!"

"Don't shout at her," Anna says.

"Forgive me," I say, aware again of my surroundings and wondering how a tall fluted glass filled with fizzing, bright yellow liquid has come to be in front of me on the table. Paula is engaged in finishing what looks like the same type of drink.

She dabs at her lips with a starched white napkin. "You completely disappeared into yourself. Are you okay? Is it the photo?"

"That?" I say, seeing that she is looking at the picture in the rectangle. "Not at all."

"So you don't recognize him," Anna says. "I think that's a blessing."

"Let me enlighten you," says Paula, pointing at the black-haired gentleman in the picture next to the likeness of Courtney, or should I say me. The notion is quite diverting, and I find myself struggling to keep my countenance.

"That," Paula continues, "is Frank. You were engaged to him. Two months before the wedding, you walked in on Frank cozying up to another woman. The woman who was designing your wedding cake," she says, raising an eyebrow, "as if infidelity weren't bad enough. Wes knew about it, but instead of telling you the truth, he agreed to lie for Frank. And Wes was supposed to be your closest male friend. Trouble is, he's been friends with Frank since high school and clearly made a choice between the two of you when push came to shove."

She regards me narrowly. "Any of this sound familiar?"

Indeed. For I know that sort of betrayal all too well. I can see myself back on Edgeworth's estate, watching as he emerges from the stables, smoothing a lock of hair from his face and brushing straw from his clothes. He is walking towards me but does not see me, and something makes me hesitate to make my presence known. And then a pretty young serving woman also emerges from the stables, her apron flecked with bits of straw, her hair, which tumbles from her cap, glinting like burnished copper in the sunlight.

She overtakes him, her hand reaching out for him, her smile confident as he turns to her. I am as still as can be, hiding behind a bush like a thief, heart pounding as I watch him stop her hand, then bring it to his lips. She colors deeply, clearly pleased with his attentions. He then hurries away, brushing bits of straw from his coat and giving his surroundings a furtive glance, for it is clear he would not want to be observed dallying with a servant. It is only when he disappears into the shrubbery and is well past me that I realize I have been holding my breath.

"Courtney? You do remember, don't you?" Paula's voice brings me back to the table and the picture of Frank and the bustle of waiters and diners and the clink of tableware and cutlery.

"Unhappily, it is a familiar tale."

"This is the first time I've seen you talk about it without tearing up," Anna says. "You've really turned a corner, sweetie."

I have not the heart to tell her that the story I have just heard is as removed from my own life as the woman I am impersonating. Instead, I venture a sip from the fluted glass. "Mmm. Champagne. And orange juice."

"At least there's something you remember," says Paula. "It's your favorite. At least for brunch." She signals to a waiter and points at her empty glass. "And mine."

"Do I generally take wine at such an early hour?"

Paula's brows contract. "And that's another thing. Amnesia I can understand. Confusion I get. But the way you talk? What's up with that? It's almost as if you were trying to sound like Keira Knightley. But without the English accent."

Anna gives Paula an exasperated look. "Do you have to be so blunt?"

Paula looks a little ashamed. "I didn't mean to be, sweetie," she says to me. "I'm just confused is all. And you know me; I say what I think. It's who I am. That's why you love me. I'm a truth-teller."

"And I'm a liar, I suppose," Anna says peevishly.

A second mimosa arrives for Paula, and she takes a sip. "No, you're just a nice person. And I'm not."

Anna smirks. "Which is why you love me."

"Don't push your luck," Paula says, at which Anna smacks her playfully, and Paula hooks her arm round Anna's neck. "You know I love you, darling."

I can't help but be affected by their obvious fondness for each other, despite the public display. Or perhaps here such manners are unexceptionable. Would that be so very disagreeable? To show whatever I feel whenever I feel it to whomever I feel it? Have I ever even imagined such freedom? Would that not be a little bit of heaven?

"And you love us, too," Paula says to me. "I can tell by that smile on your face. You may not remember us all that well, but you love us. And if not, you definitely will. I guarantee it."

Anna giggles. "Or your money back."

"But why you love Wes," Paula says, her manner more sober now, "I'm sure I don't know."

Anna sighs. "Give her a break. She doesn't remember."

I gasp. "Did I say I loved him? I was not—quite myself yesterday." Lord knows what I babbled when I took Dr. Menziger's pill.

"Don't be ridiculous," says Paula. "But you watch yourself with him. You may not remember how betrayed you felt, but we do."

"I thank you for your kind hints." I hope that my countenance does not betray my feelings, which are far more disordered by the ladies' disturbing reports of Wes than by anything they might say about Frank, a gentleman of whom I know nothing.

I think of Wes and how he looked as he slept on the chair beside my bed. Could a man with such an angelic countenance be capable of betraying a lady? Then again, what do I really know of him after such a short time? Did I not come to know and trust every nuance of Edgeworth's countenance? I would have given myself to him completely—and ruined myself forever.

"Finally," says Paula, as a huge, steaming platter of eggs and potatoes is placed before her. "I'm starved."

A platter just as large, and with food enough for three people, is placed before me, and another one before Anna. I am hungry to be sure, but this must be a joke.

Or perhaps not. For as I look round me at the other diners, I observe that almost everyone is served immense portions. From another table, a waiter removes half-eaten and discarded plates of food, most with enough still on them to make a generous meal. As neither Paula nor Anna betrays any surprise at the wastefulness, I can only conclude that such dining habits are considered unexceptionable.

"Courtney," says Anna, placing a hand on my arm, "you're not going to call Frank, too, are you?"

"Don't even think about it," says Paula, waving her fork for emphasis. "If I hear you went within ten yards of that lying, cheating narcissist, I'll give you a bigger concussion than you already have."

"I promise I shall do no such thing. Truly." I smile at them, and their countenances relax. "I can assure you that my life is confusing enough."

And that is no lie.

"Nothing confusing about it," says Paula. "All you have to remember is that this is what men do. They cheat. They lie. They stick together. So don't forget it the next time you need someone. Men are all the same. It's women who'll have your back."

Anna raises a hand. "Excuse me, I'm not saying

Courtney shouldn't be on her guard with Wes, but do we really want to make such a sweeping statement about half the human race?"

"Why do you think my mother divorced my father?"

"Well, it's not like you've sworn off all contact with the evil gender," Anna says, giving Paula a meaningful look.

"Don't start," says Paula with a warning edge in her voice. "And whose side are you on anyway?"

"Hers," says Anna. "And yours. Which is why I wish you weren't giving that—Michael person another chance."

"I told you not to bring that up." And then, to me, "Sweetie, I didn't say anything because you've got so much going on right now."

"And because she trusts him even less than I do."

Paula ignores Anna and addresses me. "He's completely over his ex, okay?"

Of course I have no idea of whom they are talking.

"What do you expect her to do?" says Anna. "Give you her blessing?" And then, to me, "She's seeing him tonight."

"Paula, I wish you a pleasant evening. And I thank you both for your kind hints."

Both ladies seem to be rendered speechless, Anna opening her mouth as if to say something, then closing it as if thinking better of it.

"Okay, then," Paula finally says, and downs the rest of her mimosa.

Nine

After announcing that breakfast is her treat and settling the bill with a shiny golden card which somehow serves as money—though the waiter gives it back to her after she signs the bill—Paula, along with Anna, extends her generosity by allowing me to sit quietly during the ride back to my rooms. "Quietly" is, however, a relative term, for music accompanies the ladies' chat during the drive. Somehow it seems that music can be had in any space, mobile or stationary, and without benefit of musicians. This is music of a sort which I have never heard, a rhythmic, pounding, repetitive sound with a man's voice that is not exactly singing, more like shouting some words that I cannot make out. Thankfully, Anna persuades Paula to soften the noise, and I am left to my own thoughts.

It is natural enough, if anything about my situation could be deemed natural, that I cannot think of the engagement of which they informed me as *my* engagement. Yet I cannot deny feeling almost injured, not by Frank, whom I do not know, but by Wes. My feelings are in all ways unaccountable. After all, I have known Wes little more than a day.

"This is what men do," Paula had said of Wes and Frank.

"This is what men do," said my mother to her

cousin Beatrice when I was but thirteen years old. It was wrong of me to listen to their conversation; indeed, I am sure they believed me asleep on the sofa, but I shall never forget the resignation in cousin Beatrice's voice as she spoke of how she had turned aside two maidservants for being with child and that she suspected her husband of fathering them.

"This is what men do," said my mother.

"Not Mr. Mansfield," said cousin Beatrice.

"Indeed, I would stake my life he does not," said my mother, and I imagine what she really meant was that she would stake his, "but it is an all-too-common tale, my dear. I shall never forget when I was but a young bride, and a particular friend had the sad truth thrust upon her. Her aunt—a lady of sterling character—urged her to bear with it, declaring that such dalliances were what we women must strive to endure, and indeed are blessings that preserve our sex from yearly confinements."

Recalling these words I see, for the first time—how did I not see it before—that what stopped Edgeworth from compromising my innocence was not, as I believed, his noble character. Or his respect for me. It was his inconstancy.

What else would have prevented him from taking me completely and making me his, body and soul, when I kissed him and held him so closely that I tremble still with the memory of it?

It was he who broke away, not I. He who said we must wait till I would make him the happiest of men, he who asked me, once again, to marry him. For I am sure that he, like all men, wished for an unsullied bride.

And it was I who was so frightened by my reckless behavior that I begged for a day or two to reflect quietly on this most important step.

And so I returned to my home and contemplated the words I had heard at my sister Clara's wedding, indeed at every wedding I had had the honor to attend, that marriage is "not by any to be enterprised, nor taken in hand, unadvisedly, lightly, or wantonly, to satisfy men's carnal lusts and appetites." That one should enter the state "reverently, discreetly, advisedly, soberly, and in the fear of God; duly considering the causes for which matrimony was ordained." One married for the "mutual society, help, and comfort, that the one ought to have of the other."

Yes, I desired to be a help and comfort to him, and that he should be a help and comfort to me. No, I would not marry him merely to satisfy my carnal lusts and appetites. But that I had those appetites I could not deny, and they frightened me. They had made me imprudent to the point of recklessness. And now they made me eager to marry him.

For had I not refused him before I knew I even had such feelings? I had disbelieved that a man who had loved before could be capable of a second attachment. I had doubted how this handsome, agreeable widower could possibly love again. And if he did love, then I wondered if he had ever really loved his wife, and thus if he could ever really love me.

Marriage, the service declares, was "ordained for the procreation of children." I knew not whether I had the courage to bear children, for I knew of too many women who had died in childbed, a fate as common as being with child. And being with child was the natural result of lying with a man. I feared the yearly confinements that were the lot of so many married ladies. My aunt Mansfield had nineteen children; the last took her life. My mother's brother had twelve. His wife lived. Even my mother, with her small family of three children, had had two more, their brief infant lives marked with gravestones in the churchyard.

But I loved Edgeworth, of that I was sure. *With this ring I thee wed, with my body I thee worship.* Any children that came of our union would be blessed by our love. I would risk everything for that love. And yes—I smiled inwardly—I would have Barnes be my emissary with Cook and her wise woman in the village who could make teas and potions that were indispensable to a lady, or so believed Barnes and Cook, whose conversation I overheard. I would avail myself of those potions and keep my family from an unreasonable increase.

And so, my answer ready, I mounted Belle and off we went. I imagined the surprise on Edgeworth's face when I appeared without any notice of my arrival. I pictured a smile of delight overspreading his countenance, like Darcy's, when I told him I was there to accept his offer. I imagined the feel of his arms around me when I kissed him to seal the bargain.

But it was I who was surprised, not he. I who found him with the copper-haired servant. I who rode back and wandered the lanes, ranting and crying out my grief so that I could return home to my mother and father with some semblance of composure in my bearing. I who lost all hope of happiness.

No, I will not dwell upon these memories.

*W*hen Paula's car stops in the street before my apartment, the ladies insist on seeing me upstairs and making sure I have everything I need. Anna urges me to lie down and rest.

"So what are your plans for the rest of the day?" says Paula, flopping on the bed next to me.

"I thought I might read."

Paula rises from her prone position and eyes the array of novels by Jane Austen on the table beside the bed. "There are other authors in the world, you realize."

Anna takes the chair next to the bed. "Don't start on her, Paula."

"I take it you are not fond of the lady?"

"Apparently," Paula says, perching on the arm of Anna's chair, "you don't remember me telling you how my high school English teacher shoved *Mansfield Park* down my throat and how I vowed never to read Jane Austen again."

"And you?" I say to Anna.

"I read *Northanger Abbey*, but I don't have time to read the other books. I barely have time to read what I'm supposed to read."

"Nevertheless," says Paula, "we both enjoyed Colin Firth when you forced us into a *Pride and Prejudice* marathon."

Anna giggles. "Yeah, and Matthew Macfadyen's pretty hot, too."

"In case you don't remember," Paula says, "your best friends are Philistines who prefer to have their great literature served up on the screen."

Anna smiles wryly. "Unless my boss is thinking of adapting it. I guess we're true loyalists to our calling."

"Yes," Paula adds, "our various employers should be proud."

Various employers. "Might I venture to ask how you are employed? Forgive me, but I do not remember."

"But of course you may, madam," Paula says, and Anna smacks her. "Ow."

"I'm a creative executive," Anna says, "and Paula's a set decorator."

"Ah." Thankfully, it sounds as if they have nothing to do with the Cyprian class.

"Which means," Paula says, "because from your blank expression I can tell you have no idea what we're talking about—which on the one hand I find alarming, and on the other hand makes you a refreshing novelty in this jaded movie town—that Anna presides over a realm known as development hell, in which books and screenplays are condemned to remain for at least as long as it took Jane Austen's works to turn into movies."

"Movies," I say, wondering what the word means and whether a screenplay is a sort of game.

Anna smiles. "Yes, but that would be purgatory rather than hell, as your description implies there is an end in sight, even one that is two hundred years in the future."

Paula says, "If I'm to judge by the permanent status of *Pride and Prejudice* in Courtney's DVD player, it appears that no wait is too long a wait for a Jane Austen movie. Right, darling?"

I nod like an idiot and smile at both of them. So the miraculous appearance of a *Pride and Prejudice* play in the glass box in my bed-chamber is known as a movie? How will I ever get by without a lexicon for all these words? It is one thing to feign memory loss; it is quite another to be without even a basic vocabulary in such a place.

"As for Paula," Anna says, "she spends her day overspending the production company's money on furniture and décor and making her minions schlep it around so that Elizabeth Bennet has a chair to sit on when that idiot Mr. What's-his-name-preacher proposes to her."

"Spoken like a true producer's spawn who lazes around feigning work at lunch and dinner meetings," says Paula.

"Excuse me," says Anna. "Some of us are actually planning to work the rest of this glorious Sunday cramming for a Monday morning meeting. Unlike someone else in this room, who—"

"Speaking of work," cuts in Paula, looking at me, "you cannot go into work tomorrow. You realize that, don't you? I mean, how are you going to function?"

I bolt up to a sitting position in bed. Anna puts her hand on my arm. "What is it, sweetie?"

"Did you say it was Sunday?"

Paula nods warily.

"Oh, dear. I have not been to church."

Paula raises an eyebrow. "When, might I ask, was the last time you stepped foot inside a church, unless it was for a wedding—" She chokes off the word "wedding." "Ouch," she says, glaring at Anna, "you don't have to kick me. Courtney, I'm an idiot."

"Do not trouble yourself. I am sure you meant to cast no aspersions on my religious faith."

"Jesus," says Paula. "You really need to rest. And don't even think about going into work tomorrow. I mean it."

"Of course," I say, curious about what "going into work" might mean and thrilled at the exotic possibilities. Never could I have imagined that the word "work" could mean anything for a lady other than sewing shirts for her husband, her sons, and the poor; basket embroidering; and making fringe. Or, in the most necessitous cases, going out as governess. "Might I ask—I was wondering—do I take pleasure in my work?"

Paula and Anna exchange skeptical glances and then both burst into laughter. "Sorry, darling," says Paula. "Don't worry, I'll call David and tell him."

"David."

"That spoiled-brat, no-talent hack you call your boss? You don't remember him either. Jesus. What are we going to do with you?"

"Stop it, Paula," Anna says, and in a more soothing tone to me, "It'll all come back soon enough. In the meantime"—she looks at Paula again—"the least you can do is let her recover in peace, without worrying about David or Frank or Wes. And maybe you should call Sandra, not David. She'll be much easier to deal with."

"No, I'll call David. He doesn't intimidate me."

"Whatever," says Anna.

I dare not ask who Sandra is, but evidently someone connected with my so-called boss. A pity that he appears to be of low character.

"Am I bound by contract to—David, is it?" I am yet to accustom myself to using someone's Christian name the moment he or she is mentioned or introduced, especially when that someone is a man—and in this case, my employer.

"You're kidding, right? Anna doesn't even have a contract. There's no such thing as job security in this town."

"So I may leave him whenever I wish."

Anna and Paula both raise eyebrows. "Sweetie," Anna says, "if that happens, I'll build an altar to that swimming pool where you hit your head and say prayers before it every day."

"Surely I can secure a more pleasing situation, can I not?"

Both ladies are saucer-eyed as they nod their heads in the affirmative. Paula opens her mouth as if to speak, but says nothing.

Anna laughs. "Congratulations, Courtney. You've rendered Paula speechless."

*P*resently the ladies take their leave, their parting orders being that I call them immediately if I need "anything, just say the word," along with their admonitions to "keep the phone charged," whatever that might mean. "You always forget," Anna explained. Or meant to explain.

It is good to be alone in my rooms—for indeed they are *my* rooms, though they are none of them very large. I pace out the three principal rooms—the bedchamber, the room with the table and chairs, and what Wes referred to as the "living room"—suddenly that term makes me double over with laughter. If there is a living room, does that mean there is a dying room as well? I suppose I would not find that comical if I were, in fact, dead, but if the dead cannot divert themselves with witticisms about death, then why bother dying at all? By this time I am laughing so hard that I must sit upon the sofa in the so-called living room, an area no larger than my mother's dressing closet. In fact, the entire breadth and depth of my apartment comprise a dwelling no larger than the drawing room at Mansfield House. Yet these meager rooms are wholly mine.

Living alone appears to be no uncommon state for an unmarried woman, for I gathered from listening to Anna and Paula's conversation in the car that each of them, although single, has her own private dwelling. This is truly singular. If you, dear Mary, could hear my words, you would accuse me of a pun.

Yes, these little rooms will suit me very well indeed. Here I need not fear my mother's feline tread and barbed remarks. Here no servant nor any other person may overhear my private conversations, if "private" could ever be a proper word for a state in which the only time I could be sure of being alone was when I went to bed. And even that I would have had to relinquish had I become Edgeworth's wife, for a wife may have her own bedchamber, but her husband shall always have admittance. Here, however, I may sleep and eat and read and amuse myself as I please, without obligation to any person other than myself. My self. My new, wholly unrecognizable self.

At least outwardly. Inwardly I am as I ever was.

No, that is not entirely the truth. I have a sense of hope that I have not felt in many weeks.

A sudden blast of music, a snatch of a song that sounds oddly familiar. Whence does it come? It stops, then begins again. Stops, then begins again. I locate the source of the music: It is the same object that Anna referred to as the phone. And the music—yes, of course—it is the music from the *Pride and Prejudice* movie. The music makes a few more stops and starts and then there is silence.

Yes, my situation is in many ways an agreeable one. To what would I look forward at home but an endless vista of days and nights sewing with Mama in the drawing room, listening to the ticking of the clock and the settling of the house as yet another night draws on, devoid of peace, and with little sleep? Though I do miss my father. And Mary. How shall I do without my dear papa and my dearest friend in the world? How shall they do without me? Though I imagine that if I am here, taking Courtney's place, then does it not follow that Courtney must be there, taking mine? What a notion! However, the only possibility is that she *was* taking my place rather than *is* taking my place, for indeed if I am now almost two hundred years after the time I left behind, then anyone alive in 1813 has long since ceased to be. The thought makes me almost dizzy. For I cannot return, that is clear. How can I go back to what is now dead? Yes, dead—and that means Papa, and Mary, and Edgeworth, and Mama, and Barnes, and Belle, and every friend I ever had. All dead.

My eyes fill with tears at the thought of Papa in his grave, everyone who ever mourned him long since dead. Ashes to ashes. Dust to dust. Long gone they may be, but to me they were alive just two days ago. It is like my old nursemaid's story of Oisin. Could it be that like Oisin, I am in the eternal land of Tir na n-Og, where three hundred years passed without his even feeling it? Perhaps then, Niamh of the Golden Hair will allow me, like Oisin, to return home. And I, like he, will be aged and withered the moment my feet touch the ground.

Not the ending I would wish for my story, however.

No, I prefer the comfort of another ending, one that I know well. And so I remove the copy of *Sense and Sensibility* from the bookcase. How lovely it is that the treasures that kept me from running mad in those dark days after breaking faith with Edgeworth are here right now to keep me strong.

If there is indeed an enchanted land like Tir na n-Og, in which one loses all sense of time and place, then such a land exists within the pages of *Sense and Sensibility*. And so it happens that when at last I emerge from the pages of this book, somehow the day has slipped away from me. I stand and stretch, moving towards the bedchamber window with its ugly exterior bars. Yet that ugliness is eclipsed by not only the orange and pink glow of sunset, but also by a brilliant display of lights, as if hundreds of candles are illuminating the windows in the houses on the opposite side of the lane, and beyond them, millions of tiny lights dot the hillside like constellations of diamonds.

What a wondrous place this is. A glorious, bejeweled city. There is so much light in the streets and hills that I can scarce make out the stars in the darkening sky.

The music from *Pride and Prejudice* starts and stops again, stops and starts. This had occurred several times while I was reading, but I easily ignored it to return to Elinor and Marianne. I look at the phone, which is the source of the music, and within its face is a picture of the actor who played Mr. Darcy! Atop his image is a small box with the words: "Wes—Answer?—Ignore?"

Wes?

Answer? Ignore? Answer what? Ignore what?

Before I can contemplate this mystery any further, the music stops, and the phone darkens.

So much the better, for I would rather remain blanketed in the contentment of *Sense and Sensibility*, contemplating the happiness of Elinor and meditating on how Marianne finds herself loving Colonel Brandon with her whole heart, than worry about the workings of an incomprehensible, and frankly quite annoying, object.

Besides, I am hungry. There being no servant, I will have to prepare something myself. I do not even know if there is a kitchen in this house, and I have seen no chimneypiece, no grate, no coal scuttle.

I venture into the room with the table and chairs in my stockinged feet and open cabinets and drawers, one after another. Plates, forks, glasses, bowls, boxes, jars. Nothing that resembles food.

On a whim, I pull on the long glossy handle of the huge white rectangular box that stands beside the wall of drawers and cupboards. I peek inside at an illuminated interior, cool air bathing my face. There are racks which are empty except for a sad-looking head of lettuce long past its prime and a few containers with who knows what inside them. At least I have discovered a larder, bare though it may be.

Ah. There is an upper door as well. Frigid air issues from the interior, refreshing upon my skin.

A giant, frosty bottle of something called Absolut. A jar, pliable as paper, of something called Cherry Garcia. I open it, dip in a finger, and taste. It is a delightful variety of ices, sweet with chewy cherries and bits of what tastes like chocolate except that it is solid and much sweeter. Must find a spoon.

Pounding on the door. A muffled voice. "Courtney? Are you there? It's Wes. If you're there, please open the door."

The pounding continues till I open the door and he stands there, fist raised to pound again and a befuddled look on his face. "Sorry. Did I scare you? I've been calling and calling and then I saw your car outside and—"

A stray curl has fallen onto his forehead, and his spectacles have slipped down his nose. His eyelashes are long and thick, and his eyes are bluer than they look behind the spectacles.

"You all right?" he says.

I remember that I am supposed to be on my guard with this man and force coolness into my tone. "I am indeed, sir."

"I was worried when you didn't pick up the phone. And so is Paula. And Anna. I've heard from both of them, and they said they called and emailed and texted and nothing. The only thing that made them seem to feel better about it was that you hadn't returned my calls or texts either." He smiles wryly. "After that, we just traded messages in which I suggested to Paula that perhaps you might not remember how to use the phone or the computer, and then she freaked out and was like, well we'd better call Suzanne, because this goes beyond common memory loss, and I said, wait a minute, I'm gonna go over there and check out the situation, and she said, no way, but then in her last message she practically gave me her permission—but without saying so—because she's in Hermosa and Anna's tied up with work and it would be a while before they could get here and —well, here I am."

"Upon my honor, they were here not more than a few—perhaps more than a few hours ago, but it cannot be so very long."

"Seven hours, according to your friends, and with your accident and all, they wanted to check in. I did, too."

Should I ask him inside? He looks so forlorn, so much aware of having no right to be here that I cannot be rude to him.

"Will you not come inside?"

He takes one of the chairs at the table, without my inviting him to sit and without any apparent awareness of his deficient manners.

"Are you hungry?" he says, and then with a wry grin, pointing to the larder, "I don't imagine you've restocked the fridge. Not that your idea of restocking means there's ever the makings of a decent meal."

He satisfies his own curiosity by peeking quickly into the larder. "Why have a fridge, I wonder? It only takes up room. How about I take you out? I'm starved."

Out at night. Unchaperoned. With a gentleman. A single gentleman. Perhaps not even a gentleman at all. And certainly not my brother, or my father, or even a cousin. Unthinkable.

"I shall be but a moment."

Ten

I no sooner retrieve the oddly shaped, orange, many-buckled reticule that Anna had thrust into my hands and proclaimed as my "bag" when we went out to dine than there is pounding at the door again.

"Courtney? You there?" A man's voice.

I glance at Wes to see if he recognizes it, and his eyes narrow. "What's he doing here?" His manner is accusatory.

"Who? Who is that?"

The pounding continues. "Courtney—open up."

"So you didn't call him," Wes says, relief softening his countenance. "I'll take care of this."

Wes opens the door to the black-haired gentleman from the picture Paula had shown me. Despite the fact that he was pounding on the door a moment ago, he lounges against the door frame as if he had merely whispered a command for it to open. Black hair falls becomingly over his forehead. His complexion is fair and flawless, and his dark, almost black eyes sparkle as they appraise me. His full lips tilt in a smile that is charming in its lack of symmetry, one side of his mouth turning up higher than the other.

"Slim and gorgeous, I see," he says, his voice rich and smooth as honey. He flashes a contemptuous glance at Wes. "And not at all neglected."

"What do you want?" Wes says, his tone icy.

Frank ignores him. "Apparently, Paula's so desperate about not being able to track you down that she held her nose and called me, wondering if I'd heard from you. Which is how I found out you hurt your head. You are okay, aren't you?" His eyes are soft, and he reaches for my hand. I allow him to take it, and he strokes the palm with his thumb, sending a thrill through my body. "I was scared there for a minute."

"You can leave now, Frank," Wes snaps. "She's fine."

Frank gazes at me, his eyes large and liquid. "Is that what you want?" Can this truly be the man who used Courtney ill? His manner is gentle, and there is so much goodness in his countenance.

"It is what you want, isn't it?" says Wes. I tear my eyes from Frank, and Wes has an almost frightened look about him.

"Hey," Frank says, "I'm talking to Courtney."

I clear my throat. "You have me at a disadvantage, sir."

"Sir?" Frank looks at Wes with raised eyebrows.

"If you will be so kind as to let me continue, sir. I do not know—I do not remember you. I recognize you only from a picture that Paula showed me. Therefore, I have no reason to wish you either here or gone. Do forgive me if my honest disclosure causes you any pain."

Frank opens his mouth as if to speak, and at first not a sound issues from it. "This is a joke, right?"

He looks at Wes as if for guidance, but Wes's gaze is stony.

"How do you not remember me?"

"Hard to imagine not being the center of a woman's world anymore, isn't it," says Wes.

"Like you would know," Frank says. "You're too busy chasing after my relationship to have any of your own."

Wes's face reddens. "Get out."

"Last time I checked, this was Courtney's apartment, not yours."

"I mean it, Frank."

"What are you gonna do? Throw me out? No, that's not the way you do things. Nothing so direct as that. No, you pour poison into everyone's ears till half my friends won't even speak to me anymore."

Wes sputters, almost laughing. "You're the one who cheated on her."

"So you say."

"Oh, please. Don't tell me you're denying this now. Isn't it a little late for that?"

"I never said I slept with her."

"She saw you!" says Wes.

"Saw me what? Saw me talking to the cake woman? Saw me touch her arm?"

Frank's words have a chilling familiarity to them. Could it be that what I saw Edgeworth do with the servant was as innocent as what Frank is claiming for his own actions? I never even confronted Edgeworth with what I saw; he had no idea I was cowering behind a bush as he kissed the hand of the auburn-haired woman. No. Impossible. What possible propriety could attach to what I saw Edgeworth do? His very countenance was evidence of his guilt as he furtively glanced around to see if anyone was about, as he brushed straw from his hair and clothing. And how the woman reached for him, almost possessively, as a lover would reach for her beloved. As I would reach for Edgeworth. No. He was as guilty as he appeared, for it was Mary's letter which erased any doubt, Mary's letter which told me of her servant who was with child. Mary's letter which sent me on that reckless ride with Belle through the woods, that ride that sent me into darkness and oblivion—and this.

"Courtney?" It is Wes. He and Frank are looking at me questioningly.

"Did I ever say I slept with her?" Frank says to me.

"If you were sensible of the impropriety of such language, you would not behave in such an ungentleman-like manner."

"I didn't, did I? You just assumed what you wanted to assume, called off the wedding, and told everyone I was scum."

"Upon my word, this is beyond anything. If you cannot speak to me in a civil manner, then please have the goodness to leave."

"You knew I wasn't ready to get married."

Wes steps in between the two of us. "Did you hear her tell you to leave?"

Frank moves as if to shove Wes, then looks as if he thinks better of it, simply ignoring him and addressing me. "And the jealousy. Always the jealousy. That's what ended this, not me."

I do not believe I am jealous by nature, but what I saw that day on Edgeworth's estate put me in a fury the likes of which I have never known.

"I'm sorry, okay?" says Frank. "I messed up. I was in the wrong."

Wes snorts. "Well, that's a first."

Frank ignores him and puts his hand on my arm. "But I didn't sleep with her."

Wes throws up his hands. "You're actually incapable of a real apology, aren't you."

"This is between Courtney and me," says Frank. And to me, "Could we talk alone for a minute?"

I look up at him, and in his countenance there is so much eagerness to be absolved of whatever he has done that I feel a little tug at my heart.

"No way," says Wes. "We're leaving, Frank, even if you won't."

How did I find myself pulled between these two gentlemen? Suddenly, the heat in the apartment is stifling; the white bodice sticks to my skin. "I must go. Fresh air." I move towards the door.

"I'm going with you," Wes says.

"So am I," says Frank.

"As you wish. Only do be civil to one another for two minutes together."

As we emerge into the street, the dazzling lights of the city provide a welcome distraction. And what a variety of light there is, from huge globes supported on tall poles lining the pavement to the blazing doorway lamps and illuminated interiors which are so bright that I can see people going about their business through the large panes of glass. And then we reach the main thoroughfare, where there are shops and dining establishments, and the light is even more impressive, the prominent signs of daytime claiming even more notice when illuminated.

Some loud whispering between the gentlemen diverts my attention. I cannot hear it all, but Frank's "the way she talks, it's like that stupid movie she's always watching" and Wes's "it's the concussion" tell me all I need or want to know. If gossip prevents them from further antagonism, so much the better for all concerned. But I really must endeavor to speak more like the people in this land, if I can learn to do so.

We stop before a dark red, dimly lit building nestled between a place called Ray's Cleaners, which proclaims its name in brightly glowing tubelike letters in the window, and another named Acme Taqueria, whose sign is less garish and from which a tantalizing aroma of exotic food issues.

"I need a drink," Frank says, motioning me towards the door of the red building, which is also red.

"I thought we were going to eat," says Wes, looking to me as if for confirmation.

"Just a quick one," says Frank, and opens the red door for me with a flourish.

Curious, I walk through the door and into another world, all plush and red and black and gold with gold fringe hanging from overhead lampshades, candle-like (but certainly candle-less) lights glowing from cherubic wall sconces, and sofas and deep armchairs everywhere, all richly covered in red velvet or brocade. The music inside is loud but pleasanter than the music in Paula's car, though as foreign in sound. The singer this time is a woman, with a haunting, compelling voice.

"Hey, Courtney," a tall man, with longish dark-brown hair oddly streaked with light-blond locks and a purple-and-gold depiction of a dragon painted onto his bare forearm, calls out to me from behind a tall bar backed with rows of sparkling bottles filled with brown and amber and green and gold liquids. He hands a glass to another man seated before the bar.

How odd for a gentleman, and most likely not a gentleman at all, but a waiter, to greet me in such a familiar manner, and without my acknowledging him first. Perhaps he is a close friend or even a brother to Courtney? I suppose I should greet him, lest I raise even more speculation. Yet that painting on his arm—perhaps it is a tattoo, like the ones I have read about in a travel diary. What sort of company does Courtney keep, and what sort of person must she be?

"Good evening," I say, hoping my smile is polite but not too encouraging.

Apparently, my hope is a vain one, for the painted man emerges from behind the bar, strides over to me, and envelops me in a hug. "Darling, your friends told me what happened. Thank God you're okay." His accent is more familiar than those I have heard thus far, perhaps English, though not genteel.

The man whispers in my ear, "So when are you going to dump that loser for good and marry me? You told me he was history, darling."

I feel my face burning, and I extricate myself from his grip. Most certainly not a brother. "Upon my word, I—"

"I know, a drink," he says, grinning broadly. "It's on me. Loser buys his own. So does the other one. You'd better hope I don't start telling tales to the girls." He's off to the bar, and so are we, it seems.

I find myself seated before the bar on a high-legged stool with a plush red seat, flanked by the two gentlemen. I learn the waiter's name, Glenn, when Wes greets him. Glenn is none too friendly to Wes, but Frank receives only a cold glance and a terse "eight" from Glen, which is apparently the price of Frank's drink. Eight shillings for a drink sounds rather steep, though what Frank extracts from his pocket is a bank-note in the amount of ten dollars with "United States of America" emblazoned on the top. I have long been curious about the former colonies, but never did I imagine anything like this.

"Your money's no good here," Glenn says to me with a wink as he places before me a large, somewhat triangular-shaped glass with a pedestal. In it is a colorless, slightly cloudy liquid with what looks like four large green olives skewered onto a thin stake of wood. I raise the glass and take a tentative sniff, and my nose clears from the fumes and my mouth waters, though I have never had such a drink in my life.

I take a tiny sip of the icy liquid—delicious. Strong and salty and tasting of olives and bracing. Perfect for the hot weather, which, now that I put my mind to it, is not hot at all inside this establishment. It is, in fact, strangely cool in comparison to the outdoors. I take a bigger sip. Glenn raises his own glass to me, and I raise mine to him and take a drink. I could easily become accustomed to this manner of refreshment.

And then I am thunderstruck. Am I actually sitting inside a public house, a gentlewoman in a public house, accompanied by two gentlemen who are neither brother nor cousin nor father, but most likely members of the lower orders and not gentlemen at all? Not that entering a public house with genteel male relations would be any less scandalous, but this is highly improper.

"Easy now," Wes says, pointing to my drink. "I don't know that vodka and a concussion is the wisest combination."

"Vodka." I savor the word on my tongue. And drink some more.

Frank lounges next to me, leaning on the bar and taking long swallows from a long-necked, brown glass bottle. "So. You don't hate me anymore?"

"Does it signify? Apparently, you and Court—rather, you and I—had a lucky escape from what all parties agree would have been a most imprudent marriage."

"Courtney, you're out of control with this weird talking. I know you hit your head and all, but you've got to stop watching those movies."

"I thank you for your kind hints."

Frank, who has put the bottle to his lips, sputters with laughter. "Concussion, my ass. You're not fooling anyone. Except maybe him." He juts his chin towards Wes.

"I have not been accustomed to such language as this," I say, and start laughing myself. Only Lady Catherine de Bourgh could speak such words and keep her countenance.

"I knew it," says Frank.

"Knew what, pray tell?"

"That you're having a little fun at everyone's expense." He brings his face close to mine and gazes intently into my eyes. I can feel his warm breath on my lips. "And that you don't hate me. You don't hate me, do you."

"Of course I do not, I—"

He brushes a strand of hair from my forehead, and the touch sends a thrill through my body. "Everyone deserves a second chance, don't you think?"

His lips move so close to mine that they are practically touching. And then he does touch my lips with his own, so lightly and softly that I cannot summon the wherewithal to push him away. And then the kiss becomes more urgent, more intoxicating, and I am drunk with it, and when he runs the tips of his fingers over the edge of my jaw, the touch instantly brings me back to another day, and I see and feel myself with him as he touches me in the same way, kisses me in the same way. And I am kissing his lips, tasting his mouth, lying with him in bed, his body stretched over mine, his skin against my skin, his leg against my bare leg. And I know with all my soul that this is not me, but it is me. My body, this body, knows that this is a memory. A memory as vivid as any memory I have ever had before. Yet it is a memory of something that never happened. It is Courtney's memory, not mine. I know not how such a thing can be; yet it is as real as any sensation I have experienced since awakening yesterday morning. How can I remember having been with this man? And in a manner far more compromising than anything I ever did with Edgeworth.

My face burns—and I am pushing him away. Almost without volition I scramble off the chair, away from Frank, away from Wes and the shocked look in his eyes, and I run towards a glowing sign on the other side of the room that says "Ladies." Perhaps it is a sanctuary, a drawing room.

"Hey!" I hear behind me. Frank's voice. I reach the door, a padded door, red of course, and pull on the handle. Inside is a wide mirror to my right with a row of wash-hand basins beneath it. To my left is a series of doors that do not reach all the way to the floor, or to the ceiling. I fiddle with the handles on one of the wash-hand basins until a cool stream of water flows into the bowl. I wet my face.

What have I done? How could I let a man kiss me, and in public? A man I do not even know. I who never kissed a man till Edgeworth, the man I loved, and we would have raised a scandal had anyone seen us in the woods that day, though he asked me to marry him. Yet I let Frank kiss me. And I feel it again, his lips on mine, his body lying on top of mine, and my arms pressing him closer to me, my hands running down the length of his torso, his—dear God, what is happening to me? What sort of woman have I become? Have I longed for a new life and had my dearest wish fulfilled, have I been transported somehow, transmigrated somehow, into this body, only to learn that I am an unmarried woman who has actually bedded a man she would not marry, that I am a woman who frequents public houses with men, who imbibes liquor and does not attend church, a woman who is godless and profligate and fallen?

The realization that I have inherited all this sin almost takes my breath away. What has become of me? How will I live with myself? And how will I ever face that man again? I must get out of here. I cannot look at him. My breath comes fast and hard, and I have to grip the edge of the wash-hand basin to avoid stumbling back against the row of doors behind me. I may be mad. I may be fallen. But I shall not faint.

"You okay?"

I hear myself gasp. I look up, and in the mirror's reflection is a young lady who has just emerged from one of the three-quarter doors behind me.

Her skin is the color of chocolate laced heavily with cream.

"Oh, it's you, Courtney," she says, smiling her delight.

Oh, dear. Another person I am supposed to know but whose countenance is wholly unfamiliar to me.

"You don't remember me, do you. I'm Deepa. You were at my party a couple of months ago?"

Her accent is like that of the actress from the *Pride and Prejudice* movie. Could she be from my country?

She frowns, a concerned, good-natured sort of frown. "We talked for quite a while, actually. Hey, you okay? You don't look okay."

I suppose the sour countenance looking back at me from the mirror must be the opposite of what "okay" means.

"I assure you I am," I say, but that is all I can get out, for my eyes begin to fill and my mouth quivers with the effort to keep back the tears.

Deepa pulls a paper handkerchief from a brown spangled reticule, sparkly bracelets jangling, and hands it to me. There are rings on almost every one of her fingers, and from her ears clear globes studded with diamonds dangle from the thinnest wires imaginable.

I take the handkerchief and wipe my eyes, and she looks upon me kindly with large brown eyes as she hands me another one. Her hair is shiny black and cut short, with jagged strands over arched black brows.

"You were unhappy the last time we met as well. And I was in a bit of a strop, too, I might add. All those people coming up to me and telling me how sorry they were about my divorce. When all I wanted to do was breathe a big sigh of relief. Though I must say, you and I ended up making each other laugh." She gazes at me searchingly. "You really don't remember, do you? You'd had a lot to drink, but I didn't think you were that drunk."

"Do forgive me," I say. "I am told I have a—concussion, and there is much I do not remember."

"No way. What happened?"

"I hit my head in a pool, I'm told."

"And you don't remember that either?" She regards me kindly. "But it'll all come back, won't it?"

I shrug.

"Hey, some things aren't worth remembering, believe me."

At that moment, there is pounding on the door, which then opens slightly. Wes peeks in and looks sheepish when he sees that there is another lady here beside me. "Oh, hi, Deepa. Sorry, but I just wanted to see if—Courtney, you okay?"

I can hardly bring myself to meet his eyes after what he saw me do with Frank, who, in that moment, strolls in and leans against the wall as if he has every right to intrude upon our sanctuary.

Deepa gives me a significant look, and my face burns. "Like I said, some things aren't worth remembering."

How much does she know about my connection with Frank?

"You do realize," she says to the gentlemen, hand on hip, "that this is a women's bathroom?"

Frank smirks. "I hadn't noticed."

Wes reaches for me. "Courtney, let's get out of here."

I am so stunned that he would still wish to escort me home that I cannot even speak.

"You sure, Courtney?" says Deepa. "I'm happy to take you home."

"Is that what you want?" Wes says to me.

All I know is that I want to get away from Frank and those—memories, or whatever they are. And from the disappointment in Wes's eyes.

"I would like to leave with Deepa."

"Pity," Frank says, eyeing me as if I were a tray of rout cakes. Then he has the assurance to take my hand and give me a soul-searching "trust me" look as he takes his leave.

"I'll call you," is all Wes says, his hands at his sides, his attitude that of one who would like to stop me but knows he is helpless to do anything but leave.

The door closes behind the two men. Deepa arches an eyebrow. "You're not still with Frank?"

"Apparently, I ended our engagement. I believe I found him with another lady."

She nods and purses her lips. I can see that she is not in the least surprised by this intelligence.

"You said I was unhappy when last we met. May I ask, was I unhappy about Frank?"

"Understatement. You said you were tired of his ceaseless flirting with other women, which had got much worse lately, and which, I might add, he was putting on a fine exhibition of at my party. I asked you why you put up with it. And you know what you said? That Frank was under a lot of pressure. And that you were so overwhelmed with wedding plans, you simply couldn't deal with anything else."

"What sort of woman would tolerate such conduct?"

"Hey, I'm not one to point the finger. I put up with that cheating sod of an ex I married and divorced. Only thing I can say in his favor is that he left me very well off. Though I was the one who left him. Best thing I ever did."

I admire her confidence, the same confidence all the women of this time seem to possess, with all their talk of self-will and marriage and divorce and independence, as if the whole world has been laid out for them to manage and rearrange as they wish. I cannot imagine any woman of my acquaintance even thinking, let alone speaking, in such a manner. I'll wager even Mary Wollstonecraft would be rendered mute in their presence.

Deepa regards me kindly. "So you're with Wes now?"

"I am not; I mean—"

"Hey, don't look so shocked."

"He is a friend." I can feel my face crimson.

"I don't know him very well," says Deepa. "He's a friend of a friend. But he always seemed like a decent guy. Sweet, you know? And easy on the eyes."

"I do like him. Very much. But my friends Paula and Anna say he's not to be trusted. That he, in fact, lied to prevent my finding out that Frank was . . ."

"Ah."

"But I do not remember any of it."

"Considering what you've been through," she says, "a good memory would be unpardonable."

I cannot help but smile at this quote from my favorite book.

"But you're sure it's true?" she says.

"I have no reason to doubt their word. Yet he is so very kind and"—I give her a wry smile—"one does not know what to think."

"So why don't you just ask him why he lied?"

The idea of confronting Wes is so unthinkable, so contrary to everything I have ever been taught about social intercourse, that I cannot even respond. Yet here I am, having only just made Deepa's acquaintance—though she says we have met before—and I cannot help but marvel at how easily I unburdened myself to her about my supposed past with Wes and Frank. I have never before been so unguarded with anyone of my acquaintance. Even Mary, whom I regard as a sister, never heard a word of what had passed between Edgeworth and me. Not that I had any mistrust of her; quite the contrary. It simply never occurred to me to speak of such things to her. The fact that she was his sister was an added obstacle, but in truth I would have kept silent even were she not his relation.

As for Wes, I hardly know the gentleman; questioning him about the past would be an impertinent freedom. And he has been so kind to me that I want to believe he is honorable. He must have had his reasons for doing what he did. Besides, this is not my life. If I do not remember Courtney's history—save that memory of Frank, if that is indeed what it was and not some wild fancy—then how real is it to me?

I meet Deepa's eyes. "That is out of the question."

"Okay then," she says, opening her reticule and taking out a comb, which she runs through her glossy black hair. "Then how about this for an idea? Something to take your mind off those two. Come with me to the club. A little music, a little dancing, a change of scenery—I promise you it will be excessively diverting."

She winks at me, and my heart lightens. A dance.

I wonder what a ball would be like in this strange land. "I am much obliged to you for your kindness, but I am hardly dressed for a dance." I regard the white trousers and sheer white bodice over the pale pink one that I have been wearing all day.

"Nonsense. You look gorgeous."

Deepa rummages in her brown spangled reticule. "All you need is a little lipstick." She produces a shiny silver tube, which she uncaps and twists to reveal a cone of a sparkly pink substance. Without further ado, she applies the pink substance to my lips. She is so close that I can smell peppermint on her breath and a sweet floral perfume on her skin. Her eyelashes are thick and black and curled; now that I think of it, I have noticed similar eyelashes on Paula and Anna; I believe it is the effect of some sort of cosmetic.

"And some mascara," she says, producing a longer tube that is dark blue with a golden cap. She unscrews it, and the cap is a wand with a bristly spiral at one end, coated with a black viscous substance. "Look off to your right. That's it; don't close your eyes." And she's applying the bristles to my eyelashes. She surveys her work and smiles broadly, revealing a dimple in one cheek. *Regard. Tu es très belle.*

Sure enough, I do look pretty. Or at least the blond, dark-lashed woman staring back at me with shiny, sparkly pink lips does.

Eleven

When Deepa and I emerge from the public house into the fresh air, I am suddenly sensible of how strong was the drink I had. No wonder, as I have had almost nothing to eat since breakfast.

Her car is sleek and black and shiny, and the first thing I notice when I take my seat is a picture of what appears to be a Hindu goddess in a stand before the front glass.

"You are from India?" I ask, hoping my question is not impertinent.

Deepa glides her car smoothly into the illuminated street. "My grandparents came from India. But my parents were born in London, as was I. I am now, however, as American as you."

American? I, an American. That is diverting.

"My parents still haven't come to terms with it. They're very English, you know. And these barbaric Americans will never live up to their standards. No offense," she says, smiling.

"There is none, I can assure you."

We arrive at a place that must indeed be the public assembly where the dance is to be held; there are young people clustered in groups outside the building, men and women talking, laughing, and smoking thin white tubes of tobacco—the women smoking as well as the men. Shocking indeed, yet the smell of the smoke is almost intoxicating. I find myself slowing down to take in the scent and even imagining myself smoking. Except that I would never do such a thing. How very odd.

None of the ladies or gentlemen is dressed for a ball, which I half expected to be the situation when Deepa insisted that my own attire was not improper. Nevertheless, it is shocking indeed to imagine a ball where women are in trousers or tiny skirts, bare-legged and most with wholly bare arms, and where the men are still without coats and neckcloths. The only indication that this is an evening party is in the abundance of spangled and glittery trimmings on many of the women's bodices; indeed, some of them are fashioned wholly of shiny or glittery stuff. And there is an abundance of sparkling jewelry.

That this assembly will certainly be like no other I have had the honor of attending is further reinforced by the pulsating, pounding rhythm—I cannot even venture to call it music—which can be heard before we even open the doors, or, shall I say, before the two solicitous men who preside at the entrance, and who greet Deepa and me as if we are royalty, open the thick black double doors for us.

We enter the assembly rooms to a crush of people and a deafening, rhythmic roar which penetrates my skin and vibrates my very bones. My fingers tingle; my chest and stomach quiver. Though my understanding tells me I should be frightened by such a cacophony, in truth it is strangely enticing and makes me want to dance in a way I have never even thought of dancing, though when we advance farther into the vast room and near the area where people are turning and gyrating in a manner that I imagine must approximate dancing, a cold stone of fear settles in my chest at the very thought of being so audacious as to stand up in this crush and attempt to move in such a manner. I am in no way equal to it.

Deepa grabs my hand and maneuvers us through the crowd to a long bar behind which are rows and rows of bottles, even more than those displayed in the public house where Glenn presides. "Have whatever you like," Deepa shouts into my ear, "it's on me." And then she lets go of my hand and disappears into the crowd, leaving me at the bar, where I am jostled by the throng and swept into their wake until I somehow find myself in the center of a circle of gyrating dancers, whose concentration on their rhythmic movements is so intense, and who seem so unaware of my presence, that soon I am sensible of my own limbs almost emulating their motions in concert with the pulsing beat. I am moving in a manner I have never moved before, hips and knees bouncing of their own volition. And then the gentleman opposite me meets my eyes and gestures with his hand to come closer, a flirtatious smile on his lips, and I am suddenly so mortified that for a moment I cannot move at all, let alone commence with this nondancing sort of dance. It is bad enough to make a display of myself alone, but to find myself dancing with a man to whom I have not even been introduced?

What is happening to me?

I somehow manage to bow my head to him and turn back towards the bar, where I spy a long shapely hand with many rings waving to me, and I see that Deepa is now behind the bar, smiling at me.

Deepa, a server of drinks? Yet apparently in this country, in this time, a server of drinks must be an unexceptionable situation for a woman of influence who wears diamonds in her ears.

"What can I get you?" she shouts at me over the din of the pounding music.

I am debating whether or not to indulge in another glass of vodka when she puts her hand out as if to stop my thoughts and then puts her lips to my ear. "I know what you should have. Give me a minute," she says, and then disappears behind a door that literally is built into the shelves of bottles and completely hidden from view.

The hidden door opens, and in slips Deepa again, a tall glass of pink liquid in her hand, which she places before me with a flourish. "Thank you," I say, my words swallowed up in the wall of sound, and take a sip. Raspberry, strawberry, lemon? Whatever it is, it is delicious indeed. Sweet and tart and astonishingly refreshing. Instantly I am full of energy and life. Deepa smiles.

When I finish the lovely pink concoction, Deepa motions for me to follow her. She lifts up a panel at the end of the bar and emerges from behind it, then waves to me. Staying as close behind her as possible, we weave through the crowd and past dancers gyrating before a stage on which are now musicians, and a female singer with long red hair cut in jagged edges over her forehead, clad in a short-sleeved, tight black bodice which ends well above her exposed navel, which is pierced with a glittering jewel, and impossibly snug black trousers which sit shockingly low on her hips. Her voice is a seductive wail. The other musicians are young men, all very thin and in tight, low-sitting trousers. One of the musicians, however, is completely bare-chested, his glistening torso and arms encircled with what looks like thorny stems painted in green and black. I have never before seen a half-naked man, let alone one upon a public stage, and I cannot take my eyes off him. He looks as if he revels in the attention as he thrusts his pelvis into the low-slung instrument which hangs from a studded black strap over his shoulder. I do not realize I am simply standing still and staring at him, no doubt with my mouth open like an unfledged bird, until Deepa shouts into my ear, "Are you all right?"

I feel my face burn with shame, and Deepa grabs my arm and continues to steer me through and finally outside of the crowd, beyond which is a door that she pushes open, and all at once we are outside the building and away from the pounding noise.

"Thank you," I say, attempting a feeble smile.

"You looked a bit overwhelmed. Are you feeling ill? Shall I take you home?"

"Thank you, no. I am well."

Her eyes search my face. "What is it, then? You can tell me. Really."

"You are very kind."

"If you don't want to talk, that's okay, too. I know we haven't known each other all that long. But I like you. And your ability to make me laugh at that disaster of a party I had two months ago was very welcome, believe me. So if you ever need a friend . . ."

I look into her large brown eyes, and I know that I can trust her. Strange as it may be, this absolute stranger, this Indian/English/American woman whom I have only just met, is someone that I know I can trust.

But how can I put into words what I feel? What can I say that will sound in any way rational to her? I think of the half-naked man on the stage, my memories of Frank which are not my memories at all, my letting him kiss me not an hour ago, my waking up as someone entirely not myself . . .

"It is just that I—I do not know who I am anymore. I have conducted myself in a manner that is wholly unfamiliar to me. And I do not know that you, or anyone, can help me."

Deepa regards me kindly. "We've all done things that give us pause. Myself included."

"I am just so confused."

"Well, you did hit your head."

"This has nothing to do with a concussion, I assure you."

I wish I could tell her of my true situation, without dancing around the matter. I drain the rest of the drink from the glass in my hand.

I pause for a moment, then say, "Deepa, do you believe in reincarnation?"

I cannot believe I have just blurted that out. It must be the drink.

Deepa laughs. "Where did that come from?"

"Forgive me. That was impertinent, and I am most ashamed."

"Whoa, don't go all Jane Austen on me. Not that I don't love the girl, but hey, I said I'd be a friend if you needed one. Which by my definition means you get to ask me about what I believe or don't believe. And by the way, the answer is yes. But may I ask to what these questions tend, as Mr. Darcy said?"

I smile. Could she have said anything to put me more at ease? "I was asking because I know someone who—what I mean is . . . Deepa, what if someone remembered having another life, but didn't just remember the other life? I mean, what if that person thought he *was* the person from the other life?"

"And this person, he . . . is a friend of yours?"

I do not know what to say. I do not wish to lie to Deepa, but neither do I wish to have her look at me as if I am insane.

"It's okay. I won't think your friend is crazy. I wouldn't think it even if he were a she. Or even if she were you." She smiles, but she is not sporting with me. She looks into my eyes, and hers are nothing but kind. "I mean that."

She takes the empty glass from me, and I realize my hands are perspiring.

"You're trembling," Deepa says, and puts her hand on mine. "It's all right. Really. Listen, nothing you could tell me about yourself would faze me. I've seen some things that—well, let's just say that there's little that would surprise me." She smiles. "Why don't we leave it at that."

I am flooded with relief to have spoken the truth—or as close as I could get to the truth—and more important, that she does not judge me for it.

"Feel better?" Deepa says.

I nod.

"Not that I'm an expert or anything, but I have heard of young children in India having vivid memories of what are supposedly past lives, and thus they are somewhat confused. But that's generally sorted long before adulthood."

"I see."

But the truth is, I do not. For I am not merely having a memory of a past life; I know with my whole being that I am Jane Mansfield and not Courtney Stone, despite all appearances to the contrary, and despite all the friends and family in the world who might insist otherwise.

"Like I said, I'm no expert," says Deepa. "But I know someone who might be able to help you." She grasps my hand. "Come."

She leads me back into the building, not into the assembly room where the music and dancers are, but through a glimmering silver curtain, behind which is another door, and down another corridor, at the end of which is a plain, unmarked door painted the same black as the walls.

"I wasn't going to do this," says Deepa, "and I won't say anything else because then you'll think *I'm* crazy." She points to the door at the end of the corridor. "There's someone I'd like you to meet. But I never know whether or not she'll be there. Sometimes she is, and sometimes she isn't. But you're welcome to try."

"Who?"

Deepa gives me a tight little smile. "If you need me, I'll be behind the bar."

I regard the door for a couple of moments, then turn back to Deepa for more instructions, only to discover that she is already gone. I get a tingling sensation in my arms and chest.

"Deepa? Deepa?" There is no answer, only the muffled cries of the singer and the wail of the guitars.

I make my way to the end of the corridor; a faint glow of light is now pulsating from the tiny space between the edge of the door and the wall. The throbbing sounds of the music are fainter. I raise my hand and knock on the door. There is no answer.

I put my hand on the doorknob and turn it; the door opens, and inside the shadowy space is a pretty young woman with a gleaming cap of dark brown hair that reaches her chin. Her long bare legs are crossed at the ankle under a little table before her. Sitting opposite her, a tall young man wearing a rumpled shirt with a turned-down collar runs a be-ringed hand through his tousled brown hair. With a flourish the lady lays down on the table a card not unlike those used by the fortune-teller at the fair I attended with Mary two months ago. There are other cards on the table in a cross formation.

"See? There's nothing to worry about," she says to the young man, who brings one of her delicate white hands, bracelets jangling from her wrist, to his lips and leans over it with a kiss. A broad smile on his face, he unfolds his long, thin form from the chair and walks past me and out the door, as if I am not there at all.

The woman with the cards trains her black-lined cat's eyes on me.

"I beg your pardon," I say, and turn round to leave, my face burning at the impropriety of having walked in on what was obviously a private meeting.

"Stay. Please," says her voice behind me, and her accent is no longer that of the colonies, but rather that of a well-bred, respectable English-woman.

Astonished by the change in voice, I turn round, only to see that the lady herself has entirely changed in person, dress, and hair. Instead of the short skirt, bare arms, and straplike footwear, she is clad in a high-waisted, spotlessly white gown of the finest India muslin, her feet shod in fawn-colored half-boots. Her hair is no longer short; it is arranged high upon her head, with little tendrils falling becomingly over her forehead and neck. Her eyes are a clear golden brown and very large indeed without all the black around them; her brows are elegantly arched. Her complexion is fine and clear, her smile sweet and engaging.

The room is entirely altered as well. The lady indicates a tea chest beside her, and a tea service, neither of which was there when I entered. The tea service sits upon a table, an entirely different table, which is lit by candles. The cards have disappeared. There is even now a chimneypiece behind the lady; the rest of the room is shadowed, indistinct.

She indicates a chair for me to sit. "Would you do me the honor of drinking tea with me?"

"I thank you, but—how is it possible that you are the same lady that I—I beg your pardon, but are you—can you be the same lady that I saw—who was here just a moment ago?"

She laughs, a high, clear, musical sort of sound. There is something altogether familiar about her, though I have never met her before. "Upon my word, you cannot expect me to answer two questions at once." She pours a cup of tea, adds a few drops of milk, and offers me the cup.

"Do sit down."

There is a something in her eyes, in the turn of her countenance, that is maddeningly familiar.

"Are you—a fortune-teller?"

"It is my belief that each of us makes his own fortune, and, as a matter of fact, tells it as well." She laughs throatily, as if pleased with her own cleverness.

"Then what are you? How did you change from the lady I saw when first I opened the door to—" I wave my hand to indicate the room, her dress, and I realize I am trembling. "What sort of magic are you working?"

My right hand reaches for my neck, fumbles for the amber cross that is not there.

"You gave it to me in payment, remember?" says she, and instantly she transforms into an old woman in a simple black dress and a finely worked shawl—she is now the same woman, the very same fortune-teller that I saw in my own time, in 1813, and I am back at the fair, inside her tent, with Mary waiting for me outside, the sounds of the merrymakers obliterated, though the fabric of the tent is thin. The air is heavy with the sweet scent of roses, though there are no flowers in the tent. The fortune-teller is holding my amber cross, gazing at it admiringly, the golden chain spilling over the edge of her wrinkled hand. "That will do very well," she says, and the word echoes—"well . . . well . . . well . . . well . . . are you well, Miss Mansfield . . ."

". . . Miss Mansfield, are you well?" she says again, and I am once again in the twenty-first century, in the little room at the end of the corridor in the club, not in the tent at the fair in my own time, and the lady has once again assumed the form of the young gentlewoman in the India muslin gown. Her golden-brown eyes regard me with kindness and concern.

I back away from her little table, my heart pounding in my chest. "What is this?"

"Do forgive me for frightening you," she says. "You are quite safe, Miss Mansfield. There are no dark arts here."

"You know my name—my real name."

"Of course, my dear," she says, and sips at her tea. "We have met before."

"Then I am not imagining any of this. You are

she—the very same fortune-teller from the fair—and also the young lady with the cards and the short dress—and—how can this be possible?"

"No less possible than your being in this body rather than the one in which I formerly had the pleasure of meeting you."

"I cannot make out how such a thing has happened to me."

"Did you not wish for a different life when first we met? Did you not wish to be someone else? Indeed, I remember well those words you spoke in my tent that day at the fair."

"Are you saying that I wished my way here?"

"And did I not warn you against riding your horse in summer?"

"Yes of course, but—"

"And here we are," she says smiling, her eyes glowing with warmth. "For are we not 'such stuff as dreams are made on'?"

"But this is no dream. And I am not asleep."

"True. But you are most certainly not awake."

"I beg your pardon, but what sort of joke is this? One is either asleep or one is awake."

"Just so."

"Then if I am not asleep, how could I be anything but awake?"

"A very good question, my dear, and I shall do my best to answer it for you. But first, do please sit down again, and drink your tea before it gets cold."

She indicates the untouched cup before me.

I take my seat, and my hand trembles as I raise the cup to my lips. The tea is still warm, strong and black and scented with the fragrance of roses. I drain the cup, and instantly I am steadier. All the fear drains away as well.

"There. You are in much better looks already," she says, smiling at me. "Now, as to your question: Most of us walk through our daily lives as if we were asleep. We regard not what is before our eyes. We see not how we construct fantasies of our own and others' intentions without having the smallest knowledge of what we, or they, are truly about. We are all imaginists, storytellers if you will, and the pity is that none of us recognizes his sorry state."

"Imaginists? I must say that I am still very much in the dark."

"Indeed. Well, then, I shall endeavor to explain. Let us consider, for example, this woman whom you have become. Courtney Stone."

"I know nothing of her."

"Exactly!" She laughs. "And yet you have constructed a story about her life. One that paints her as imprudent at best, and fallen at worst."

"I have reason to think that she is not what a young lady ought to be."

She arches an eyebrow. "Why? Because she has done what you so very nearly did yourself?"

"What do you mean?" I say, but my cheeks

flame with the memory of being with Edgeworth in his woods, when I nearly gave up my innocence to him.

"It was he, not you, who said the two of you should wait."

"You have no right to speak of such things."

"Why, then, did you come to see me? To hear the truth, or to engage in polite conversation, the substance of which is nothing? Have you not had enough of such discourse in your life?"

She gazes at me kindly, and her eyes are those of the old woman at the fair, the fortune-teller who spoke of my parents, my friends, my life, as if she had access to my most intimate thoughts. The woman who frightened me so terribly with her knowledge of my life that I left her tent trembling and promised myself never to indulge in such silliness again. And so I determined to disregard everything she said, including her warning that I not ride Belle in summer.

I rub my arms against a chill that has overtaken me.

"You see, my dear," says the fortune-teller, "this story you have constructed about Courtney has only one point of view: yours. You are entirely asleep to her point of view—her wishes, her feelings, her intentions. You know nothing of her, yet you presume to write her story as if you do. That is the very essence of arrogance, is it not?"

I feel my face grow hot. "How should I know her point of view? She is nothing to me."

"Then I shall give you one more example, Miss Mansfield. Two persons with whom you are intimately connected and whom you believe you know very well. Your parents."

"Are you saying I do not know my own parents?"

"Indeed, you appear to know as little about them as you do Miss Courtney Stone."

"Nonsense."

"I know that you believe your mother to hold your father in contempt, and that she never loved him, despite his constancy and love for her."

I feel that same chill which I felt that day in my own time, in the fortune-teller's tent, when the lady saw so clearly into my most private thoughts.

"I would never speak of my mother in such a manner. And what has this to do with my situation here?"

"I am merely trying to illustrate, Miss Mansfield, that your so-called knowledge of your parents' hearts is as much of an imaginist's fancy as your so-called knowledge of Courtney Stone."

"I know what I see."

"Yet it is not the whole story. Your father is scrupulously kind to your mother, but love her he does not. He still mourns the loss of a young lady of his youth named Miss Allcott, whom he was not permitted to marry. Your mother knows of his past, and though she did not love him when they married, she grew to have a strong affection for him. She could never reconcile herself, however, to being unloved by him, much as he tried to hide it behind his unfailing kindness. And so she turned bitter and feigns an indifference to him that she does not, indeed, feel. She is eaten up with jealousy and makes both of you suffer for it."

My father in love with another woman? My mother suffering jealousy over my father, the man whose politenesses she scorns? Impossible.

Then why do I feel as if the world has turned upside down? I grip the edge of the table. "I do not believe it."

"Of course you do not. You, after all, have written their stories. 'True stories,' we like to call them. What a ridiculous notion!" She laughs, high and clear like a bell.

Then she regards me with some concern. "My dear," she says, "you look as if you need a cordial very badly. I am sorry to have laughed so heartily at what must be shocking to you indeed, but it had to be done. Not the laughing, but the telling. How else are you ever to awaken?"

"I am awake," I say like a petulant child.

"No," she says gently, "but I have hopes you will be."

She produces a stoppered crystal decanter and pours some ruby liquid into a tiny glass, which she places before me, next to my cup of tea.

"You have not the opportunity to walk in your mother's shoes, Miss Mansfield. But you do have the opportunity to walk in Courtney's. You must own that there is nothing like it for understanding a different point of view."

Indeed. For I see myself again, in the public house not one hour ago, tingling with desire for Frank, allowing him to kiss me, then pushing him away and running from my shame and from the pain in Wes's countenance, and I shudder at the memory.

"I did not wish to walk in Courtney's shoes, no matter what you might have thought I said."

"One should choose one's words most carefully, Miss Mansfield. Did you not ask for a different life when last we met? 'A very different life,' I recall you saying."

I cannot deny that I spoke those words.

"And did you not also wish to do something important, to be part of a noble purpose?"

Indeed, though I said nothing of the kind to the fortune-teller that day in her tent.

"Well, this is your chance, for there is nothing nobler than to give up one's self in service to another," says the lady.

"I do not understand."

"Surely you did not think your wish would come without a price. For there is much work to be done here. Look at the state of this life you have inherited. Courtney has banished two gentlemen from her life, both of whom keep turning up, despite the best efforts of her friends and, I might add, what she regards as her own better judgment."

"What she regards . . . Are you saying it is *not* her better judgment?"

"That part of the story, my dear, is for you to determine."

"But how am I, who know nothing of this world and all its ways, to be of any help at all?"

"You may have come here with a limited perspective, but it is certainly a fresh one. And I do believe that Courtney—and you—are in need of a fresh perspective.

"Drink," she says, and her kindly tone impels me to obey. I lift the glass to my lips; the fumes of the ruby drink open up my breathing passages in a most pleasant manner; its fragrance is that of warm blackberries on a hot summer day. I consume the drink in one swallow; it is indeed a most agreeable restorative.

The lady smiles approvingly. "Think of it this way: What makes a story true is not that it really happened, for truly it is your word against mine, or your word against Courtney's, or Courtney's word against Frank's, or Wes's, and so on, and which one of us—or them—is really lying after all? What makes a story true is that there is the truth of human nature and self-reflection in it, the awareness and the awakening to the fact that we indeed know nothing and that nothing we think is true is really true, that indeed we have made it all up. Like Miss Elizabeth Bennet, who realized that much of what she had assumed about Mr. Darcy, and even about her most intimate friend in the world, was the product of her own imaginings. Yet the most memorable words she spoke, and the truest of them all, were this: *'Till this moment, I never knew myself.'* Myself! You see? Myself. Not someone else."

"*Pride and Prejudice* is my favorite book in the world. How wonderful that you know it well."

The lady's smile has a hint of mischief this time. "Nothing wonderful about it at all. I am pleased that these works are at your disposal; you won't find a steadier friend or wiser counsel. Unless, that is, you come to see me again."

"Am I to stay here forever, then, in Courtney's life?"

"You mean shall you sit *'like patience on a monument, smiling at grief'*?"

"You speak in riddles, Miss—may I not know your name?"

"Would you not prefer the answer to the riddle?"

"Of course."

"Well then, when at last you awaken, the answer shall be yours."

"I do not—"

"Do call on me again," she says, rising majestically from her chair, the candlelight no longer on her face, which is now obscured by shadows.

"This was a most delightful reunion." And with a curtsey, she withdraws into the shadows.

And as sure as I know she was here, I now know she is gone. If there is another door by which she has left, she has done so without a sound.

I sit there for a couple of minutes, and in that short space of time, the fire is dying down and the room growing cold. The candles are mere sputtering stubs. I rub my arms against the chill, and the room is swallowed in absolute darkness. I fumble my way to the door and open it.

Dim light from the corridor spills into the room, revealing a completely different setting! There is no chimneypiece or table or tea service or chairs, merely some shelves stacked with boxes and a bare floor.

With trembling hands I scramble out of the room, closing the door behind me, and lean against the wall. Have I imagined the entire encounter?

No. She is as real as the beating of my heart in this chest in this body that is mine but not mine at all. She is as real as the love I felt for Edgeworth, the love that still pierces my heart.

Why do I think of him now? But of course I would think of him, for when I went to the fair with Mary, her arm linked through mine as we strolled towards the fortune-teller's tent and she said, "Shall we try our luck, Jane? Oh how delightful to have our fortunes told!" I acted as if it were a mere diversion. But it was Edgeworth who was foremost in my mind. It was Edgeworth I had seen betraying me. It was he whose very name was agony for me to hear. And so I entered the fortune-teller's tent, leaving Mary outside. And I wished with all my heart for a different life. I wished with all my heart to be somewhere, anywhere else. To be someone else. If only that were possible, I thought.

And here I am.

Twelve

I make my way through the crowds of dancers and throngs milling around the bar in search of Deepa. She is nowhere to be seen, but I trust she will return. I station myself before a railing on a sort of gallery which overlooks the bar, so that I might have a better view. I hope she returns shortly and will not mind taking me home, for I am feeling the effects of all I have experienced in this long day and would like nothing more than a quiet room and a comfortable bed.

The musicians are no longer on the stage, and while there is still music playing, no doubt from one of those clever little music-producing objects, it is not nearly as loud as the music played by the band. Much as I am relieved by the respite from noise and fascinated by the spectacle of dancers and revelers below, I cannot stop thinking about what the fortune-teller said. Which is that I have work to do. That there is a purpose to my being here.

But how might I, who knows nothing of Courtney or of this strange time in which she lives, bring order to her life? I who could not even resist the advances of a man who is but a stranger to me.

As if to emphasize that thought, I see below, near the bar, a couple locked in a kiss so ardent that they appear to be swallowing one another. No one seems to be shocked by the display; indeed, the ladies and gentlemen around them seem not to note them at all, or at most give them a passing glance and return to their own business.

Such things would be unthinkable in my world, but this place is unlike my world in every way; that much is clear. And as much as I rejoiced today in having my own set of rooms and the prospect of an independence, I fear that I may not be strong enough to withstand this degree of moral profligacy. My conduct with Frank tonight and those disturbing thoughts—or memories—of doing much worse have shaken my very sense of who I am.

Suddenly, I am startled by a tap on my shoulder; I turn round, and it is Wes. What joy it is to see his gentle countenance alight with a smile, until, that is, I remember that he was witness to my shameful dealings with Frank. And then I cannot look him in the eye.

It is bad enough that Wes saw me kissing Frank—but does he truly know the extent of my sins?

He puts his mouth close to my ear. "I was hoping I might find you here. Are you okay?"

I nod, still unable to look at him.

"I know it's none of my business. But you're not really going to give Frank another chance, are you?"

I can feel the blush rising up my neck. "I have no excuse for my conduct."

"So you're not going to . . . ?"

"I am most ashamed."

The fortune-teller did say it was up to me to determine whether or not it was in my—or Courtney's—best interests to keep Frank from my life. And Wes as well. *That part of the story,* said she, *is for you to determine.* But I know that any man whose very presence incites me to nearly throw away my reputation—or whatever shreds of it remain—is someone I must avoid at any cost.

As for Wes, there is indeed so much goodness in his countenance that I feel safe with him. Despite what Anna and Paula say he has done. And yet . . . if I can see the wisdom in Paula's and Anna's warnings about Frank; and indeed, Frank himself admitted he did wrong—should I not give their warnings about Wes due consideration as well?

"You have nothing to feel bad about, Courtney. He saw an opening, and he took it."

And I allowed him to do so. But I do not speak those words aloud.

"You are very good," I say.

I allow myself to meet Wes's eyes for a moment, and his eyes betray nothing but kindness. The kindness that a compassionate man would bestow on a ruined woman. Unless—and I can only hope it is so—he does not know to what extent Courtney has compromised herself with Frank; if only I could drive those images of lying with Frank from my brain, but I cannot. They are so real, so vivid, that my ability to think of those images as Courtney's life and not my own is dwindling by the second.

Again I cannot meet Wes's gaze. I cast my eyes again to the bar, and there is Deepa. I wave until she sees me and smiles, a dazzling smile even from here.

And then I see another lady, a young, black-haired woman standing several feet from the bar and gazing up at me. Or Wes. I cannot tell. But there is something about her pale, heart-shaped countenance with its uptilted eyes that is oddly familiar, though of course I have never met her before.

And then Deepa appears in the gallery, and I see that Wes, too, is gazing below at the lady, who is still looking up in our direction.

"Had enough festivities for one night?" asks Deepa with a smile, and I nod, smiling, too. Wes breaks his gaze at the lady below and turns his attention to us. "Great, then let's roll," says Deepa. "Take care, Wes."

"Bye, Deepa."

She nods to me, slings her bag on her shoulder, and turns towards the stairs.

"Good-bye," I say to Wes, and he reaches out to clasp my hand.

"Don't be so hard on yourself, Courtney." He squeezes my hand.

I am almost overcome by his kindness, and I can only nod at him, then hurry down the stairs towards Deepa's retreating form. As for the strangely familiar lady who had been staring up at us, she is no longer there.

The ride home with Deepa is largely silent, save for the music in her car. She pats me on the arm a couple of times and glances over at me with a reassuring smile, but she asks nothing about my meeting with the lady, and I say nothing, though I dearly wish to do so.

When she stops her car before my house, I venture, "Shall I tell you about the lady I met when you left me?"

"You do realize," she says, looking into my eyes and dropping her voice to a whisper, though we are the only two creatures in the car, "that what happened tonight is not something you should discuss with 99.9 percent of the population? The same goes for saying that a certain person is from another life. Some things aren't for everyone, you know? Don't ask, don't tell." She attempts a light-hearted smile, but I can see she is quite serious.

I regard her with awe. "I suppose I am too apt at times to wonder whether something is merely the fancy of my imagination—even when I know it is not—but clearly you have had your own dealings with the lady." I pause, wishing for information but not wanting to seem impertinent.

"No offense," says Deepa, "but that's not something I discuss. I almost didn't even send you down that hallway tonight. The one time I did say too much—and to the wrong person, I might add—I didn't see any trace of the lady, as you call her, in the club for six months. Besides, if I talked about her, I'd reduce her to a mere story that no one would ever understand anyway. And then she'd never come back, and it would be as if she never existed."

I say nothing, but I believe I do understand. What would Mary say, after all, if I returned to my own country, to my own time, and tried to tell her what happened to me here? She would never believe me, and I would hardly believe it myself.

"So," says Deepa, "what did you think of Awakening?" She smiles slyly. "Aside from what we don't talk about?"

"Awakening?"

"Duh. The club."

"Awakening." The irony of that name is not lost upon me. "It was—exciting. Different. Have you been employed there long?"

"Actually, I own a controlling interest in the club. Have done since my divorce became final two months ago. When you and I first met."

I think of the mix of gentlemen and ladies I saw at the club. "May I ask the criteria for membership?"

Deepa laughs. "You are too funny, Courtney."

I laugh along with her, though I have no idea why, and I take my leave, thanking her most sincerely for her kindness.

"Let's do it again soon," she says, and I wave my good-byes with a warm feeling in my heart. I believe I have made a true friend tonight.

As I run up the stairs, I am struck by Deepa's having received a controlling interest in the club as a result of her divorce. That Paula's words at breakfast indicated a lady might divorce a man for *his* adulterous behavior was astonishing enough. That a lady might even gain financially from the business is beyond anything. Certainly my mother's cousin, whom I heard her comforting all those years ago, had no such options. She, like all ladies similarly situated, could only live out her life in misery and dependence while her husband made a fool of himself.

Would my mother have divorced my father if she could? I cannot imagine such a thing. She would never want the world to know she was unloved, if indeed that is the truth. No, even if I can believe my father carrying around in his heart the lost love of his youth—and attempting to picture my spindly, thatch-haired, careworn father as a youth, let alone a love-struck one, is a feat of imagination indeed—I cannot believe my mother ever loved my father. That fortune-teller may be able to prognosticate a fall from a horse, but I'll wager she is as much a storyteller as she claims I am.

And yet . . . she is indeed the same fortune-teller with whom I met in my own time, and in my own country. And I cannot deny that she knew then, as she knows now, more about my life than I have ever disclosed to another soul. And thus I cannot so easily dismiss anything she says.

I unlock the door and welcome the solitude of my rooms, the quiet of which emphasizes the ringing in my ears. I fill a glass of water and sink into the soft cushions of the sofa to reflect upon the strange happenings of this night.

There is much work to be done here, said the lady. *There is nothing nobler than to give up one's self in service to another. Look at the state of this life you have inherited.*

My stomach rumbles, reminding me that I've barely touched food since breakfast with Paula and Anna. I cannot very well do my work on an empty stomach, let alone examine the state of this life I have inherited.

And so I retrieve the papery jar of Cherry Garcia ice cream from the fridge, as Wes called it, and settle back into the sofa.

Which is all I can manage right now. My mind has had its fill of noble missions and two-hundred-year time shifts for one night.

Although . . . I retrieve the pile of novels by Jane Austen from the table beside the bed. *Emma* is what I need right now. There will be time enough tomorrow to deal with what the fortune-teller said.

I open the thick volume, eager to delve into a wholly new story.

Thirteen

Someone is pounding on the door, and I bolt from the sofa with a start. I have slept in my clothes, *Emma* nearly finished, the empty jar of ice cream on the low table. I am loathe to receive company in such a disheveled state but dare not ignore such insistent pounding, as if one could.

"Who's that?" I croak, ear to the door.

"It's Sandra, sweetie. Open up."

Sandra? Ah, yes, Anna and Paula did mention someone named Sandra at breakfast yesterday. A connection of David, my supposed employer. I open the door, and there stands the sweetest-looking creature, ephemeral and slight, like a fairy princess with long, silky dark-blond hair, enormous blue eyes in a delicate countenance, and the loveliest smile. She looks to be no more than one and twenty.

"How are you, sweetie? We've all been worried. David of course has been beside himself, but you know how he gets." She rolls her eyes. "You'd think the man could live without you over the weekend. If I were you, I'd use his new-found realization of your indispensable qualities to get yourself a raise. As if you could ever be paid enough for what you do."

Her voice is surprisingly deep, like Mary's but smooth rather than rasping. The similarity is enough to make my heart ache for my beloved friend.

Sandra's large blue eyes search my face. "You do look a bit out of it; are you okay?"

I smile. "Perfectly."

"No pain?"

"Nothing I regard."

She opens her mouth as if to say something and then lifts her eyebrows as if thinking better of it. "How 'bout I run you a shower and start some coffee." I follow her into the bathroom, attending her closely as she pulls aside a curtain to reveal a recessed bathtub, turns on a cascade of water, and then closes the curtain again.

"Hop in," she says. "You deserve to be waited on for once. I'll even pick out your clothes and drive you to the office. If you don't mind, that is. Of course if you prefer to drive your own car . . ."

My own car. I drive my own car. The very thought is thrilling, but I would not know the first thing. Sandra must be David's servant, and he has sent her here to escort me to my place of employment. I, with a place of employment. A profession of my own.

But Paula had said I was not to go to work today. Oh how I wish she or Anna or Deepa were here to advise me as to how I shall get through this situation.

Well, I must soldier on. And I must own I am brimming with curiosity about my place of employment.

I smile at Sandra. "I would prefer to be driven. I am most obliged." She looks at me somewhat quizzically and then dashes out of the room. I disrobe, then test the water with one foot; it is the perfect temperature. I step in behind the curtain and am immediately soaked by the steamy water-fall. Heavenly.

An array of tall containers on openwork white shelves catches my eye. Two sorts of something called shampoo. Conditioner, whatever that might be. Body wash. All quite exotic-sounding. Ah, something familiar at last: two cakes of sweet-smelling soap. I could use the soap to wash my hair, but I am curious about the bottles, which are of a pliable opaque substance and covered with print praising the "miraculous" and "revolutionary" properties of the various concoctions. There is so much to read that I could become a boiled-red wrinkled thing before I accomplish anything.

Fortunately, I forestall such a fate with the very next bottle, whose set of directions as to the washing of hair are so minute that I laugh as I massage the fragrant stuff into my scalp. Would someone actually apply the mixture onto wet hair and fail to wash it out were he not otherwise instructed?

I do not remember the last time I felt so clean; it is nothing like a long soak in a tub with water that soon becomes as dirty as the body within it, and thus there is nothing to do but stew in one's filth and remove it as best one can with a towel.

I turn the knobs I saw Sandra operate, in an attempt to shut off the flow of water, the result being a momentary scalding and an involuntary shriek from myself before I manage to achieve my ends.

A quick knock and Sandra peeks in through the steam. "You all right?"

I grab for a towel to cover myself. "Indeed. It was merely a bit of hot water."

Another eye roll from Sandra. "First a raise. Then a place where things actually work. But first we need to get *you* to work before David has a stroke. He's called three times while you were in the shower. I told him if he called again, you'd be even later, so I think that might save you from him till you get there."

"Thank you."

True to her word, Sandra has laid out an ensemble for me on the bed. Shiny black trousers, along with a tiny black bodice without sleeves. The scantiness of the bodice is bad enough, but—

Sandra lays a hand on my arm. "Something wrong, sweetie?"

"Am I in mourning?"

Sandra looks at me, openmouthed, and then laughs. "I should hope not. But when has that ever stopped you from wearing black?"

Sandra pulls from the closet a white flowing dress dotted with blue flowers, not full-length, of course, but one that might hang to the knee or a bit above. It is sleeveless as well.

"How's this?" she asks.

I cannot show my legs; I can hardly imagine showing my arms.

"Perhaps I might pair the black trousers with something a bit colorful? And with sleeves? Half-mourning is preferable to full." I smile in what I hope is a conciliatory manner, but she looks as puzzled as before.

"Right." She pulls out a claret-red, long-sleeved bodice with a fold-down collar and buttons. "At least you won't freeze in the air-conditioning. Or have to worry about shaving legs." She glances at a watch, a very feminine item that is more a piece of jewelry than a watch, and such a clever idea to have one fastened about the wrist. "Which would make you even later."

"Of course," I say, opening the door for her so that I might dress in private and wondering what she means by "air-conditioning" and "shaving legs." I can now navigate my way around the undergarments and trouser fastenings on my own, but the lexicon of this society is still a mystery.

When I emerge from the bathroom, I look well, having finally succeeded in applying mascara without poking my eye or looking as if I smeared my face with ashes. Sandra awaits me with a ring of keys in hand, her bag slung over her arm.

"By the way," she says, pressing something on a boxlike object in the window, which silences the loud rushing noise I have been hearing since I emerged from the shower, "your landlord really should do something about this poor excuse for an air conditioner. I was going to offer to blow-dry your hair for you," she says, indicating an oddly shaped brown object lying on the table, "but no way in this heat."

It is indeed hot in the room. A trickle of perspiration runs down my back; I hope it does not show. I also hope that the powder-fresh antiperspirant/deodorant which I discovered in the cabinet, and which I applied to my under-arms as the label instructed, does its office.

No matter, for within mere minutes we have made it past the wall of heat awaiting us outside and into the plush seats of Sandra's iridescent dark-gray, instantly air-cooled car, which drives away with barely a sound. This, I realize, must be what she meant by air conditioning.

In fact, it occurs to me that Paula's car and Deepa's, too, must have been cooled in a similar manner; both were, I believe, far cooler than the air outside, though I did not mark it at the time. Perhaps, as the fortune-teller said, I really am asleep to certain things. What else, I wonder, am I not noticing, especially when there is so much to capture my attention in this strange world that I can hardly attend to Sandra's polite inquiries as to my comfort and the state of my head, and her gentle admonishments that I not allow David to pile too much on me all at once. Instead, I am almost wholly engaged in gaping out the front and side glasses at the rush of exotic brush-headed trees, speeding cars, and oddly shaped buildings rich in glass and gleaming masonry. Though I cannot dispel the disconcerting sensations generated by Sandra's references to inadequate salary and disobliging landlords and the inferior state of my apartment. I cannot help but conclude that the woman I am supposed to be, Courtney Stone, lives in such a penurious manner that a servant sees fit to advise her on it. Such a reduction in circumstances—for clearly the absence of a servant of my own is indication enough—is mortifying indeed for a gentleman's daughter.

Yet—can a woman who earns her own bread

and is driven to her place of employment, who is attended by a pretty and engaging servant in a car which is clearly superior to that driven by Paula or Deepa, truly be considered poor? Can a woman who has such an abundance of garments, who keeps her own carriage, who commands the use of rooms, not merely a room, of her own be anything but rich? Perhaps not rich in landed, freehold property, such as befits the owner of Mansfield House, nor rich in the manner of Edgeworth, who has two estates and a house in town—but rich as an unmarried woman might be rich. Rich in independence and voluntary solitude and self-will. Rich in determination to discover what riches await me in this wondrous and mysterious adventure called work.

"Here we are," Sandra calls out cheerily as she turns the car into a drive which descends below the level of the street into a veritable underground house of cars. I cannot believe how many cars are stabled in this brightly lit place, which seems to exist solely to house them. Sandra selects a parking space, as she calls it, and soon we are in a moving room, like the one in Dr. Menziger's building. When the door opens, some of the people exit, and I move as if to exit as well, but Sandra grabs my arm.

"Not yet," she says.

The door slides open three more times before Sandra makes a move to leave the room, this time seizing my hand to make sure I do not stay behind. I am greeted by a chorus of voices as both young gentlemen and ladies call out to me, some seated at desks, others rising from their chairs, many with strange objects protruding from their ears.

"Hey, Courtney," "You're here!" and "Didn't think you'd make it in, dude" are among the variety of greetings, all accompanied by smiles, a few by impertinent winks from a couple of the gentlemen, one of whom says, "The wet look is hot on you," causing my face to heat up without my really understanding why. There is a persistent sound of some sort of machine going brrr-brrr-berrrrup, brrr-brrr-berrrrup, which seems to cease momentarily when one of the ladies or gentle-men taps the device in her or his ear or lifts a rectangular object from a boxlike thing with winking lights and begins to talk into it. I see; this must be another sort of phone, though much larger than the one which is mine, or which I have seen Wes, Paula, and Sandra use.

Sandra propels me past the greeters. "Give her some air, people," she says good-naturedly, when suddenly she stops moving and I am swept away by a gale force of a man with one of those strange objects in his ear and who appears to be having a conversation with both me and it at once. (My clue to the latter is his propensity to touch the object in his ear when he speaks to it rather than to me.)

Sandra, too, is swept into his wake, and even kisses his cheek, his only response to which is to put his arm briefly around her slim waist and pat her hip with one of his enormous hands. She seems to regard it not, though I am disgusted by such an unseemly treatment of a servant.

"Go easy on her," Sandra warns him, giving me an encouraging wink before disappearing into one of the rooms made of glass that appear to line the wall of this vast, bustling space filled with large tables and chairs, people talking into the air or I assume into the objects in their own ears, staring into glowing boxes, and clack-clack-clacking their fingers on objects that appear to have all the letters of the alphabet on them. I am so caught up in the spectacle before me and distracted by the myriad of greetings that I do not immediately catch all that the human hurricane is saying.

"Lance? David." He's speaking into the air again, his head cocked in a way that makes him look very silly indeed. "Let's get this wrapped up, okay? Two more weeks, and I'm out. Tick tock. So, are you up to speed yet? Hello . . . Courtney?" He snaps his fingers in front of my face, which is how I realize he is now talking to me. "The day marches on and I'm already buried. I need you to go through my calls and emails. You with me? No, Lance—unacceptable. Are you?"

He's staring at me, and though the temperature in the room is chill and crisp, I am perspiring. His eyes examine me from behind their black wire spectacles, and their gaze is chill as well.

And then he breaks into a toothy and most disarming smile and instantly envelops me in a tight hug. "Mr.——" I try in vain to extricate myself. "David, I——"

He lets me go and rolls his eyes. "No need for a lawyer, okay? You gave me a scare, that's all. And you're okay now, right? Great!"

We've now arrived at what I assume must be my worktable, for he is shuffling through about six exceedingly untidy stacks of papers and unearths a pile of smallish pink lined papers, which he waves at me. "The temp they sent couldn't roll calls or even enter my calendar," he says, indicating the pink pages with contempt. "This was her idea of keeping track of things. Take care of it and sync up my BlackBerry, will you?"

Am I now to pick fruit? This is a degradation indeed.

He tosses onto the table an object that is rounder and fatter than the phone I have (and which I now realize is still attached to its cord in my apartment). I pick it up; it says "BlackBerry" in small white letters above a windowlike square. I start to laugh.

"I'm glad someone finds this amusing," he says, his tone quite the opposite of glad. "Now get Angelo for me. Please."

"Where shall I 'get' Mr.—or Miss—Angelo, is it?"

"What?"

"Where would you have me go?"

"Get him on the phone, for Christ's sake!"

Dear God, I am a servant. There cannot be two opinions on this matter. The abuse, the tyrannical manner. "If you cannot speak to me in a civil manner—"

"Courtney, this isn't funny."

"Indeed it is not. I thought I had respectable employment, but I find instead that I am a mere servant."

"For Christ's sake, Courtney. If you were a servant you'd do what I asked, not stand here trashing a job that anyone would kill to have."

A snort of derision from one of the young men manning a nearby worktable calls my attention from David, and his from me.

"Sorry," says the young man, cheeks flaming.

David addresses me in a lowered tone. "How do you think that makes me feel? Do you have any idea how much I depend on you?"

The large boxlike phone on my worktable begins emitting the brrr-brrr-berrrrup sound. Repeatedly.

"Well?" His arms flail about.

"Sir?"

"Pick up the damn phone!"

My hands are actually trembling as I reach for the boxlike instrument, but as I begin to lift it—

"What's wrong with you?" he screams.

The box slips from my moist palms back onto

the worktable; if only I had a handkerchief. The back of my bodice is now drenched in perspiration, a most inelegant state for one who wishes to assert a modicum of dignity. "Sir, I will not be talked to in such a manner. Good day to you."

And with that I turn on my heel and, head held high, retrace my steps.

There is utter silence among the watchful ladies and gentlemen, save for the odd sounds the various box phones emit.

David's voice calls out to me. "You can't do this to me. . . . Courtney? Please . . . Sandra? Sandra!"

I make my way past the gentlemen and ladies at their desks, avoiding their curious looks and holding my head high, till I reach the wall from which Sandra and I were transported to this room. I wonder whether I might summon the conveyance myself.

"Courtney, what did he do?"

It is Sandra, her gaze sympathetic. I can only shake my head, and then, unaccountably, I am weeping. She makes a move as if to put her arm around me, but I forestall her with a raised hand. What humiliation—first to be publicly set down by the likes of such a creature, and then to lose control of myself, again in full view of who knows how many people.

It is trying enough to pretend I really am this person whom everyone knows as Courtney Stone when nothing about her is in any way familiar to me. But then to be singled out and scolded by such an ill-bred, ungentlemanly person. It is not to be borne.

Sandra offers me a handful of paper handkerchiefs, and I take them gratefully. "Forgive me," I say, pleased that at least my voice is steady. "I am perfectly well again. If you would be so kind, I wish to go home now."

"I'm sure he was an ass—he always is—but you know he doesn't mean it."

The same words my father used many a time when I was a child weeping over my mother's scoldings that I was the most unmanageable child that ever was seen, her prognostications that I would never amount to anything as a young lady, and furthermore, her declarations that I would never make a good marriage because no man would tolerate my headstrong ways.

"She does not mean it, Janey girl," he would say, reaching out to smooth a stray lock of hair from my forehead and offering me his handkerchief to wipe my tears. "She does not mean it."

"No," I say to Sandra. "They never do."

"Can we sit down and talk about this?"

"To what purpose? My mind is made up. I shall quit this place. Now."

All my life, I have had to bear with my mother's ire, her lack of affection, her disappointment at my very existence. I had to bear with it, for I could not walk away from her as an unmarried woman any more than I could walk away from her as a helpless child. Not unless I married, or went out as a governess, which she would never allow, and which, to own the truth, I imagined would likely subject me to worse indignities than those I endured in her house.

But now, when I have somehow landed in a world where women, single women, may live on their own, without the rule of their parents, without the dominion of a husband or a brother or even the protection of a lover, where they may be employed and earn their bread, and in professions other than that of a governess or servant or worse, how should I do anything but quit this scene of degradation?

"You're serious," Sandra's voice brings me back to where I am standing. "But how will you live?"

I look Sandra in the eye. "I do not know. I must own that I do not even know how I am to go home."

"I'll drive you, of course." Sandra presses an illuminated circle on the wall repeatedly, and within moments the doors slide open and we are back inside the conveyance. I follow her to her car, and soon we are back on the road.

After several minutes of silence, Sandra says, "Are you sure you won't reconsider?"

"I certainly shall not."

"I'm supposed to overlook his faults; after all, I'm in love with him. But you—I can't say I blame you."

This is intelligence indeed; she cannot be David's servant. I cast my eyes as surreptitiously as I can towards her hands, but I spy no wedding ring. Could I be sitting next to the mistress of my former employer?

"I'm sure I could get him to turn your last advance into severance and maybe get him to throw in another week or two. I think I can scare him into that. And a reference. But beyond that—" She shakes her head.

"You are very good."

Thankfully, Sandra lapses into silence for the remainder of the journey home; I am too full of what has just happened to be fit for conversation. In fact, I am not even fit to think of what has come to pass with my so-called job. The speed of her car, and indeed of the other cars on the road, gives me a powerful curiosity to know how such a machine works. What mysterious force powers it? What causes the cunning illuminations which light up this city by night and day? It is impossible to be in this world and not long to know. The question, however, is how to inquire about such things without revealing a most shocking degree of ignorance.

I observe Sandra driving as well as I can; however, I am no closer to understanding what she touches with her foot to move and stop the car than I was when I watched Paula driving.

Sandra halts the car before my house, then puts

her arms about my shoulders and hugs me tightly. When she releases me, her eyes are wet with tears. Though our acquaintance has spanned but a few hours, I feel a little tug at my heart. By the time she allows me to alight from her car, she has extracted a promise that I will "keep in touch" and call her if I need anything.

As soon as I settle into the sofa with *Emma* opened before me, it occurs to me, thanks to a violent protest from my stomach, that I've not made a decent meal since yesterday morning. Perhaps I shall rifle Courtney's bag for money and then venture to the cook-shop next door to the public house where Frank and Wes took me. I can almost smell the scent of the exotic cookery. I hope Courtney's bag yields money enough for a meal; I know neither the value of currency in this land nor the cost of food.

To think that I should be searching the contents of my purse to see whether I will go hungry today. At home I had only to ring the bell for Barnes or have a word with Cook, and a delicious meal would appear.

What if Sandra's fears for me are not unfounded? Not only do I lack the smallest knowledge of what it costs to run my own household, I have not the least idea of whether my income in David's employ was merely sufficient for those needs or more than adequate. In short, I have no idea whether I am in cash, have money in the funds, or should soon be hiding from the duns. For if Courtney has been as profligate with her money as she was with her reputation, then my prospects are sad indeed.

With no father, no brother, and no husband at hand, I have not the smallest notion of how to discover if I am indeed beforehand with the world. I am, however, determined to find it out.

I know I should neither rest nor eat until I know what I can afford, but truth be told, I am more eager to know how these miracles called cars work, and how these wonders which light up the world get their illumination, than I am to know the extent of my fortune. And I am more anxious than anything to put some food in this noisy stomach.

No sooner do I reach for my bag to find some cash than there is knocking at the door. "Courtney?"

It is Wes's voice. There is a strange surge in my chest, as if he is my dearest friend and I am to see him again after many weeks. I know not whence this feeling comes; I only know that I am rushing to the door and opening it.

"Sorry to keep barging in like this," he says, "but you never answer your phone, or your email, and you do still have that concussion." He searches my face. "Court, are you okay? Is it true?"

I feel my face burn with shame. He knows that I have done much worse with Frank than allow him to kiss me.

"Is it, Courtney? Did you really quit your job?"

I practically collapse against the wall in my relief.

Silly goose. He truly does not even seem to judge me for what he saw me do last night. As for anything else he might know, well, I cannot feel quite so comfortable with such a thought, but of course he is too much the gentleman ever to remark on such a matter.

Wes takes my arm and leads me to a chair in the kitchen. "It's gonna be okay," he says, pouring me a glass of water. "I had a feeling you might have been stubborn enough to go in today—or sufficiently guilt-tripped into it—so I called the office. And Jay said you'd quit."

He puts the glass in my hand. "Here, drink this down." He sits opposite me, his eyes earnest, and puts a hand over mine. "If it's any consolation, Jay says you're the buzz of the office. They can't stop talking about what a stand you made. All I can say is, it's about time."

I cannot help but warm to the praise. "I am happy you approve. And please do not concern yourself; I am perfectly well, I assure you. I think I am merely hungry."

He grins. "Stay right here, and I'll be back in a half hour or so with your favorite from Acme, okay?"

"O-kay." I smile. That might be just enough time to finish *Emma*.

Fourteen

*L*ess than an hour and a half later my mind is sated with the joyful ending of *Emma*. What a glorious book, which well deserves to be placed alongside its sisters, *Sense and Sensibility* and *Pride and Prejudice*. Though its heroine was indeed a little too well pleased with herself, that is, till her own awakening to the truth. Again I am reminded of the fortune-teller's words. But I did so admire Emma's contentment with her single state. Nothing would have tempted her from it—and did tempt her from it—but the deepest affections.

Not only am I glowing with the satisfaction of having read a most delightful novel, but my belly is comfortably full of the most delicious food I have ever tasted. Mexican food, Wes named it, and chicken mole is the name of the dish—my favorite, according to Wes, and I have no difficulty believing him.

I put down my fork after having consumed less than half the meal, the portions being as large as those in the restaurant where I breakfasted with Paula and Anna. Wes scrapes the rest into a covered dish and stores it in the refrigerator, a truly ingenious invention of this time. I can only imagine the joy of Cook if she had such a convenience in our kitchen. How she always lamented the amount of food which spoiled or which she was obliged to cook in order to avoid its spoiling.

But while the refrigerator prevents waste, I gather that one is actually expected to discard the very platter and cutlery that accompanied the meal, as Wes is doing that very thing.

"The knives and forks are flimsy, to be sure," I venture to Wes, "but disposing of them in such a manner seems terribly wasteful."

"Tell me about it," he says. "The joys of living in our disposable society. I don't know why they just throw utensils in the bag without asking first. And Styrofoam containers, no less. Do you believe anyone still uses Styrofoam? I mean, how about cardboard, guys? You'd think they never heard of global warming. Or reducing our carbon footprint. At least it'll be recycled."

I attempt a concerned nod to cover up my ignorance and he stops, as if catching himself, smiling sheepishly. "Sorry. I'm ranting. Your turn. You say something."

Ah. The opening I had hoped for. "Now you mention it, there is something I wish to say to you. But it has nothing to do with the wasteful-ness of our meal."

He smiles wryly. "Fair enough."

"I wonder if you might . . . what I mean to say is, would you be so kind as to recommend how I might, well, learn how certain things work?"

"Not sure I understand." He regards me with a

questioning eye, and I resort to a small falsehood to gain my point.

"I believe that such explanations might help me regain my memory."

"Oh," says he. "But what do you need explained?"

I hesitate, fearing he may think me mad.

"It's okay, Courtney. You can ask me anything."

His manner is so encouraging and gentle that I find myself blurting out, "I do so very much wish to know how a car works."

There. I've said it. And he does not look at all shocked. On the contrary, his smile is rather pleased. Perhaps he, like most of his sex, does not object to an opportunity for demonstrating his superior knowledge to an ignorant female.

"I can explain that to you pretty well," he says, "but let's try it the fun, do-it-yourself way. On your computer." With that, he leads me over to the table in my bedchamber with the glowing box that is not unlike those in my former place of employment. So that is what it is called.

He seats himself to my right, and I must say his scent, which is reminiscent of lemon and freshly laundered linen that has dried in the sun, is both pleasing and distracting. I school my thoughts to focus on the rectangular screen, as he terms it, before me. He tells me to click on something called Google, which makes me giggle, but it dies quickly in a most embarrassing gasp when he puts his large, gentle hand over mine and places it on something called the mouse—causing another laugh to bubble over—and manipulates my fingers to click and point until, sure enough, the word "Google"—what a silly-sounding word —appears on the screen.

I barely hear Wes's softly spoken instructions as to what I am to type onto the screen, I am so alive to every touch of his large, beautiful hand on mine, the pressure of it, the feel of his palm on the top of my hand, the pressure of his fingers atop mine. His hand is beautifully shaped, a sculptor's hand. It is reshaping my hand, this hand that is not mine yet is, transforming it into—

"Courtney, you're trembling," he says, and leaps up to get me another glass of water. "Are you okay?" he asks, placing the glass before me.

I will my hand to steady as I pick up the glass but do not trust myself to bring it to my lips. Silly goose.

"Should I offer you something stronger?"

Why should I be so undone by a mere touch of the hand? "What happened to your admonishments last night about not mixing vodka with a concussion?"

"Since when do you ever listen to my advice?"

He is altogether too charming. I feel my face flush. "Perhaps a bit of something stronger would set me to rights."

"I suppose a little couldn't hurt," he says,

already reaching for the colossal bottle in the upper part of the fridge and pouring a tiny glassful, "long as you drink down all of that water with it."

I give him what I hope is a saucy smile. "Yes, sir." Dear me, I am a shameless flirt. But I don't care. Do I not deserve this little taste of vodka? Have I not done a good day's work in quitting Courtney's unsuitable situation with that dreadful David whatever-his-name-is?

I raise the glass to my lips. "Will you join me?"

"Oh, what the hell." He grabs another glass and pours himself a drink. "To you," he says, and consumes the entire thing.

For my part, I shall only allow myself a ladylike sip, which is enough to spread a pleasing warmth through my bones. My hands hover over the keyboard, as Wes called the rectangular white object topped with raised alphabets and numbers. Keyboard—just like a pianoforte—and all at once my fingers move as if of their own accord. It is indeed like playing the pianoforte, for my fingers know where to go on the keyboard of this strange device as well as they know where to go on the keyboard of the instrument in my father's house.

"See! I knew you'd remember." Wes is jubilant.

I am even moving the mouse and clicking and pointing in a manner that reveals all sorts of heretofore hidden lists of words and pictures on the screen with just a touch of my finger. This is truly diverting. I know not how I could possibly be so proficient at playing this keyboard without any memory of ever having learnt it. I click and point, and my hands instantly summon pictures and words. Could it be that these hands will remember other things as well, things I cannot possibly know or even imagine? The very idea of it is an exciting adventure. Here I am, almost two hundred years after my own time, sitting before a machine I could never have dreamt existed, and my hands know exactly what to do.

Wes's voice rouses me from my thoughts. "You might want to check your email. I got at least five messages from Paula and Anna complaining you're either not checking or not answering."

Without a thought, my right hand automatically guides the little arrow on the screen to one of a row of symbols at the bottom of the screen. I click on it, and a little rectangle appears: "56 new email messages." Instantly, the rectangle disappears, replaced by a screenful of single lines of text that appear to represent a summary of mail delivered to me, but where are the actual letters?

Some of the names in the "From" column are unfamiliar; several are from Paula, Anna, and Wes. There are about ten from David.

"That's a lot of mail," says Wes. "Looks like you haven't checked it since Friday."

"Would you be so good as to tell me how I might fetch the letters? And their cost?"

"What?"

"Or perhaps the senders have had them franked?"

"Courtney, I have no idea what you're talking about. Oh, sorry; I thought because you were pounding away at those keys that everything had come back. Here." He gently removes my hand from the mouse and moves it around the table. "All you have to do is click on whichever email you'd like to read—but you don't need to read that one," he says, indicating the latest one with his name on it. "Just throw it in the trash."

"I certainly shall not," I say, directing the little arrow to the email in question—what a strange word, "email"—and clicking the mouse, causing a message of sorts to appear on the screen:

Courtney, guess I thought we'd put all that behind us. But it looks like Frank isn't the only one you want to avoid. Can we talk? Wes

Wes clears his throat. "Speaking of mail, there was so much of it in your mailbox downstairs that it was practically spilling onto the floor. So I brought it up and put it on the table when I picked up the food. Couldn't help but notice you had a couple of those pink envelopes in the stack."

"Indeed," I say, wondering how much reassurance would be proper for me to give Wes in light of this letter.

"Do you want me to dig out those letters for you?"

"Wes, I am sorry if my flight last night caused you any pain. It was not my wish. I was confused, and—"

I am once again mortified at the thought of my conduct last night.

Wes puts his hand on mine. "I'm sorry you read that one. I sent it from my phone last night, before I found you at Awakening."

"Oh." I venture a glance at his face and am instantly warmed by his gentle gaze.

"We don't ever have to talk about it again if you don't want to."

I give him a grateful smile.

And then I realize his hand is still on mine, and I feel myself blushing. As if reading my thoughts, he looks down at his hand and removes it, clearing his throat.

"I think I'll have another drink," he says, pouring himself half a tiny glassful of vodka.

He offers to pour more into my glass, but it is then I am struck by what he said about the letters. "Do you mean to tell me that I receive mail on paper as well as mail on this computer?"

"Is that a serious question?"

"There are fifty-six letters in this computer, and another stack, you say, of letters on the table. How many would you say were in that stack?"

"I don't know; maybe thirty."

"Today is Monday, is it not?"

He nods.

"And since Friday I have received almost ninety letters? Assuming there is no post on Sunday, that is thirty letters per day. How can anyone find time to earn her living, keep house without servants, and read and answer thirty letters per day?"

"Since when have you had servants? Wait, don't tell me."

"I meant it only by way of illustration." I really must watch my tongue. As I run my eyes over the long list of email messages, it occurs to me that I may have the chance to learn much about Courtney's life, her connection with Wes—and everyone else—from her letters. And perhaps even more from a journal, should she keep one.

Best to be direct. "Do you happen to know if I keep a journal?"

"I did buy you a blank one for Christmas. You don't remember that either, do you. I only bought it because you said you wanted to start writing things down. I have no idea if you ever used it. It was shiny, orange fabric, with embroidery and sparkly things on it." He runs a finger along the spines of the books on the bookshelves, stopping when he reaches the lowermost shelf. "Here it is!" He brings it to me.

I open it to the first page, which bears Courtney's name, address, and some numbers. Before I have an opportunity to peruse the journal, the little phone atop the bookcase emits the music from the *Pride and Prejudice* movie.

Wes looks over towards the phone. "You're not gonna get that?"

Would I even know how?

He seems to read my thoughts, for he steps over to the thing, picks it up, and shows it to me. "See? It tells you who's calling. It says 'Paula,' with her telephone number below the name. See here? You have two choices: Finger-click 'Answer' or just 'Ignore.'"

I point to the word "answer" and press it with my finger. Wes places the phone in the palm of my hand and guides it to my ear.

"Say hello," he whispers.

"Halloo!" I shout, hoping she can hear me.

"Whoa, can you turn it down a notch? That hurt my ears." It is Paula's voice, or rather, a sort of ghost of Paula's voice.

Wes motions to me. "Just talk normally," he whispers.

"Sorry," I say to Paula, but how can I be talking to Paula? How can this disembodied voice be hers when she is not in this room, or even in the other room?

"Where have you been, Courtney?" It sounds as if she is standing in a windstorm. "Anna and I have been calling and calling and emailing and texting and it's like you're blowing us off or something. I was forced to call Wes, who told me about your job. Bravo, girlfriend! You haven't changed your mind and started panicking, have you?"

"I have not."

"Good. Anna and I are taking you out tonight. There's no way we're letting you sit home and start second-guessing yourself like you always do. Dinner. Drinks. Whatever you want."

I suppose now that she has paused to draw breath, I should say something.

"S'okay, darling. You're in shock. We'll be there at eight, okay?" Her voice is muffled, and there is a crackling sort of noise around it.

Perhaps the miracle of talking to someone without their being physically present comes with a price: noise. Indeed it is a small price to pay.

I wonder how far away a person can be and still have a conversation with me.

"Where are you?" I ask.

"Sorry, the service sucks on this stretch of the 110. I'll see you at eight, okay?" More tissue paper crumpling and windstorms raging.

"Okay," I say, and the next thing I hear is not Paula's voice but a short sound followed by silence. I remove the phone from my ear and look at the pane of glass upon it, which says "Call ended." I can hardly believe I have actually had a conversation in such a manner, yet it is true. I smile, feeling almost like a bona fide citizen of this world.

Fifteen

*W*es takes his leave shortly after I inform him of my evening engagements with Paula and Anna, but not before he alludes to the aforementioned pink envelopes by saying that if I need help with them, I can count on him. He also informs me that there are messages for me on my answering machine—yet another machine in this land of machines—and shows me which so-called button I need to press to listen to them. I thank him and promise to take care of all of that directly, but as soon as he goes, I turn my attention back to this marvelous thing called a computer, where I set about pointing and clicking and absorbing as much information as I can about phones, cars, refrigerators, lights, and movies. A good deal of what I read on the screen I do not understand, as there is so much in the modern world, and thus in the modern lexicon, that one must know in order to understand, and these screens of information are written for those who are fluent in the lexicon, which I am not.

Nevertheless, after I don't know how many minutes or hours, I feel a degree less ignorant than I was when I began. I know, for example, that electricity is what fuels the wondrous machines in my apartment and the lights in the city. I know that gasoline, or gas, is what fuels the car, and that movies consist of a succession of tiny images—twenty-four of them in a mere second—created by something called a camera, a word not wholly unfamiliar to me, having read about the camera obscura employed by the great painters.

I now also know that England battled Napoleon for another two years before enjoying a final triumph over him, that Napoleon's madness was exceeded by two world wars—a horrid term—and that England and America have long been allies. And how can I look up English history without also searching for my own dear village? Is it possible that I could find it? Yes, there are screens of information on my village, and it is indeed the very place, for there is an eighteenth-century drawing of the church and high street next to a recent photo, which does not look all that different from the drawing, if you do not count the row of cars or the tall poles with electric lighting.

Finally, I notice a clock at the top of the screen, and I realize that I have little time left to open the mysterious pink letters as well as change my clothes.

Aside from determining that the pink letters are demands for payment, I can make neither heads nor tails of them. "Final shutoff," they say. But of what? It takes me some time to determine that one of them is a notice to shut off electricity. Ah, well. I suppose the worst that could happen is that I shall have to light a candle at night, and be hot in summer, neither of which would be new to me, though I grant the weather here is, at least from my limited experience, a good deal warmer than it is in my own country.

Questions of comfort aside, I cannot abide the thought of being in debt to anyone. My poor father was most scrupulous about never exceeding his income and held in contempt our so-called betters who used to flee to France, leaving their debts behind. Therefore, I must determine the extent of my resources and settle these matters posthaste. And, truth be told, I would not like to be without the computer, as I value its vast repository of information, so useful to someone in my situation. Besides, I would so much like to see the *Pride and Prejudice* movie in full. To have machines, one must have electricity. In fact, I do believe electricity is indispensable.

I remember that I must listen to the messages of which Wes spoke earlier. I press the button he indicated, and after an inhuman-sounding voice announces a date and time, I hear: "Courtney, it's Mom. Why haven't I heard from you? It's been over a week. Are you okay? If you're avoiding calling me because you don't want me to know you're broke again, don't bother. I saw this coming, but you wouldn't listen to me. Do you ever listen to me? And don't think I'm sending you any money, because I'm not. Call me back, okay?"

Call her back? The very thought is terrifying. Though I have never heard the lady's voice before, the very sound of it has given me a pain in my stomach.

I press the button again. There are two more messages from the same lady, each increasingly frantic, each proclaiming her steadfast refusal to send money.

Well, at least this message tells me that if I am unable to pay the bills, I will need to go somewhere other than to family for help. I hope it is not as bad as Courtney's mother thinks, and the pink envelopes suggest, it may be.

But how shall I determine the extent of my fortune? Perhaps I might ask Wes to help me discover if any funds exist beyond what is in my purse at this moment, though I am sensible of the delicacy with which I must approach such a subject. He is, after all, not even a relation. But did he not offer his services with respect to the pink letters? I dare not approach Paula or Anna, who would no doubt take a fright at what they would consider to be my lack of memory. As for Deepa, I do not think she knows enough of Courtney's history to be of much help in that regard.

I look again at the other pink letter, and I make out that it is for the shutoff of telephone service, which, I believe, would be no disservice at all. No one would be able to intrude upon my peace and demand that I speak with them even when they cannot be bothered to pay a morning call as civilized people do.

Then again, at least I have the choice to answer or ignore the summons. Although I do hope that if ever I choose to ignore a call, the caller would have as little idea of my true state as she would if the footman said, "Miss Mansfield is not at home." Perhaps the phone and the computer, therefore, have done away with the need for servants.

Ah, well. I suppose that if I am to be a bona fide lady of the twenty-first century, I should have the requisite accoutrements, including a phone.

Yes, I shall ask Wes for his counsel in these matters. Furthermore, initiating that request will be an opportunity to test my newfound knowledge of how to operate the blasted thing. In the meantime, I take the pink notices, replace them in their envelopes—so clever this extra envelope that is quite separate from the letter itself—and position them under the stack of mail on the table, far from the prying eyes of the two ladies who should be here at any moment.

I am now, after being whisked away in Paula's round blue car, in Anna's apartment, which is at least four times as large as mine and graced with a spectacular view through bar-less windows of astonishingly tall buildings, all lit up like fairy castles. Anna is bustling in the kitchen, which is separated from the living room by a sort of half-wall with a counter and tall stools, where Paula sits while Anna mixes up a drink concoction in something called a blender. Paula is wielding what I now know is called a remote control, pointing it at an enormous rectangular screen which is situated above a chimneypiece and is, like the smaller screen in my own apartment, emitting images as lifelike as those of the *Pride and Prejudice* movie, yet the scenarios keep changing as Paula presses buttons on the device. This must be television—TV—which I also read about while looking up movies and how they work.

Paula switches from a smiling woman with shiny red lips, cooking fish in a pan and talking about spices, to two nearly naked men wrestling each other to the floor while an audience roars, to a young man finishing a song and fidgeting nervously while a group of men and women seated at a table cruelly mock his performance, to a bare-breasted woman being fondled by a man, to I don't know what because I gasp in spite of myself and cover my eyes momentarily.

"There's never anything on," says Paula. "I don't know why I bother except that I can't resist this giant screen. I end up downloading everything I want to watch anyway. TV is just crap."

"Yeah, yeah, tell me about it," says Anna. "The end of the world as we know it, as everyone at work likes to say. 'The death of TV is the death of movies, everyone wants to download on demand,' blah blah blah, who cares."

She turns on the blender for another two seconds, then shuts it off and pours a bright yellow concoction into large stemmed glasses.

"Mango vodka smoothie," she says, handing me one.

"You don't mean that," Paula says.

"I do. I'm sick to death of this business. I'm always thinking about what else I might do with my life."

"Yeah, right. Ten years from now, you'll be running a studio and I'll be designing your big blockbusters instead of the crap I've been working on."

"You wish." Anna smirks.

Paula grabs a tea-cloth from the counter and swats Anna playfully on her rear with it.

"Ouch!"

"So, Courtney," Paula says, warding off a retaliatory swipe of the cloth from Anna, "what are we gonna do about your future?"

It is with difficulty that I tear myself away from the drama unfolding on the screen.

"Courtney?"

"Oh. Do forgive me."

*A*nd thus we embark on a discussion of my employment prospects. More precisely, I say as little as possible while endeavoring to gain as much useful information as I can, and, thankfully,

Anna shuts off the TV, which has been engaging too much of my attention, despite my efforts to train my eyes on the ladies and not on the screen. So far, they have been bandying about terms like "leveraged lateral move," "maximizing relationships," and "career networking," none of which I comprehend, while I sip at the delightfully sweet and potent drink.

"So it's all settled," says Paula. "You start emailing your contacts, and Anna and I will put out some feelers with ours. You'll be set in no time."

"Sounds like an excellent plan." I smile but have no idea what they could possibly mean by my "contacts," let alone what I would email them.

"There's something else," Anna says, glancing furtively at Paula, who is sitting to my left at the long bar. "The way you've been talking the past couple of days might not work to your best advantage."

Paula holds up a hand and cuts in. "Let's get it on the table, okay? It's clear the concussion and the breakup have done a number on your head. Everything I've read, along with the little Suzanne told me, says it'll pass. But in the meantime you'll only make things worse if you keep watching Mr. Darcy on an endless loop or have contact with any of those Jane Austen Society nutcases—and please don't tell me you are, 'cause I don't even wanna know about it. Wake up and

187

smell the twenty-first century, sweetie. People just don't talk like that. So stop it already. And for God's sake, read a thriller or a mystery or, better yet, a magazine or a newspaper. Something from our modern era. There's a lot more to read in this world than Austen, you know."

A Jane Austen *society?* An entire society of people who love the authoress as much as I do? I can hardly contain my delight, but I endeavor to compose myself.

"I am much obliged to you for your hints," I say.

"See what I mean?" Paula throws up her hands. "You won't even try."

"Leave her alone," says Anna. "We can't possibly know what she's going through."

"I promise to say little and listen more," I say, and I mean it. Perhaps the more I listen to the way the ladies and others around us converse, the more I will be equal to emulating it.

Paula looks as if she is not at all reassured, but she sighs and then pours herself another drink. I am sipping mine with care, as I have need of all my faculties.

Paula takes a long drink from her glass. "Another thing we want to talk to you about. Wes."

Anna is nodding her head.

"You're a big girl," says Paula, "but I really don't think your head is screwed on straight right now. Where do Wes's loyalties lie? Not only was his covering for Frank inexcusable as your supposed friend, but according to Frank, Wes's coveting of his best friend's fiancée was more than a little creepy."

"According to Frank . . . ?"

Do they know that I saw him last night, that I . . . ?

I swallow hard and attempt to compose myself. "When did you last speak with Frank?"

Paula waves her hand dismissively. "Don't get all bent out of shape. I called him late yesterday afternoon, when I was looking for you." She juts her chin towards Anna. "We both did. I can't stand him, but he was pretty concerned about you."

"How is his concern of any consequence?"

I can feel him whispering those words in my ear: *Everyone deserves a second chance, don't you think?*

"He was also concerned about you trusting Wes," says Paula.

"Ah. And is Frank to be trusted?"

"I didn't say that."

"Yet you trust his opinion of Wes."

"Wait a minute," says Anna. "Wes knew where Frank was the night you broke up. Yet he not only said nothing, he agreed to cover for Frank."

"I don't want to fight about this," says Paula. "I'm only looking out for you. And so is Anna. Okay?"

I nod at her. "Okay."

"Good," says Paula. "Let's make a plan for tonight."

But I cannot truly give the ladies my full attention, because there are too many unanswered questions. The biggest one is this: If Wes truly is Courtney's friend, then why would he choose to protect a blackguard over her?

I suppose a strict sense of honor could have obliged Wes not to betray Frank, if Frank indeed sought his confidence. However, should not a sense of honor towards a lady, and a lady who is a friend, supersede the claims of another gentleman? But perhaps Wes felt he had no right to speak ill of the lady's husband-to-be.

This is a conundrum indeed, especially because I have only the secondhand accounts of various parties, none of them disinterested, to guide me.

Perhaps Wes did know just how far Courtney had gone in risking her reputation and therefore believed it would be better for her to marry Frank than not.

After all, had I discovered Frank's inconstancy in my own time, and in my own country, it would not signify if I'd found him abed with seven other women. This man would now be my husband. The alternative would be ruin. For once a lady made the choice to bed a man, there was no turning back. Unless he abandoned her, which Frank clearly had not.

Yet no one in Courtney's circle seems to think

her choice to break the engagement an imprudent one. Quite the opposite. But then again, they cannot know that she—that I—and he—or can they?

Does Wes know? If he knew, that is, if he does not already know, then he would never have the feelings which Paula and Anna seem to think he has. Or had. For no respectable man would ever wish to court a lady who had ruined herself in the way that Courtney ruined herself with Frank.

I cannot answer any of these questions. I cannot know if the laws of honor have any meaning whatsoever in this future time and place. And most of all, I cannot help but think of what the fortune-teller said, that I do not know the whole story about anyone.

Yet I must somehow ascertain how the marriage state is regarded in this world. I have seen and heard enough to puzzle me exceedingly. But how shall I conduct such a study?

"Should we take that smile as a yes, Courtney?"

The two ladies are looking at me, and I realize they have been trying to get my attention.

"Anna really wants to see that film," Paula says, "and I don't mind as long as we go out after, and as long as we head to the Arclight right now. I need a good snack bar and good projection."

"You okay with that?" Anna says.

"Perfectly okay," I say, and the ladies smile. I have read enough on the computer about movies and films to feel a thrill of anticipation, although I have no idea what the Arclight is. I keep my silence, not wishing to betray my ignorance, and once we are in Paula's car, I settle in to enjoy the drive and marvel at the spectacle of more tall buildings.

And then, an enormous, honeycombed dome of a structure that is somehow like St. Paul's but without the cathedral looms before us. "Great," Anna says, smiling. "Still plenty of time."

We emerge from an immense parking structure and make our way towards a large building with vastly tall glass doors and a carpeted floor. Inside, there is a sort of shop to the left and what appears to be a restaurant on the right. We, however, move straight ahead to a bank of counters. When Anna approaches one of the counters, takes out money, and says, "Three for the ten o'clock show," I realize that this is the place which sells tickets for the movies.

Tickets in hand, we ascend an enormous stair-case. Everything is on a colossal scale here, including the food, with which Paula loads us up at a long counter. A smiling young woman stand-ing behind the counter hands me a lightweight container filled with white-and-golden things that look like blooming buds. "Small popcorn," she announces as she places the container in my hands. I taste a buttery, perfectly salted piece and smile at Paula. Anna chews on long, flexible, raspberry-colored sweets, and Paula dines on a mustard-covered sausage, a huge container of popcorn, and a box of bonbons. "I haven't eaten since dinner last night," she says, a little smear of mustard in the corner of her mouth. Equipped with featherlight trays, we carry our food to our seats and settle in, and I sip on a deliciously icy-sweet drink called a Coke.

When the theatre fills up, the lights dim, and I am immersed in the spectacle before me. Moving images of gigantic proportions appear on the screen before us. The screen dwarfs even the one above Anna's chimneypiece; it must be twenty feet high. The sound is all-encompassing and almost staggeringly loud; the faces are as tall as a house. I can see the individual eyelashes on the woman's face!

Now the same woman is looking down from the roof of a terribly tall building. She sways as she looks down, and I, looking down with her, get a sickeningly dizzy feeling in my stomach. Hands catch her round the waist from behind; she gasps—I gasp with her. She turns round and her face is transformed with joy as she recognizes the man embracing her. I, too, smile my relief. And then it has ended, and large letters proclaim, "Coming Christmas Day."

Instantly, that image is replaced by several cars hurtling towards one another and narrowly missing calamity. Then we see inside one of the cars, where two dirty, disheveled men laugh and drink from brown bottles. A third man in the rear seat displays his—ah—hindquarters to his traveling companions. The audience laughs its approbation. I know that what I see before me is no more real than a theatre play, though if an actor bared his bottom onstage I would most certainly take my leave. Strangely, I have no desire to make such a statement now, nor, apparently, do my companions. When I steal a glance at Anna, she turns to me and rolls her eyes, and it gives me pleasure that her sensibilities are not unlike mine. Paula, however, is trying in vain to suppress a smile.

Anna says into my ear, "I don't know why they're promoting testosterone-fueled schlock with a romantic comedy."

"Ah," I say, having not the smallest notion of what she means.

And then, the rapidly changing little stories on the screen come to a close, and Anna whispers, "Here we go." With that, our movie begins.

Almost as soon as it does, the heroine is driving her car and another car crashes into it, and the impact and sound are so violent and so real that I bite my lip and fight the urge to grab Anna's arm. But I remind myself that these are actors and that the catastrophe I am witnessing is one of the "special effects" I read about.

After a few more minutes, having accustomed myself to the thunderous noise and enormity of the images hurtling towards me, I begin to lose my sense of sitting in a theatre and become wholly involved in the drama unfolding before me, not unlike those rare moments when I have seen truly good acting on the stage.

Despite the opening crash of cars, the story is, for the most part, a comedy, as I can tell by the laughter from the audience, and there are even a few times when I comprehend the humor myself. But there is much sadness in the story as well, as it follows the life of a young single woman who has just ended her "relationship" with a "boyfriend" whom she discovered was "cheating on her." So many new words I am learning.

"I don't know what Anna was thinking," Paula grumbles to me under her breath during a scene in which the heroine is weeping over her boyfriend's inconstancy.

"Sorry, Courtney," Anna whispers a moment later. "Do you want to leave?"

"Not at all," I whisper back.

Indeed, such a story is just what I need, for I hope it will give me a key to the arcane courtship practices of this future world and thus a better understanding of Courtney's life.

In one scene, the heroine attempts to hide her tears while in a shop with her recently engaged best friend, who is planning her wedding. The shop is filled with long white dresses and long white veils. Wedding dresses. White must be the fashion for brides. Which puts me in mind—dear me—of that white gown I put on when first I awoke in this world. No wonder Wes and the ladies were shocked to see me in what was to have been Courtney's wedding dress. For unlike my world, where white gowns are worn on many occasions and a wedding gown, no matter the color, may be worn again and even trimmed afresh, here a white gown means one thing only. Especially here, in this world of short dresses and ladies in trousers and everyone wearing black.

After the heroine leaves the dress shop, she returns to her own apartment and allows herself to weep in a most heartbreaking manner whilst throwing large publications called *Bride* and *Modern Wedding* into the trash.

I steal glances at my friends and see that they are in no way oppressed by what they are watching. Their countenances reveal a touch of sadness when the actors are sad and an echo of happiness when they are happy. They eat their food and drink their drinks. And why should they not, I tell myself. It is, after all, not real; it is a story, vivid and lifelike, yes, but no less a story.

The most astonishing part of the movie is when, after a long discussion as to whether the heroine will or will not "have sex" with the new young man she has recently begun "dating"—"have sex" sounds like it is of as little consequence as "have cake"—the movie actually shows the heroine and her new boyfriend in bed together, half-clothed.

I half-cover my eyes, peeking out to see if Paula and Anna are as shocked as I. But as usual, they are thoroughly engaged, little half smiles on their countenances, and there is even a burst of laughter from the audience at one moment, the humor of which evades my understanding.

The aftermath of the heroine's tryst with her boyfriend is a detailed discussion of the event with her aforementioned best friend. Which makes me wonder if the true nature of Courtney's intimate connection with Frank is as hidden from Paula, Anna, and even, heaven forbid, Wes, as I had hoped it might be.

I do not indulge very long in those worries, for the hero declares his love for the heroine (but does not make an offer of marriage), the theatre is once again illuminated, and I am following Paula and Anna out of the theatre, the two of them passionately engaged in debating the various merits of the story and acting and effects.

As for me, I leave with more questions than answers.

Sixteen

*H*ome again. I managed to persuade Paula and Anna that I was merely tired, not ill, but the truth is that I simply craved the quiet of my rooms after the sensory onslaught of the film and the subsequent race down illuminated nighttime roads. The bright carriage lamps of hundreds of speeding cars—headlights and taillights, as I remind myself to think of them—red moving away, white coming towards us, made for a dizzying display that, in combination with the movie, left me spent and wishing for nothing more than the quiet comfort of a dimly lit room.

I am determined to find out if the movie—with all its having of sex and planning of weddings—is a true portrayal of courtship and marriage in Courtney's world or merely the writer's fancy.

First to be perused is Courtney's journal. I open the orange spangled book and rifle through its lined pages. The first several pages have been ripped from the book; only the jagged edges remain.

After that are some blank sheets, then this one:

Guests: final count 150
Florist: no baby's breath
Dress: fitting Sat.
Weymouth Cakes: deposit by Monday

Then dozens of blank pages until this one, in the same flowing hand:

What kind of person gets caught with his hands on another woman and the first thing he says is Wes was supposed to tell you I was at a meeting? Were the two of them laughing at how gullible I am? Would Wes have admitted it if Frank hadn't told me? What a stupid stupid fool I am. How long has Frank been hooking up with this skinny lying cake-baking witch who'd better close up shop or I'm gonna ruin her in this town. How could he do this to me I'm so humiliated I just want to die.

More blank pages, and then:

E was adorable and so young and such great sex but I feel empty again. Definitely won't call him. Meaningless sex not what I need right now. Keep thinking of Frank packing up his stuff in my apartment and how I wanted him to touch me and hated myself for wanting it. Wes keeps calling and texting. Why doesn't Frank call? One feeble attempt and he's done. Why would I even want him to I am so pathetic.

There is nothing more in the journal, but what little there is has shocked me exceedingly. Clearly, she believed Frank and Wes to be cruel as well as dishonest. And not only had she bedded Frank, but also someone named E.

It appears the conduct of the heroine in the movie was more realistic than I had hoped. Are more women like this? Perhaps there is something in Courtney's bookshelves, a conduct book perhaps, that will have an answer.

An intriguing array of titles catches my eye, including:

STOP GETTING DUMPED!
All You Need to Know to Make Men Fall Madly in Love with You and Marry "the One" in 3 Years or Less

A title that would sell many dozens of copies amongst my circle.

THE MARRIAGE GAME:
How to Win Big

So it is a game now, is it? I suppose a game is better than a market.

WOMEN WHO LOVE MEN WHO CAN'T COMMIT

Commit what, a crime?

I pull the books from their shelves. Something that feels like a soft folio with slick paper is jammed into the space between the bookcase and the wall. I manage to extricate it. Aha—it is a bride magazine like the ones in the movie. I page through the magazine—its existence alone is proof that marriage is of prime importance in this world.

And yet, by the time I close the last book several hours later, eyes burning and brain unable to comprehend even one more printed sentence, I am teetering between giddiness and a queasy sensation, as if I have drunk too much wine. How to make sense of it all?

In my world, Courtney would be ruined. But here, women have sex before marriage, and with as many partners as they please. Those who would wait for marriage are deemed prudish or odd or exceedingly daring or religious, depending on the author's viewpoint.

"Have sex." At least that expression is preferable to "hook up," which brings to mind being lured to one's death like a fish.

Which seems not to be too extreme a metaphor after all, for despite women's engaging in marital intimacies without the protection of an actual marriage license, they have an abiding fear of the consequences of taking that momentous step. To wit: a plethora of rules and formulae as to how to assess the man's "commitment quotient" before having sex, how many "dates" one should have before actually engaging in sex, and how to ensure that sex does not reduce one's chances of marrying.

Therefore, while women value their so-called sexual freedom, they are fearful of giving away too much too soon, thus obviating a man's reasons for marrying. Which sounds like freedom for men and not for women, in my humble opinion. And which sounds like being ruined is almost as much a risk in this world as it is in mine.

There is, I must say, one astonishing aspect of the business that does indeed represent a degree of freedom, namely that women may engage in sexual relations without the consequence of pregnancy, both before and after marriage. Therefore, marriage is neither, as the church service proclaims it, for the procreation of children nor a remedy against fornication. Marriage is, I must conclude from the bride magazines and the movie, for the extravagance of the celebration, the richness of the dress, and the impression it makes in the eyes of the world.

Or is it? In truth, is not the finery and the splendor of the celebration as much a lure in my world as it is in this one? Does not the idea of marriage eclipse the truth of it? I may not have attended a grand celebration with 250 guests, such as those described in the wedding magazines, but I cannot count the times I have heard of an old schoolfellow who was in raptures over wedding clothes and new carriages and all manner of details that have little to do with real happiness in the married state. Nor can I count the times I have then heard of, or even seen with my own eyes, a quite altered creature in the form of the married woman from what I had seen in the bride to be.

Notwithstanding the importance of external

trappings, marriage for love is as important as it ever was. In fact, women of this century even feel they are entitled to love.

My eyes are weary from hours of reading; I really should retire before the sun rises. Though I may no longer have a situation for which to arise in the morning, I shall not ever let it be said that I am without employment.

*B*y the time I have awoken and dressed myself, it is a little before eleven, and my stomach clenches at the sound of the expected rap at the door. It is time to broach the dreaded subject, but how, I ask myself for the twentieth time, as I open the door to Wes and force a cheerful smile. Though my cheerfulness is not wholly forced; I am truly happy to see him.

Try as I might to be on my guard, as Paula and Anna desire me to be, there is something so artless in his manner that I cannot sustain any distrust. Nevertheless, I must learn once and for all why he chose to lie for Frank rather than be truthful with Courtney. For if there is work for me to do in Courtney's life, as the fortune-teller said, then is it not of the utmost importance that I make a study of Wes's true character?

And so I invited him here. I am duly proud of myself for not only having used the phone to do so, but also for learning how to make coffee with a machine. It seems there is nothing I cannot find out from my oracle, the computer. Wes, however, has come supplied with coffees for both of us, plus flaky pastries stuffed with strawberry preserves. Nevertheless, he kindly tastes some of the coffee I have prepared for him and proclaims it delicious.

"So," Wes says, wiping his mouth on a paper napkin, "are you going to tell me what this 'delicate matter' is that you mentioned on the phone? I keep telling myself you're not gonna give me the ax if you're sitting here having breakfast with me, but I imagine that your closest advisors have urged you to do otherwise."

I feel the blood drain from my face.

"Are you okay?" he says, his own countenance now solemn. "Whatever it is, I can take it."

I take a deep breath. "I am sensible of the kindness you have shown me. You have watched over me, been solicitous of my comfort, and I am truly grateful."

Wes puts his hand on mine, and the warmth of it is electrifying. "I'm the one who's grateful, Courtney. That you let me back into your life is more than I ever dared hope for." He gazes deeply into my eyes, and for a moment I can hardly breathe.

"You know I'd do anything for you, don't you?" he says.

"I believe I do . . . which is why it is particularly awkward for me to ask what I must ask."

"Whatever it is, I'm here for you."

There is so much gentleness in his eyes, in the turn of his countenance, that I cannot form the words to ask him why he was willing to lie for Frank. I cannot. No. I cannot bear to see the pain in his eyes if I question his honor, he who has been so good to me. And what are Courtney's words in a journal to my own experience? No, there must have been some misunderstanding, and it will all come to light when the time is right.

But there is something else that I would like to ask him, something delicate indeed yet easier to broach.

"In truth," I begin, "I am in need of your advice. You see, I do not know how I am to ascertain the extent of my—ah—money matters. There are some bills which I would like to settle without delay, and I do not know; that is—"

"Oh," he says, and looks almost disappointed. "The shutoff notices." What, I wonder, did he imagine I would ask him?

And then he gives me an encouraging smile. "I can help you with that. How long do you have?"

"Well, if only I could determine how much money I have."

"Sorry. Of course. You don't remember your passwords. Let me see what I can do." And with that he seats himself before the computer and tap-tap-taps his fingers on the keyboard. "This could take a few minutes," he calls over his shoulder. "It's okay, Courtney. Whatever it is, we can handle it."

We?

Yesterday I might have thought such a turn of phrase impertinent, but today I do not care. In fact, I like it very well indeed.

"In the meantime," he adds, "why don't you look through the bills and see what needs to be paid first, okay?"

I am even calmer by the time I decipher the bills and see that I have been granted ten days to pay for electricity and five for phone. Then, Wes gestures to me to join him at the computer; he has found out where my passwords are stored and directs my attention to the screen. But I am so distracted by the citron scent of his skin as he leans in close to me that I must force myself to focus on the numbers on the screen.

"That's your balance," he says, indicating a sum that is over three hundred dollars. "Doesn't look great."

I do some quick mental calculations. "But that is at least eighty pounds."

"More like two hundred pounds, but what does that have to do with anything? Pounds, euros, dollars, or rupees—you'll probably need most, if not all of what you have in the bank to cover your phone and power bills. If it covers them." He hands me a little rectangular book. "I found your checkbook in the top drawer. You might want to see if there's anything in it that hasn't cleared." He points to the screen. "I don't mean to talk down to you, but you do grasp that you may not even have all $317.25, right? I don't see any recent deposits. Did you get your final check from David?"

"No, I—"

"Maybe you should see if Sandra can speed things up a bit?"

"She did actually say something about asking David to throw in, as she phrased it, an extra week or two, but she was not sure."

"Excellent."

"And there was something about turning an advance into severance, but I did not fully comprehend . . ."

Wes groans. "If he gave you an advance, he may not owe you anything. Let's hope she comes through for you. In the meantime, how are you set for cash?"

I go to retrieve my bag, and Wes takes the checkbook back from me. "Here, let me see if I can make sense of this while you get your wallet." He turns a few pages, looks at the screen again, and frowns. "Long as you wrote everything down, it looks like your balance is about a hundred dollars less than what's on the screen. If Sandra's getting you a check, it can't come too soon."

I show him the contents of my wallet: It seems the extent of my fortune is the two hundred dollars in the bank and another twenty-seven dollars in my bag.

He reaches into his pocket and pulls out a wad

of bank-notes; I put out my hand to stop him as he offers them to me.

"Please, Courtney. Take it. You'll pay me back. I don't want you walking around without any money. Or running up your credit cards." He takes my hand and presses the bank-notes into it.

"I cannot possibly—" I am too overcome by tears welling up in my eyes to say more, but I manage to get the bank-notes back into his hands. "You are very good, but I assure you I am in no trouble whatsoever."

"What about the shutoffs?" says Wes. "Why don't you let me write you a check; you'll pay me back soon as you get on your feet again."

"I have several days, and it will have all worked itself out by then. Truly."

"Are you sure?" He points at the shutoff notices, which are strewn on the bed. "Should I have a look?"

"I assure you I've not yet reached that level of incompetence, sir." I smile at him with what I hope is an abundance of self-assurance.

Wes grins back at me. "I like it when you call me 'sir.'" He stands up, stretches. "So . . . you have a plan?"

"Plan?"

"For your next job. What's in store for the multi-talented Courtney Stone?"

"What would you advise?"

"Well, we already know you're skilled at hand

holding, enabling, and ego fluffing. Not to mention supplying a raft of creative ideas you almost never get credit for."

"Not a very agreeable picture, to be sure."

He smiles. "I think you should go in a different direction."

"I would have to agree."

"So in the meantime, while you're figuring that out, how about you work for me?"

"What?" I realize I do not even know what Wes's profession is.

"Just temporarily. And don't worry; I don't expect you to help me build websites. I just need someone to help organize my receipts."

"Certainly not."

He looks almost hurt. "Why not?"

"Because—" I can feel my face flush. "Do I even have to—because it would be most improper."

"You're not serious."

"Where I come from, everything I've been doing, everything I am doing now, goes against what I have been taught. Everything, from living like this"—I wave my hand to indicate the apartment—"to receiving morning calls from a single man without another person present." I cannot even look him in the eye. "How can I make you understand? It is not that I do not enjoy the solitude and independence, but it is all so very . . . unprecedented. In truth, I do so very much enjoy our conversations." Why do I feel the blush spreading all the way down my neck? "But surely you must realize that if I were to be employed by you, I would not be your equal. It would be like Jane Fairfax going out as governess and unable to mix with the family on equal terms. Can I speak any plainer?"

"Who's Jane Fairfax?"

"Oh. I thought perhaps you had read *Emma*."

"I will if you want me to. . . ."

"That is not the point. What I mean to say is that one is not, cannot, be on an equal footing with one's employer."

"That is the most antiquated thing I've ever heard. Courtney, I'm asking you to do me a favor. To work *with* me, not for me, okay? Truth is, my accountant's gonna kill me if I don't get my receipts into some kind of order. But I've got so many jobs, I don't have time to do it myself."

Is it possible that he is making me a reasonable offer? I start to pace the room. "And you are not simply acting out of pity?"

"I'm the one who needs pity. If you can't help me, I'll have to hire a complete stranger, give that person access to my confidential files."

Certainly, I would not wish to be overly scrupulous and refuse a friend who has been unstintingly kind to me, regardless of what mistakes he may have made in the past. And working with such a man would be a far more agreeable prospect than risking the possibility of being engaged by another such as David.

"I shall give it some thought."

A rhythmic, syncopated song starts to play, and Wes pulls his phone from his pocket. "Sorry. I have to take this," he says, and strides into the kitchen to take the call. I find it fascinating that everyone seems to have his own personal sound signal—ringtone, it is called.

As I bid good-bye to Wes, who apologizes for having to go and meet a client, I wonder whether my promise to consider his offer stems purely from a desire to reciprocate his kindness, or to spare myself from poverty. Certainly not an easy question to answer.

I decide to distract myself from such grim musings by trying my hand at the clothes washing machine that stands in a tiny room off the kitchen, next to the outdoor staircase. I cannot deny that I am most particularly tempted to work for Wes—and yes, it is for, not with, regardless of how he gilds his words—because I fear being without money.

It is easier to be principled when one is sitting on a pretty little fortune than it is when one is necessitous and poor. Which is why it was all very easy for me to refuse two unexceptionable offers of marriage before Edgeworth came along. I was then surrounded by every comfort, every luxury, with the protection of a landed, respectable family. But here I am, with little in the way of a character to protect and no income to speak of. I have not even sufficient funds to settle the electric and telephone bills. How shall I pay the rent and buy food?

I do not know if I could face a lifetime of poverty in America in the twenty-first century. There is very little dignity to the state of poverty, no matter the age, for I did not fail to notice several bedraggled persons in rags on the streets of this wondrously modern city, which seems to have eliminated every inconvenience of my time except that of poverty. I hope that Sandra persuades David to pay me for an extra week or two. And that the money arrives quickly. I do have some days before the shutoffs occur. And I do not think I should be in Wes's employ, tempted as I am to rely once again on his kindness and generosity. No, I do not wish to risk spoiling a friendship which has become most dear to me in these few days which already seem like a few years, so much has happened. I shall find employment some other way. I must.

I shall not think of this any longer. I shall be mistress of myself. At least, that is, till my clothes are clean.

*I*t is but a couple of hours later that I deposit a pile of washing upon the bed's soft red coverlet. My satisfaction in having learnt how to use the washing machine has an alloy, for despite my certainty of having followed every instruction on the lid of the device, I am left with a miniature version of a white dress that I now hold in my hands. I suppose I might pull apart the dress and make a set of handkerchiefs. Or a fichu. If, that is, I could but locate a needle and thread. I have seen neither a workbag nor a needle-case. Not even a thimble in this house.

It is only upon folding the pile of garments that I discover they, too, come with instructions. It appears that each garment requires a different washing temperature and method of drying. I do hope there are a greater number of literate people in this time than there were in mine. Otherwise a great many people will find themselves with doll's clothing.

With the washing now put away, I believe I deserve a reward: the *Pride and Prejudice* movie. Besides, I have Googled "credit cards" and discovered yet another means of buying necessities until I have an income. Granted, it is also the means of sinking further into debt, but if I must borrow, I would rather it be from a bank than from my friends. No, I shall not think of this anymore today. Instead, I reach for the remote control for the DVD. I have become so adept at mastering the manifold devices of this world (indeed, my fingers seem to know what to do more than my mind does) that it is but the work of a minute before the disk is in place, the movie beginning, and I am snuggled atop the coverlet, cool drink in my hand. This is surely a most agreeable way to spend the rest of the day.

Y̧ou must allow me to tell you how ardently I admire and love—" Suddenly, Mr. Darcy disappears into blackness, and I am awakened from my hours-long/days-long/what-is-time-in-such-a-state *Pride and Prejudice* reverie. I work the remote control to no avail; the screen is still and silent. What can this mean? Indeed, the room itself is now silent—and as dim as a nighttime room in this city can be with the curtains open and the streetlamp outside enabling me to pick out its major features without bumping into furniture. Even the computer screen is dark. I fumble around attempting to turn on the lights, the air conditioner, the movie. All in vain.

And then I remember the shutoff notice. But how can that be possible? The letter stated clearly that there were ten days to pay before the electricity would terminate.

I fumble in the darkened kitchen for candles; finally, I find a few in a drawer and light two with the flame from the stove. I carry one of them over to the pile of mail on the kitchen table and peruse the letter from the electric company, dripping wax on the pages until I find the part that says ten days. There, it must be a mistake, for I only just received the letter the day before. So how can it be that—I examine the letter more closely, and I see that the date at the top of the first page is eleven days ago. How can that be when I just received the letter yesterday? Ah, yes; the mail had been in a pile, Wes said, and this is my fourth day here, and who knows how long Courtney let the mail sit unopened, and besides, who knows how long it takes for a letter to reach its destination and . . . oh, none of that is of any consequence when I am sitting here in the dark.

Why did I have to inherit such a disordered life? Here is a woman who cannot make prudent choices, neither in matters of the heart nor in matters of economy. Well, well. Listen to me. It is all well and good when I look into the mirror and am thankful for this shapely form and this delicate complexion. Or look round this modest apartment and want to fall upon my knees with gratitude that it is a place I can wholly call my own, without dependence on any person's whims or pleasures. Is it not right that if I am to enjoy the benefits of my new person and situation, with all the attendant helpful friends, clever devices, and splendid book collection, I should take responsibility for the disadvantages as well? For how can I lay claim to one and not the other?

In any case, it is fruitless to repine when the most pressing question is how shall I get the lights back on and is that even possible and when shall

I see the end of this movie and . . . ? I have to laugh at myself now, for truly I am become a lady of the twenty-first century who feels herself ill-used indeed when deprived of electricity for a whole five minutes. I, who knew nothing more than candlelight just four days ago. Four days and 196 years.

What shall I do for relief? I dread Wes's discovering my state of affairs, for he would no doubt settle the bills with or without my permission, as would Paula and Anna. How fortunate I am to have inherited such affectionate friends, but I dare not be a burden on anyone who is not a blood connection. I do so wish I could contrive the means to settle it all myself.

What, indeed, would I do were I to find myself stranded in my own country, in my own time, but far from home? I would apply to my father, of course, by post, and he would manage it all and keep it from my mother. Strange that on my first morning here, Wes asked if he should call my mother but said nothing of my father. Perhaps Courtney has no father. And clearly her mother is not a person I can turn to in a time of distress. I must clear my mind somehow. Walking. That always restores my spirits, provides me with commonsense ideas. I snatch my bag from the table and run down the stairs.

Seventeen

I walk the two blocks towards the principal street where all the shops are, though I've no intention of spending what little money I have, and luckily I dined earlier on the remains of yesterday's dinner, that lovely chicken mole, so I have no need for food. Not yet.

Just before I reach the main road, a car catches my eye. Well, not the car itself, for its brown bulk, dulled by a veneer of dust, is plainer than most of its neighbors. No, what commands my attention is behind the car's large front glass, lit up by the streetlamp above it: a tiny stuffed lion hanging from the mirror—and I know it is a lion even before I get close enough to see its features. And suddenly I, as Courtney, am holding that little stuffed toy and offering it to Frank. It is his birthday, and the little lion is a present. I am sitting on a tall stool at the bar, in the public house where Glenn works, the place that all at once I know is called The Fortune Bar. And I know, with all my being, that what I am seeing in my mind's eye is a memory, even though I also know that it is not my memory. It is Courtney's memory. I am in the bar with Frank, and my stomach is tightening with hurt because he has refused the present.

"Come on, admit it," he says, his full lips smiling. "This is a present for you, not me. You know, like those red lace panties I got you for Valentine's Day. Definitely a present for me. How 'bout you hang this little guy off the rearview mirror and he'll protect you from all those clueless drivers and rapacious meter maids. I like that word . . . *rapacious*. How come we don't use words like that every day?"

"Because we don't want to sound like pretentious wankers?" says Paula, who has suddenly materialized in a cloud of sheer, pale blue fabric, a frothy scarf and a matching frock, a saucy smile on her glossy red lips, and lands on the vacant seat between Frank, who is standing, and me.

I whisk the stuffed lion out of sight and into my bag. Frank glares at the intruder.

Paula's eyes are wide with mock innocence. "Did I say something wrong?"

Frank says, "I suppose using British profanities when you're from Wisconsin isn't pretentious."

Paula inclines her chin towards Glenn, who grins from his station behind the bar and raises his glass to us. "He's been teaching me."

"Excuse me, ladies," says Frank, making his escape and heading over to the other, presumably more hospitable end of the bar, where he begins conversing and smiling with another tall, handsome young man with spiky brown hair and thin arms.

"Be nice," I hiss at Paula. "It's his birthday, for God's sake."

A tap-tap-tap at the side window of the car jolts me from this strange memory. I am now actually sitting inside the car with merely a vague sense of having opened the door and taken a seat while wrapped in the memory of Frank's birthday. And, as if that memory has conjured the man himself, Frank's grinning face lowers into view on the other side of the window. Tap-tap.

Feeling a flush of anger which no doubt crimsons my face, I insert the key that I have been clutching in my right hand into the lock beside the driving wheel—the steering wheel, I correct myself—and turn it. The engine roars to life.

Tap-tap. I glance to my left. Frank's face is a question; his lips form words I cannot make out, do not wish to make out. I turn and face the front window; I do not owe him anything. And who is he to have the assurance to call on me and intrude upon me at all hours after having betrayed me?

Me? He betrayed Courtney, not me.

But I am she, am I not? Like it or not, impossible or not, I am she. I see her in the mirror, I answer to her name, I live in her home. Those who are true to her are true to me. And those who are false to her are false to me.

My right hand moves the gearshift to D—Drive. I have watched Paula and Sandra do this, but till this moment I did not realize that D was for Drive. Till this moment I knew not which pedals my foot must depress in order to move and brake. I know not how it is so, but my hands and feet know exactly what they need to do to drive. My hands turn the wheel towards the street; the car rolls an inch and—

Pounding on the side window. A muffled "Courtney!" My right foot touches a pedal and the car rolls even more. A whizzing roar, the blast of a horn, and my foot slams on the brake as a speeding two-wheeled vehicle races a mere inch beyond my door. A woman sits on a pillion behind the driver, long blond hair streaming from a helmet; my blood courses furiously through my veins, and my hands freeze on the wheel. For a moment I cease breathing, and then it comes fast and hard as my body trembles.

I could have killed them.

The woman turns round and jabs her middle finger in my direction before facing forward again, and then they are gone.

I move the gearshift to P and turn the key to the left. The car is now as silent as the devices in my home. How could I possibly think myself capable of driving such a powerful, complex, wholly foreign vehicle?

Frank taps on the window again. I turn to him and his countenance is suffused with kindness. I acknowledge him with a nod and pull the door handle. He stands up, waiting for me to emerge. I stumble slightly as I alight from the car; I am a bit dizzy, it seems. He quickly supports me with an arm round my waist, and I don't resist. The flare of anger I felt a moment ago no longer feels real; it is but a ghost of that strange memory.

"Are you all right?" he says. "Here, give me the keys, and I'll take care of the car."

He leads me over to a wall that separates a grassy garden from the pavement. "Here, lean against this for a minute; I'll be right back."

True to his word, he moves the car back to where it was before I almost drove it into two people. I shudder again at the narrowness of their escape, and he is again by my side. "Here, let me walk you home."

"That is most kind—I mean, okay, thank you." And then I remember the lack of lights in the apartment. How will I explain that to him? "I mean, thank you but no, I am perfectly able to walk home on my own."

Frank smiles down at me. "Don't worry; I won't try to come up. I'm not that presumptuous."

I turn my face away. He is as impertinent as he was the other night.

"Sorry, Courtney. I was just making a stupid joke. I'll wait on the sidewalk till you turn on the light so I know you're okay."

This certainly will not answer.

"In truth," I say, summoning some cheerfulness into my voice, "I would like to walk a little before I go home."

"Not by yourself you don't. This is L.A., not

Mayberry RFD. Let me just walk beside you. Wherever you want to go."

I nod my assent, and we continue towards the main road in silence.

"You don't even have to speak to me," he says, smiling mischievously after a couple of minutes without any conversation. His countenance takes on a more serious expression. "Though I'm hoping you will."

I do not answer. Much as I am loathe to admit it, he does have the ability to soften me with a look, a quality of which I believe he is very well aware.

"Or better still," he adds as we near the red door of The Fortune Bar, "you can let me buy you a drink, which I'm sure you could do with after your ordeal." He pauses. "You still don't have to talk to me."

A drink does sound lovely right now.

Strangely, I have a sense of coming home as I enter the overly trimmed yet comfortable establishment and settle into one of the curved, padded red benches at a corner table while Frank repairs to the bar to fetch us drinks. Everything about this red and black and golden place feels familiar, and familiar beyond having been here once before —the little sculpted angels which serve as sconces on the walls, the velvet chairs, and most of all, the tall, welcoming form of Glenn, who is on his way over with a broad smile, his blond and brown locks oddly becoming and distinctly Glenn.

"Darling," he says, leaning over to enfold me in his arms—and this time I am pleased rather than concerned about how it might look; even the purple-and-gold dragon on his arm is comfortingly familiar. "So happy to see you. But what are you doing with the ex-fiancé from hell?" He raises an eyebrow and shakes his head. "If you need me to whack him over the head with a cocktail shaker, just say the word." He winks and heads back to the bar, just as Frank arrives bearing two glasses and slips into the bench a discreet distance from me.

"He could at least try to hide the fact that he hates my guts," Frank says, looking ruefully after Glenn. "I'd stop tipping him if I weren't afraid he'd spit in my drink."

"Perhaps he does that anyway," I say sweetly, then clap a hand over my mouth, astonished at what came out of it.

"Very funny," he says, and I cannot help but laugh. "Really, Courtney. You have no idea what it's like to have everyone hate you. And why do you get to be the only injured party? You're the one who called off the wedding, not me. I would have gone through with it."

"Rather like having a tooth drawn."

"What's that supposed to mean?"

I drink deeply from my glass and regard him carefully as I throw as much indifference into my air as possible. "Are you saying we should have married?"

He sputters and coughs, practically choking on his drink. "I—I'm just saying I'm not the only one who wasn't ready."

All at once I see that this man, who could have been my husband, this person with whom Courtney was supposedly violently in love, is a child.

He drains his glass and regards me. "You know I still care about you. Can't you at least stop acting like I have the plague?"

"I don't know what you mean."

"You nearly clipped a motorcycle trying to escape from me."

I shudder. "That will never happen again."

Frank laughs. "Glad to hear it." He motions to a long-legged young woman with closely cropped red hair and a tray of drinks, but she is smiling flirtatiously at a man at the next table and appears not to see Frank. "Can't catch a break in this place," he scowls. "Speaking of which, could you try to cut me a little slack behind my back as well? The role of village pariah is getting old."

"I shall do my best."

I catch sight of Glenn, who is leaning against the bar, arms folded, shaking his head at me.

I ease out of the bench. "I really must go."

"Okay," he says, "but I'm walking you home."

I do not contradict him this time.

When we reach the house, he reminds me to turn on a light to signal to him that I'm okay.

"Actually," I say, "I will light a candle in the window. I find that candlelight is easier on my eyes since the concussion."

Frank's full lips curve into that slightly crooked smile as he looks deeply into my eyes. "Sounds romantic."

I can feel the heat spreading from my face down my neck. He leans down, and his lips brush the tip of my ear, sending a thrill through my body. "How 'bout I come up and light some of those candles for you," he whispers. "I meant what I said the other night about a second chance. I miss you, you know."

I almost cannot breathe. Is he about to . . . ?

His hand reaches for mine and clasps it, fingers caressing the top of my hand. "We were so good together," he breathes, his lips close to mine. "You remember, don't you."

This body remembers, this body which arched itself under his, the weight of his body, the touch of his lips. Dear God, what is happening to me?

"You're trembling," he murmurs, wrapping his arms around me. He whispers into my hair. "Let me stay with you tonight."

Ah. Now I understand. He wants nothing more than to get into my bed. To think I have almost been taken in.

"I do not," I say, extricating myself from his grasp.
"What?"

"I do not remember." And that is almost not a

lie, save for those bodily memories, or whatever they are—I shudder inwardly—and that incident with the little stuffed lion.

He strokes my cheek with the back of his fingers. "I could make you remember."

"No," I say, backing away from him. "You have no right."

"I don't get it. How come Wes gets another chance, but I don't?" He gives me a hurt look. "I said I was sorry about Amy."

"And that, I suppose, should make the heavens part."

"For God's sake, Courtney, I didn't even sleep with her." He looks down at his shoes, then meets my eyes again. "But I am sorry."

I cannot believe I am discussing such things with anyone, let alone with such a man. "I'll wager that whatever it is you're sorry for, it is not something one does when one is engaged to be married. Not that it is anything to me. I remember almost nothing about you."

He looks at me as if stupefied. "You really don't remember."

I do not contradict him.

"Yet you're angry at me anyway."

I am angry. More angry at myself than at this vain, selfish creature who nearly charmed me into believing he had real feelings for me. But I shall not give him the satisfaction of knowing my heart. "You are mistaken. I am merely indifferent."

"You really don't remember me," he murmurs, as if to himself. "That's just not possible."

I regard him coolly, unwilling to allow him the satisfaction of knowing just how far his words outstrip the truth.

"Courtney—" I turn to go upstairs, but he takes my hand. "Maybe if we spent some time together, it would come back. Actually, I think you should move in with me. I don't mean you should give up the apartment. Not yet, anyway. But why don't we see how it goes? Get to know each other again. A fresh start."

A bubble of laughter escapes me. "You must be joking." I pull my hand from his grasp and start up the stairs.

"If things work out, we can talk about getting engaged again," he calls after me.

But I do not answer him.

"It's Wes, isn't it?"

I do not look back till I am inside, candle lit and placed in the window. It is then that I peer outside at his solitary form looking up at me, hand lifted in a wave; then he turns away, and I watch his figure retreat into the nighttime gloom, relieved to be out of his orbit.

To think I had believed, even for a moment, that he was about to offer me marriage, not a chance to bed him again and be his mistress who must still work and pay her own rent and can be thrown off without a moment's notice unless perhaps he decides to make her an honest offer again. What a bargain.

Yet it is most unsettling how drawn to him I was down there in the street. Before, that is, I came to my senses. Certainly, now that I am safe within my rooms, I feel nothing but relief at his departure. But for a few moments, there was that pull, like a bird flying too close to a cat. That I should be taken in for even a moment, despite everything I have heard from Wes and Paula and Anna, despite what I witnessed of Frank's own conduct myself, and most of all, despite his own confession of guilt, is beyond anything.

Were those Courtney's feelings down there in the street, or mine? I can see why Courtney would be drawn to him, for she did, after all, share with Frank what should only be shared in marriage. And she did, by all accounts, truly love him. And he, in his own words, would have gone through with the wedding. Not every man would do the same.

Though indeed, he must now consider me damaged goods after all. Else he would not have made such an insulting offer.

For the first time, I am sensible of how brave it was for Courtney to break her engagement. Perhaps her choice would not be a prudent one in my world, but it is certainly a wise one.

Eighteen

I am unpleasantly reminded of the limitations of reading by candlelight, especially when there are but two candles in the house. Thus I am sent earlier to bed than I desire and am up at first light to devour as much as I can of the next Austen novel in my possession, *Mansfield Park*. This particular volume affords me not only the delights of a new story, but also the chance to learn something about the author herself, for there is a good deal of information about her in the front of the book, including an account of how she accepted an offer of marriage from a very rich man, a friend of the family. Although the marriage would have saved her, her mother, and her sister from poverty, Miss Austen did not love the gentleman and thus refused his offer after all. A courageous act in light of her age and situation, for she was nearly twenty-seven at the time, her prospects were bleak indeed, and her friends surely disappointed. At least Courtney had the approbation of her friends for breaking her engagement.

I wonder if Miss Austen's path and mine ever crossed in town, or in Bath. Perhaps I might have attended the same assemblies in the Upper Rooms or bought ribbons in the same Bond Street shop. What would I not give to have had the good fortune to meet her! And how I wish I could have had the means to tell her how famous and beloved she would be almost two hundred years after her death.

By the time I leave my bed, the sun is high in the sky, and the heat in the apartment is already at a disagreeable level, even with every window wide open. Were it not for the bars, I would be tempted to thrust my head outside, not that I imagine it would do me any good. Courtney's native climate is a hot one indeed.

I make my way into the kitchen on bare, blue-nailed feet (which no longer shock me; I think I might even like them a little) and open the refrigerator. Good God. I cover my nose, which is assaulted by a sulfurous odor. It seems the sad-looking head of lettuce has expired in the heat and is now become a rotting corpse.

Horrible. I hold my breath and grab a paper towel with which I remove the slimy thing, then dump it in a paper bag, which I hasten out of the apartment and down the stairs to the large receptacle outside where I saw Paula dispose of her coffee cup. I am not even aware that I have done all this clad only in a long shirt which exposes my legs to the middle of my thigh until I return to my bedchamber and catch sight of myself in the mirror of the open closet. A mere five days in this society, and already I am putting my charms on exhibition for all the world to see.

What would Mary say if she saw me expose

myself—literally—in such a manner? Not that she would recognize me. Not that I recognize myself.

Ah, Mary. I do miss you. If you were here, I would make you know that this is me.

Good lord, it is hot in here. A cool shower would be lovely; I cannot even imagine getting dressed without one. I shed the nightshirt and step into bracingly cold water; I could stay in here all day, glorying in the delightful refreshment and the marzipan scent of the body wash. Heavenly.

As I dry this well-formed body with an enormous, fluffy white towel, I am struck by the difference between this body and the number of remarkably thin, almost half-starved-looking ladies in the bridal magazine I perused the other day. All of the women were of a style of beauty that is quite different from these rounded arms and legs and the gentle swell of this belly. This body is not fat, but it is by no means like the women in those pictures, who are thinner than even the slim body I left behind, with its small breasts and columnlike form. My mother's favorite dressmaker always said that I had the perfect figure for the high waists which are all the fashion, but I always longed for more womanly proportions.

In this future world, however, it seems that the more starved a woman looks to be, the more her collarbones and elbows protrude through her skin, the prettier she must be.

No wonder Anna referred to Courtney's litany

of complaints about her personal size. Poor Courtney; were she in my time she would be considered an ideal of beauty by many a man and woman. I, however shall make up for that neglect by showering praise every day upon this beautiful form which I have inherited.

As I rifle through my clothes for something suitable to wear, my stomach rumbles. Something I imagine women who would not otherwise go hungry voluntarily endure, as there was a great deal of talk in the magazine of the methods used to achieve the desired starved look, which, of course, involves actual starving. That is a practice I shall certainly not adopt, as long as I have money enough for food. I have had nothing at all to eat since yesterday afternoon. How blessed I am to have money in my bag that will buy me a meal at one of the restaurants along the road, and some money left in the bank, but I am no closer to having the smallest notion of what I shall do when that runs out than I was yesterday. I cannot think of such things now; I must dress and buy food. And a supply of candles.

I find a long, flowing skirt in the closet and top it off with a sleeveless white bodice. It is, after all, abominably hot, as Mary would say, and it's not as if every woman out there isn't baring both arms and legs. I have to laugh, for I believe my little blunder of running outside before in only a nightshirt has relaxed my heretofore strict notions of proper attire.

I am about to walk out of the apartment when the phone, which I've forgotten in my haste and left sitting atop the bookcase, explodes with the joyous music from *Pride and Prejudice*.

"Mom," it says on the screen. "Answer. Ignore."

My stomach tightens at the thought of speaking to this unknown person who has been leaving me increasingly angry messages. Nevertheless, she is supposed to be my mother, no matter how unknown she is to me, and thus it would be unfilial to refuse her call.

Oh, dear.

"Hello?"

"Courtney—thank God. First I don't hear from you for two weeks. Then I call your number and it's disconnected. What the hell's going on there?"

Perhaps answering the phone was not the most prudent idea after all.

"Well? Are you all right?"

"Perfectly—Mother."

"Since when do you call me Mother?" Her voice is deep and has a rapidity of expression quite unlike that of my own mother, whose calm clear tones and careful enunciation can be quite deceptive.

"Ma-ma?" I venture.

"Have you been drinking?"

"I hardly think—"

233

"What happened to 'Mom'?"

"Forgive me—Mom. Of course." Stupid, stupid. It was right there on the phone. And in her messages.

"Just what are you up to, Courtney?"

"I was only going to walk to Sunset Boulevard and buy something to eat."

"You're not at work? Did you lose your job? Is that why your phone's disconnected? Oh my God, Courtney."

I summon as much calm and command into my voice as possible. "I left my job. It was the right thing to do." Despite my efforts, I am trembling by the end of this little speech. Clearly, Courtney's mother has the power to unsettle me as much as my own does.

"Without lining up another job first? Are you out of your mind?" She drops her voice to a whisper. "How much do you need?"

"Where are you?" I realize I have dropped my voice as well.

Still whispering, she says, "I don't want Don to know I'm sending you money."

Don? She cannot be talking of my father.

"Not that it's any of his business," she says, "but you know how it is."

I do?

"His kids are like vultures, and I don't want him to think—"

"That I'm picking at your carcass?" I cannot

believe that just came out of my mouth. And who is Don anyway?

"That's disgusting," she says. "And unfair. Don's been very good to me. And you, I might add. It's not his fault your own father forgot he had a family. But you'll never give him a break, will you?"

Oh, my. What sort of family is this? Courtney's father—my father—abandoned his wife and child? And is her mother married to Don? Or is she—?

"I'm sorry, Courtney. I shouldn't have brought up your father."

"No. It is I who should apologize."

"Let's just forget it, okay? You know I'm not made of money, but you're my daughter, and if a mother can't help her own daughter, then what kind of mother is she?"

"Please do not trouble yourself. I'm certain I will find a new job very soon."

"In this economy? You should listen to me and forget about the movie business. Assistant. That's a make-nothing, go-nowhere job if there ever was one. I know, I know, you have friends who moved up. Well, good for them. I'm tired of seeing my daughter treated like dirt. Assistant. It was all well and good when they changed my title from secretary to executive assistant back when that first became fashionable, but that didn't mean I got to stop fetching the coffee, and it didn't mean I was ever getting my boss's job. Of course when you work in a law firm, that's not an issue, but at least it paid well. Why didn't you listen to me and get an MBA instead of a degree in English, of all things?"

I, a degree?

"You could have gone to law school. And now it's too late; you have to start thinking about having kids—Oh, boy. I really stuck my foot in it, sweetie. I'm so sorry. I know you're devastated. God. I'm just so upset that you're out of work on top of everything else."

"I'm—okay—Mom. Truly."

I have taken a degree. I. A woman. Oh how I longed to be like my brother and go to Cambridge. I would treasure the opportunity for learning, whereas he saw it only as a means of being free from the restraints of home.

"Courtney! Are you listening to me? When have you ever quit a job without having another lined up? That's it. I'm coming out there."

"No!" I know not whence that came, but I do know I must prevent her coming at all costs. I force some calm into my tone. "Truly. I am perfectly okay. I assure you."

"I can't keep sending you money forever, you know. Truth is, I'm about tapped out. I know I said I'd never mention it, but that $2,000 in deposits I laid out for your wedding is money I'll never see again. You need to find a job. Fast. Which is why you should let me help you. Give me two weeks in L.A. scouring the want ads and reworking your résumé and I promise you'll have results."

Despite the heat in the apartment, my bones chill with fear.

"But the expense of traveling, would it not be—"

"Don has plenty of miles; flying won't cost a thing."

"Miles." I have no idea what she's talking about, especially the part about flying, and I dare not inquire. I have only a terrifying vision of this strange woman who claims to be my mother sprouting wings and then tapping on my windowpane.

"And of course I'll stay with you."

No. This cannot be happening. Shall I tell her about Wes's offer, or would doing so seal my fate?

"Mom. There is no need for that. I assure you that I will have a new job within a week."

"How do you figure that?"

"I have a plan." Of course I have no such thing. "And please, Mom, do not send me money."

"Are you sure?"

Of course I'm not sure. I have not even money to pay the electric and telephone bills. But I know that I cannot trade my independence for pecuniary assistance.

"All I ask is one week, and if I am not employed by then, I will do whatever you wish."

"I'll believe that when I see it." She pauses. "All right, then. One week."

Thank heaven. I feel as if I have been holding my breath. "And Mom? I'm touched by your generosity. Truly."

And I am. Despite my terror at having her appear at my door. Or window.

"Don't disappear again, Courtney. I love you, you know."

Suddenly, my throat is tight with unshed tears which blur my eyes. It is all I can do to choke out "Thank you." And with that I end the call, vastly relieved. And just as guilty as I feel after every conversation I have ever had with my own mother about the grim state of my future. If only she could see how that future turned out.

If I do not get out of here, I shall end up on the floor having hysterical giggles. I grab my bag and hurry out of the door.

Nineteen

The glare of the sun is blinding, the heat a solid wall. I rummage inside the bag, hoping I possess a pair of dark spectacles like the ones I have seen Anna and Paula wear, and which I now see on almost every driver in the street. My fingers close around a pouch which contains a pair of dark spectacles—sunglasses, that is what they are called. Lately, it is as if a vast internal lexicon has opened up in my brain, providing to me names of things I never knew of before.

I put on the sunglasses. Ah, yes. The bright world is now pleasantly so. When I reach Acme Taqueria I marshal my courage, for in my world it would be unheard of for a respectable woman to enter an eating house alone. Indeed, it would be unusual to see a genteel woman, accompanied or not, in such a place. But this is not my world, and few if any of those rules apply.

I stand before the door of the restaurant, longing for the coolness I know awaits me inside yet unable to move myself out of the heat. I survey the several configurations of diners at the various tables. Women. Men. Women and men together. A lone man. But not a lone woman.

But it cannot be wrong for me to dine here alone, for did I not say to Courtney's—my—mother that I was about to venture out for food? She did not even inquire if I was accompanied, let alone by whom. She cared only about employment and money matters.

Then why are there no unescorted females within?

I am about to turn round and go home, despite the grumblings of my stomach, when a familiar voice calls out.

"Don't go in. Come out with me instead," it says.

I turn towards the voice. It is Deepa, alone in a car. "Get in, girl. It's bloody hot out there."

I was never so relieved to see anyone as I am to

see Deepa's smiling countenance, her perfect teeth bright white against her lovely brown skin, and as soon as I'm settled into the cushiony, cream-colored seats in her car, I know I am safe.

"I can't believe I didn't get your number the other night," says Deepa. "So I stopped by your place, just like an old-fashioned Jane Austen morning call"—she turns momentarily towards me, her eyes sparkling mischievously—"but madam was not at home. Lucky for me running into you on Sunset."

I smile at her. "Lucky for me as well."

"So," she says, "shall I assume your hesitant manner in front of the restaurant indicates you're not as starved as I am?"

"Not at all. I'm famished."

"Excellent. Can you wait forty-five minutes for a meal? I've got this wild idea to drive out to the beach, where it's got to be at least fifteen degrees cooler than this inferno, but it didn't sound like much fun doing it on my own."

"The beach. That would be lovely."

I haven't been to the seaside since Brighton, and that was four years ago.

"My treat," she says.

"But I—"

"No, I insist. This is my adventure, and I'm happy for the company."

She cannot possibly know how straitened my circumstances are; no, this is not the impulse of pity. It is an act of real friendship. She has sought my company, and not merely for a fifteen-minute formal morning call, but for a journey to the seaside. I shall accept her generosity and repay it when I can.

We are on the road not ten minutes when I catch sight of something that nearly makes me gasp aloud—a bona fide airborne machine with wings like a bird, high up in the sky, cutting through the heavens like an arrow.

Did Deepa see it as well? She does not look as if she has noticed anything extraordinary. Could it be that in this world, a flying wonder in the sky is as commonplace as a carriage was in mine? What a miraculous creation! Somehow I manage to tear my eyes from the sky and respond to Deepa's kindly asking me how I've been since that night in the club.

By the time we leave the freeway—another new word I have learnt—and turn down a street, at the end of which beckons a twinkling blue sea, I have seen two more flying machines. And I don't quite know how it happened, but I have also ended up telling her about the loss of my job, the refusal of my mother's offer of money, and the threat of a visit from her (and it was then that I realized the airborne machines must be what she had in mind when she talked of flying).

"In all fairness," I say, "she is quite generous to make such an offer, so I should be ashamed of myself for dreading the prospect of a visit. I mean, I *am* ashamed of myself."

"You're kidding, yeah? Listen, I love my mother as much as anyone does, but whenever she descends upon me, she positively puts everything in my life under a microscope. And she never likes what she sees. You did the right thing by turning down her cash. There are always strings attached, believe me."

I could not be more delighted with a companion if Mary suddenly appeared before the imposing hotel made of brick and what looks almost like Bath stone, where we alight from the car.

"What do you think?" says Deepa as we enter the building. I am so absorbed in the airy lightness of the vast space that I can only murmur my approbation. A curved double staircase inlaid with colorful tiles leads us to a vast columned area filled with sofas and deep, cushioned chairs, where young men and women sit sipping drinks. The walls are lined with books, and there are even desks with little lamps, giving the feeling of a library in a grand estate rather than a public place. But no library, of course, leads to a bar where two smiling women with long blond hair serve drinks. One wonders if the ladies were chosen for their looks, like footmen, as they are of the same height and figure and complexion.

These wonderings are but fleeting, for the source of the brilliant light that permeates the vastness of the grand room comes into clear view as I walk closer towards the bar, and I behold what takes my breath away: a veritable wall of windows, semicircular in shape, which must be twenty feet tall and reveal a spectacular view of the ocean and strand. And this, I realize as Deepa leads me to a table before one of the immense windows, is where we are to dine!

Deepa laughs. "At a loss for words?"

I can only nod and smile. Sailboats bob in the shimmering vastness like children's toys while other, sail-less boats speed through the waves. An astonishing juxtaposition of old and new, for the sailboats could have come from my own world, while the ones without sails or oars are as foreign as a carriage without horses. Equally fascinating are the wheeled machines, with one wheel in front of the other, upon which scantily clad men, women, and children glide happily along curved pavements that straddle the sand.

And then, as if the magnificent display before my eyes were not enough, another winged machine not unlike the ones I saw earlier soars past, high up in the sky. If only my father, who marveled at the ascent of the aerial balloons in Bath, could see such a miracle.

And in that moment, it is as if the floor has fallen away and I am unmoored; I am almost overcome with the momentousness of witnessing such marvels, of being in a time, in a world, where such things are possible, and indeed where they appear to be everyday facts of life, if I am to judge from the nonchalance of the other diners who face the windows and doubtless see the same spectacle that is before my own eyes. Courtney's eyes. If it weren't for Courtney's eyes, I would not be here seeing these wonders. And in this moment, I am fervently grateful to her for allowing me a glimpse of her world.

"Are you going to look at the menu, or do you already know what you want?" says Deepa.

In truth, I am unable to take my eyes off the windows long enough to focus on the menu.

She laughs. "I'm too hungry to wait. How about I order for both of us?"

I smile my assent. And she does. Drinks, too. "The orange margaritas are to die for," she says.

The drinks arrive, along with a basket of rolls that smell as if they have just emerged from a hot oven. I slather one of the rolls with butter, which melts as the knife touches the bread, and I close my eyes as I chew the first bite, it is so good.

Now I must taste the drink as well, and I take a large swallow. Delicious and like nothing I have ever tasted.

"Careful, darling." Deepa smiles. "That's some serious stuff. You might want to eat the whole roll before you dive in."

But I can't help myself. The margarita is so delicious, so tart and sweet and salty and refreshing, that I drain the entire glass before I have even a second bite of the bread.

"Or maybe not," says Deepa, laughing.

*F*ortunately, the waiter returns to place a plate of food before me, and I take a large bite of something called a hamburger, which is dressed with a sharp yellow melted cheese and fried onions.

It's heavenly, but it is also too late. I am already in liquor.

"So," says Deepa, putting down her fork. "Any ideas what kind of work you want to do?"

"Ah. An interesting question. If only I had an answer." The waiter puts another margarita before me, and I take a healthy swallow of it before I see Deepa shaking her head at me, and I put it down, feeling sheepish. "My mother says I should have gone to law school. Or had an MBA. Or had children. But it is too late for any of that, it seems."

Deepa laughs. "So she crushed you between the rocks of guilt and fear. A technique my own mother has mastered."

"I suppose it was a little like Scylla and Charybdis. But what would she say, I wonder, if she knew that Wes offered me work?"

Deepa arches an eyebrow. "Did he? What sort of work does he do?"

I shrug and start to giggle. "I have no idea."

"I seem to recall it's something to do with computers."

"Indeed." I think of Wes's big hand covering mine as he showed me how to use the mouse. I take another sip of the drink and giggle.

Deepa moves the glass away from me. "I believe you're a little drunk."

I put my hand over my mouth, mortified.

"So are you going to work for Wes doing who knows what?"

"Certainly not."

"Good move," says Deepa. "Too complicated."

"My thought exactly."

"Yeah," she says, taking a sip of her margarita. "He fancies you."

I almost choke on my food and cough so hard that Deepa reaches over and thumps me on the back with the flat of her hand.

"You okay?" she says.

I reach for the margarita glass and take a large swallow. I nod.

"Anyway, if you work for him, he might feel too awkward to do anything about it, and he's too cute to pass up for a job, if you ask me."

"You really think he . . . ?"

"Oh, come on. Anyone can see how he looks at you." Deepa gives me a sly grin. "You're blushing. Does that mean you like him, too?"

Is it possible that Wes really does have a regard for me which is more than kindness and friendship? But that would mean Wes truly does not know the extent of my history with Frank. No matter what those books in Courtney's rooms implied, no respectable man would ever connect himself with a woman who had . . . And even the books themselves warned of the consequences of giving oneself to the wrong man too soon.

"Courtney? You look like you're a million miles away." She smiles at me kindly and places a hand on my arm. "I'm sorry if I hit a nerve. It's none of my business."

"No, not at all." But I can feel myself blushing even more and occupy myself with the view through the windows and the parade of smiling, scantily clad people walking, riding two-wheeled machines, and gliding on boots with wheels.

"How about we stop looking at the world through glass and experience it instead?" She gestures to the waiter. "I'm thinking a walk on the beach, maybe a swim?"

Now she has my attention in full. "But I had no thought of entering the water." I scan the beach for bathing machines, but there are none. Nor are there dippers leading ladies and gentlemen into the water for their three immersions. "How would we?" Yet scores of people apparently see the lack of bathing machines and dippers as no deterrent to their pleasures, as they run into and out of the waves entirely unattended and without an apparent thought to modesty. Indeed they are frolicking, splashing, and even swimming whilst wearing tiny bathing costumes which barely cover their most intimate parts, and most of which appear to expose more flesh than would the one Wes showed me when first I awoke.

Despite the disagreeable thought of wearing such a garment, the apparent delight the sea bathers take in their exercise makes me long to join in the fun. And I did so wish to bathe in Brighton, though my mother deemed it improper to bathe in a place where men and even a few of the women, some said, immersed themselves in the nude. No matter that I would of course don the long and singularly undaring flannel dress favored by the great majority of sea bathers. No matter that the beaches were separated as to sex, and the bathers were anything but visible to the shore from the protection of the bathing machines, which, now that I think on it, is a perfectly absurd name. The very idea of calling a horse-drawn box from which to undress and descend into the water a "machine" is as ridiculous as imagining the nearly naked sea bathers on this beach desiring to hide their bodies behind one.

I can only imagine my mother's face if she could see what I am seeing. Yet no one here appears to give the sea bathers a second look, except, that is, for one Venus-like lady who emerges from the sea in a scant costume divided into two sections, seawater streaming from her willowy form. More than a few male heads turn to admire her.

Well, fortunately, I have no such costume with

me. "I have only these clothes," I say to Deepa.

She arches an eyebrow. "You're not getting off that easy. Come on." And, quickly settling the bill, she takes me by the hand and leads me into a women's restroom, where she opens the large, shiny white bag she has been toting and pulls from it two quite diminutive garments, one bright orange, the other a pale yellow. She holds up each one against me.

"What do you think? I couldn't decide which bathing suit I wanted to wear, so I brought both. I've even got an extra sarong with me." She pulls out two long bolts of varicolored fabric. "I'm taller than you, but this one's got little ruchy-stringy things that adjust the fit." She indicates the pale yellow one. "I think you could wear it just fine."

"But I—" The thought of parading into the sea in such a state of undress makes my stomach clench with fear.

"Come on," she says, "you'll look great in it." She waves the bathing suit before my face. "And with this tied around your waist," indicating the yellow-and-white length of fabric she referred to as a sarong, "you'll be absolutely gorgeous."

I hold up the sarong against my waist. I suppose a full-length, makeshift skirt makes the tiny straps and backless form of the bathing suit a little less objectionable. A very little.

"Try it on," says Deepa, waving me into one of the little stalls.

After much maneuvering and Deepa's coming to my rescue, I am now wearing the yellow bathing suit, the sarong tied round my waist. I almost cannot believe I am going to leave this room with a bare back and bare arms, but Deepa tugs on my hand in a manner not to be resisted. Wearing the sunglasses and ducking my head, I allow Deepa to lead me out of the building and around the back to the beach, where she kicks off her shoes, and so do I, and then we are making our way across the sands.

We weave our way through children playing and clusters of men and women, young and old, lying or sitting on large, brightly colored blankets, reading books, eating, chatting, or simply watching the waves.

As we get closer to the water, I feel a thrill of anticipation, for I have never been in the sea, never even so much as put a toe in the ocean.

And then, Deepa pauses to remove her sarong, which she spreads upon the sand, anchoring it against the breeze with her shoes and the large white bag. She starts off towards the water, then turns and looks at me questioningly. But I am rooted to the spot. Does she expect me to remove my sarong and follow her?

Deepa strides over, a big smile on her face, and before I can protest, she actually unfastens the knot of my sarong and takes it from me.

"No!" I cross my legs and put my hands on my thighs in a feeble attempt to cover myself.

"What's wrong, Courtney?" she says, her eyes kind. "Are you okay?"

"I . . . I . . ." I am so frozen with fear, despite the heat, that I cannot form a sentence.

"Did I do something wrong?"

"All these people, and I—" I look down at my nearly naked state and raise my eyes to Deepa.

"Darling, who made you so ashamed of that gorgeous body of yours? You look fabulous. And you're still wearing twice as much as almost anyone on this beach. It's the most modest suit in town."

She gives me a dazzling smile and holds out her hand to me. "Come on, let's get that body of yours into the ocean. Then you won't care what you're wearing."

And then the delighted laughter of the sea bathers rises over me in a wave, and I am giving Deepa my hand and running with her towards the wide ocean and the azure-blue sky and we are in the water to our ankles, the sand pulling at our feet. We wade in deeper, still holding hands, like two little girls on their school holidays. And soon we are waist-deep, and we are jumping with the waves and laughing our delight. Deepa says, "Come on, let's swim out," and I say, "I don't know how," and she looks at me a long while and laughs and says, "And this from the woman who hit her head in a swimming pool," and she lets go of my hand and plunges into the waves. A big wave is about to break over my head when I find myself diving into it and emerging with strong clean strokes that transport me across the water, and all at once I realize I am swimming. I, who have never swum in my life, am swimming as well as any sea creature. And I swim and swim and float on my back and glory in the azure-blue sky with the soft white clouds and the sun warming my face and the water cooling my back. This is heavenly indeed.

Twenty

After I have no idea how long, so enchanted am I by the lovely buoyant waves and sparkling sea, Deepa swims back to me and suggests we take a "breather." I swim effortlessly to shore and emerge from the waves, seawater streaming from my hair and skin, and give only a passing, habitual thought to modesty as I make my way to the sarongs which are now our blankets. Deepa stretches out on her back upon her blanket and puts on her sunglasses. I do the same beside her, the bright strong sun drying me and lulling me into a near doze. Oh, how I love the sea.

Deepa offers me water from a large bottle she has in her white bag, and as I take a long drink, I am fascinated by the sight of two structures off in the distance to our right, one a gigantic turning wheel, the other a tubelike thing that snakes along what I suppose must be a rail. Both are stationary yet moving structures, some sort of machines. I dare not inquire as to what they are but am relieved from my suspense by Deepa, who says, "Ah, yes, the Ferris wheel."

Named after Edward Ferrars, perhaps?

"First time I rode it," she says, "was when I was an eighteen-year-old girl on my first trip to America with my parents."

"How exciting," I say.

Deepa takes off her sunglasses, and her eyes have a faraway look. "I had sneaked out of our hotel on the beach to meet a guy. He was all of twenty years old, very exotic, though as it turns out, he was no more exotic than I am. Anything American was exotic to me. Anyway, he took me to the pier. And when I looked out at that vast expanse of ocean from the top of that wheel, the tanned arm of this golden California boy round my shoulder, I was instantly in love."

"And so you married him?"

Deepa laughs. "I fell in love with L.A., you silly girl. Not him. I was all set to go to university in England, but I decided to apply to school here. Eventually, my parents gave in, I graduated from USC, and they've never stopped regretting it."

"And you?"

"I love it here. Especially now without the unhappy marriage. Which was to an entirely dif-ferent guy, I might add, and years after I took my degree." Deepa smiles at me. "You know, I'm glad you and I met after my divorce. That you're part of my new, postmarriage life. A new friend for a new life."

"A new friend for a new life. I feel that way about you, too."

Deepa squeezes my hand, and we watch the waves in companionable silence. Presently, she says, "Wanna go? If we leave now, we might avoid rush-hour traffic."

Rush hour. Another new term to decipher. And so I silently bid the beach good-bye, promising to return, and drive back in Deepa's car. And this time, when she stops her car before my house, Deepa presses her card into my hand, kisses me on both cheeks, and extracts from me a promise that I will call her very soon and come to the club whenever I like as her guest.

Happy as I am in my newfound friendship, I cannot say I am happy to find myself at the door of my apartment, and as I tarry in the doorway, I once again feel the weight of my situation. Surely it will be no cooler within my set of rooms than it is out here, which is considerably hotter than it was at the beach. And without the distraction of new surroundings and the pleasure of Deepa's company, the promise I made to Courtney's mother about finding employment presses upon my mind. In fact, my head is beginning to throb again.

I sigh as I open the door and brace myself for the oppressiveness of the heat, but no such unpleasantness awaits. Instead I am greeted by coolness, blazing lights, and the sweet sounds of the music from *Pride and Prejudice.*

How can this have happened?

Somehow, inexplicably, the electricity is restored. I cannot begin to speculate how this has come to be, but I shall enjoy it for as long as it lasts. Now I may settle in for a delectable evening of movie-viewing in a cool room, enjoy a cold drink, and tomorrow I might even venture to stock the refrigerator with food, since I now know I might use my credit cards, and there is a grocer's within an easy walk of the apartment.

Just as I arrange myself on the bed and start watching *Pride and Prejudice*, a blast of thunderous music obliterates any other sound.

> *I'm gonna keep on lovin' you*
> *'Cause it's the only thing I wanna do. . . .*

The very floor beneath my feet vibrates with the sound. The source must be downstairs, the same source from the day I arrived, when Wes and the ladies took me to see Dr. Menziger.

What is this music? There is something disturbingly familiar about it—but how?

> *I'm gonna keep on lovin' you*
> *'Cause it's the only thing I wanna do. . . .*

. . . and all at once it is another day, and I am here, in this apartment, and the music, this same music, is blasting from downstairs. I am here with Frank. Not with him exactly, but watching him. I am watching him pile books and CDs into boxes; that one is mine, I think, but I don't care, for he is moving his things out of this apartment, and I am watching him, bereft, angry about the intrusion of the music, knowing our relationship is over, that he betrayed me, but yet I cannot stop watching him, wanting him, longing for him. And I cannot blot from my mind the picture of myself lying in bed with him, under him, the weight of him on top of me.

Pounding on the door jolts me out of my reverie, and I scramble to my feet and rush to answer it. It is Wes.

I feel my face crimson with confusion at the sight of Wes. I can hardly raise my eyes to his countenance, to the clear, sweet goodness in his eyes, a goodness that deserves more than the inconstancy of a woman immersed in improper thoughts of that worthless—what am I thinking? It is as if Wes were my lover and I have just been abed with another man.

Wes's voice jolts me from such thoughts. "Guess my truce with Mr. REO Speedwagon is over," he shouts above the roar of the music.

"What?"

"Your neighbor." He points downward. "I'll talk to him."

"No—he is my neighbor. I shall do it."

"But you hate the guy."

"All the more reason to make peace, then. Do come in."

He does, and I drink in his citron scent as he walks past me into the kitchen. He turns round to give me an encouraging smile, and I nearly melt. Was Deepa imagining an attachment on Wes's part, or did she really see something that I did not? Ladies often fancy they see more than is there when they are anxious for their friends' marriage prospects. Ah, well. I must tear myself away and deal with the business at hand.

And so I take a deep breath to marshal my courage and descend the steps, steeling myself for an encounter with I cannot imagine whom, but certainly not the balding, round, shiny-faced man who answers the door without a word of greeting and blinks at me from behind smudged spectacles.

"Sir, I am very sorry to intrude upon your privacy, but I wonder, would it be possible—might you consider playing the music a bit more—piano? Although it is not very loud down here, my apartment is so filled with sound that I cannot carry on a conversation without shouting."

His face is impassive, his arms crossed.

"And what's more," I add, rather lamely, "I was hoping to watch a movie."

To which he replies, in a falsely deep voice with a thick accent, perhaps Russian, *"You must allow me to tell you how ardently I admire and love you."*

I cannot help but smile, and his lips twitch as if wanting to follow suit. "Why, yes," I say. "How did you know?"

"My walls are as thin as yours."

"Oh, dear. I am very sorry to have disturbed you."

Now he looks well and truly astonished. "You know, I almost start to believe that cock-and-bull story your boyfriend told me about you hitting your head."

I feel myself blush, more pleased by my neighbor's assumption than I would like to admit. "He is not my boyfriend, sir, though I did indeed hit my head."

"No matter. Though I like him a lot more than the other one, who, you'll pardon my saying so, was a piece of . . . In any case, I did use the headphones the one who is not your boyfriend gave me." He shows me a pair of circular silver cup-like things connected by a curved piece and places them on his head momentarily, as if to demonstrate. "Excellent sound, I must say. He's not cheap, that not-boyfriend of yours. In any case, I was only just playing my music without them because you were not at home. At least I thought you were not at home."

"Might I inquire how you would know I was not at home?"

"Because I can hear those high-heeled shoes of yours clomp-clomp-clomping on the wooden floor above my head just like you hear my music pound-pound-pounding in your feet. And so you see, Miss Courtney Stone, this is what we call a two-way street, no?"

"Indeed I am very sorry to have disturbed you. Might I make amends?"

Now he raises both eyebrows, and his full lips form a kindly grin. "How hard did you say you hit your head?"

"I do not exactly know."

"No matter. How about this: We both agree to play our music and movies pianissimo? And if we need noise, we use the headphones. Or I make sure you are not at home, and when you come home and the music is too loud, you knock or call and I turn it down. And what do you say to a no-shoes rule in your apartment? Or a carpet? That would do just as well."

I can just imagine how my mother would respond to the suggestion of a no-shoes rule. She who punished me for running on the lawn barefooted when I was a little girl. Then again, I can only imagine what she would say had she seen me not only sea-bathing, but swimming like a fish. And practically naked for all the world to see.

I giggle at the thought and give my neighbor a smile. "No shoes? What a delightful idea."

"Happy to oblige," he says with a little bow.

I bid my neighbor good-bye. Vladimir is his name, I realize, as I ascend the stairs to my apartment. One of those things I should not know but know anyway. I find myself whistling a melody—that of Vladimir's song, the one I supposedly hate—and I have to laugh at myself, at Courtney, at the futility of endless war with our fellow creatures. In this case, a good memory is indeed unpardonable. How could I be angry with someone who is only the phantom of a memory which is not even my own? And how satisfying it is to have taken charge and solved my own problem instead of relying, once again, on Wes. Or Paula. Or Anna. Or Deepa. If I am to be an independent woman of these times, then I suppose there is no time like now to begin.

I let myself into the apartment—after removing my shoes, that is—and join Wes, who rises from his alert posture on the sofa, his eyes searching my face.

I smile at him, and the tension leaves his features. "That smile, and the sustained quiet, tells me your parlay was a success. I'm impressed."

"He was quite reasonable. He'll use the headphones if I remove my shoes." It is then that I find myself staring at Wes's feet. Oh, dear.

He follows my gaze. And laughs. "Oh." And kneels down to remove his shoes.

"I hope it is not too much—I mean, I had not

thought of how such a rule might affect my friends."

He puts up a hand as if to forestall further apologies. "No problem. I'm proud of you, Courtney. Especially after you said you'd sooner move out than ever try to talk to that man again."

"You deserve some of the credit as well for giving him headphones. I would not have thought of that."

Especially because I have only just discovered what headphones are.

"It was very generous and thoughtful of you," I add. What a dear man he is.

He shrugs, but I can see his countenance is suffused with pleasure at my praise. "I had that brilliant idea when I took you home from the hospital. You needed rest, and they happened to be in the car. By the way, I gave the old man next door a pair, too; not Bose like I gave to Vladimir, but a decent pair of earbuds." He smirks. "There was nothing I could do about the rooster next door, however. He was above any kind of bribe. Besides, he lends a certain sort of pastoral charm to our urban landscape, don't you think?"

"He makes me think I'm back in my father's— I mean, he reminds me of living in the country."

"When have you ever lived in the country?"

Must choose my words a bit more carefully. "I—well—anyway, giving away your headphones was most generous of you. Which puts me in mind of another matter in which I suspect your generosity is the author."

His countenance is most endearingly innocent.

"Surely the lights, the air conditioner? You must have had a hand in it."

"Busted." He ducks his head and blushes most charmingly. "Last night I couldn't reach you on your cell or email, so I called your landline and got the recording that it was out of service. Then I drove by and saw the candle in the window. I know I shouldn't have done it without asking you, but I was afraid you'd say no. So I paid both bills."

"Wes, I cannot—"

"Please. Let me. Besides, there's not much I could do about it now. It's all paid for. Though the phone will take another day to be reinstated. At least now that the electric's on, you can charge your cell phone, which I suppose is dead, too, and that's why I came by again today, just to see if you're okay. There just wasn't any way to reach you by phone."

He thrusts his hands in his pockets and looks down at his feet for a moment before meeting my gaze. It is then that my eyes fill with tears.

"Courtney? You're not mad, are you?"

"Sir, your kindness oppresses me." My voice is shaking, and I pause to draw breath and compose myself.

Wes's eyes are kind behind his spectacles. "I'm

not so sure I like you calling me 'sir' anymore if you're going to be so serious about it."

I smile at him. "Please do not think me ungrateful. I am. I cannot begin to express my gratitude. You are very, very kind. I do insist on repaying you, as soon as I secure employment."

I hope it was not imprudent of me to refuse my mother's offer of money. But how was I to know I would be in Wes's debt?

I clear my throat. "Speaking of which—" This is more difficult than I thought. "I have thought about your offer of employment and—"

He puts up his hand as if to stop me. "I'd like to make you a much better offer."

I can hardly breathe. He cannot mean—could he? Is he about to make me the only offer that a gentleman ever makes to a lady he holds dear?

My heart is pounding so loudly I can almost hear it.

"Court, are you okay? You're all red."

"I—I'm just thirsty. It was very hot outdoors."

He rushes to the kitchen to get me a glass of cold water. "Here. Drink this down." He smiles ruefully. "I thought you were scared I'd offer you a worse job than helping me with my tax files. Don't worry—I found you a better job."

Stupid, stupid girl. Of course he wasn't going to make you an offer of marriage. Shall I ever learn the language of this world? Thank heaven he cannot read my thoughts, which set my face to burning again. I look down at my lap and touch the icy glass to my cheek. Quite soothing.

"Let me buy you a coffee. An iced coffee, if you like. And I'll tell you all about it, okay?"

I manage a smile. "Only if you allow me to buy the coffee."

For that is what independent women may do with their non-boyfriend gentlemen friends, is it not?

Twenty-one

Within five minutes, we are standing before our destination, a squarish, dark brown and bright yellow façade with a rough texture to the walls, a cheerful-looking place with its fresh paint and large, gleaming windows—Wes's new favorite place, he proclaims; recently opened, best coffees in town—and I catch sight of my reflection in the glass of the door. Yes, it is my reflection, and I am ever more comfortable in thinking so. At this moment, I cannot help but smile at that reflection, for as the door opens and the heady aroma of freshly brewed coffee greets me, I realize all at once that this is a coffee-house, and who would have imagined that I would ever enter a coffeehouse, something no lady would do in London. And here I am, doing so as an unchaperoned, unmarried woman in the company of an unmarried man. And an unmarried man whom I find ever more handsome and charming.

No, there is not a missish thought in sight. Nothing shall spoil this moment.

The coffeehouse is nothing like those my brother has boasted of frequenting. Here is no noisy den of gentlemen smoking pipes, transacting business, and arguing over politics and news. No, the only noise, apart from the staccato music which is not unlike what Paula plays in her car, is visual. Tattooed and bejeweled young men and women with slim figures and wildly dressed hair of multiple hues drink sedately from large cups. Some read books and nibble on pastries; others huddle in murmured conversation. Still others ignore all else while tapping on laptops—another new word I am proud to have at my command.

As Wes and I queue up for coffees, there is a slight fluttering in my stomach, for this is the first time I am to pay my own way, and I wish not to appear to disadvantage. I have already studied the denominations of all the currency in my purse; now I train my attention on the young men and women in the queue before me. I watch carefully what they do and, in particular, I observe that they put an extra note or a few of the larger coins into the glass bowl next to the money machine—the cash register, I somehow know it is called.

As we approach the front of the queue, the waitress, a lovely, long-limbed girl with pale skin and enormous, light-brown eyes fringed with thick lashes, greets Wes with a sparkling smile.

"Sharon," he says, and kisses her on the cheek. Her hair, which is a rich chestnut, is piled loosely atop her head and fastened with what looks like an enameled stick.

"And who is this?" she says, favoring me with her smile, and her manner is so engaging that I relinquish the silly impulse I had, for just a moment, to be jealous of Wes's intimacy with her. Not that I have any right.

Wes introduces us. She puts out a hand and shakes mine warmly, and I am instantly won over by the sweetness of her smile and the genuine friendliness in her eyes. Besides, it is not improper at all in this world for a single man to kiss the cheek of a single woman. And I remember, with an inward smile, how shocked I was that first time I entered The Fortune Bar and Glenn enfolded me in his arms.

"So, Sharon," says Wes, "I heard you're giving this all up." He makes a sweeping gesture with his hand.

She sighs. "Don't think I won't miss the place. Best job I ever had. Really."

Wes smiles at me. "I swear I didn't pay her to say that. Sharon here's off to law school. Gonna be some hotshot attorney."

Sharon rolls her eyes and then trains her warm smile on me again. "Not exactly. I'm setting my sights on public policy law, which can be decidedly unglamorous, especially when you're starting out. Anyway, it's been a few years since I was in a classroom, except for cramming for the LSATs, and I've got a lot to do before I start my new life."

"Sam must be heartbroken," says Wes.

She laughs. "He'll live."

After we order and I proudly pay for our coffees and muffins, adding what I hope is a generous tip to the glass bowl, Wes and I settle into a couple of cushioned armchairs near the window.

Wes sips his coffee and sighs contentedly. "I love this place."

I lean back into the chair. "It's very comfortable."

He looks down into his cup and pauses before meeting my eyes. "Think you could spend four or five days a week here?"

"I don't understand."

"Sam, the owner, is a good friend. I told him all about you, and the thing is—he'd love to give you Sharon's job, sight unseen. That's how much he trusts me. And Sharon. She'd be training you. I know it's not the most prestigious job in the world, but it's not a long-term commitment. Sam knows it would only be an interim gig for you. All he asks is that you give him a little notice when you find something else."

"I—I don't know what to say."

"Think about it. You don't have to decide right now. Tomorrow would be good, though."

I, a server of drinks in a coffeehouse. How could I, a gentleman's daughter, consider for a moment accepting such a situation? Serving drinks for wages. Taking tips. Carrying a tray.

I watch Sharon laughing with a young man as she removes empty cups and plates from his table and stacks them on her little tray.

No. I cannot give it another moment's consideration. I, stoop to a situation that my own housekeeper would spurn to consider? It would be insupportable. There cannot be two opinions on this matter.

Or can there?

"You're insulted, aren't you," says Wes, a little defensively, and it is then that I realize I have put my head down and am cradling it in my hands.

I meet his eyes. I do not wish to appear ungrateful. But is appearing ungrateful worse than being ungrateful? And who am I, in my penurious state, to reject any sort of paying work?

I can feel the blush spreading from my neck to my cheeks. "I just—I don't know what to think."

"Courtney, there's nothing wrong with working in a café. I did it one summer. And look at Sharon. She's our age, top of her class, on her way to being a lawyer, but even if she weren't, she'd have a decent gig here for as long as this place stays in business. What's wrong with that?"

What could I possibly say that would make any sense to him? That I am not who he thinks I am? That I am a gentleman's daughter who was educated to believe that such work would be a degradation?

No, he would never understand, even if I could get him to believe that I am not Courtney Stone, that I am someone else from a different world and a different life, a life with inflexible lines between different spheres of society.

"No offense, Courtney," says Wes, "but is there anything more demeaning than being an assistant to someone like David? I'd rather work here any day. Especially for Sam. Do you know what he told me when he opened a few months ago? That he wanted to feel like he was serving coffee to guests in his own home. And he wanted his employees to feel that way, too. That's his vision of a workplace."

Serving coffee to guests in his own home. How many times have I presided over the tea in the drawing room at Mansfield House, making the tea and offering it to our guests, refilling their cups with coffee, and helping them to cake? That was no degradation; it was my duty and honor to show hospitality.

Could I not do the same here, or imagine that I were doing so, even if I am paid a salary to engage in such feats of fancy? Could it be any worse than that endless interval after dinner with the ladies, feigning interest in endless tales of lace trimmings, spoilt children, and petty gossip? Is there any real shame in earning my bread in such a manner? What could truly be undignified about honest labor?

Wes is right; serving coffee and tea and muffins to strangers in this coffeehouse—this café—is no less dignified than catering to the whims of that David creature. Far more dignified, I'll vow.

"Yes," I hear myself saying almost before I realize I have decided to say it. "I'll do it. And I thank you for offering it to me."

Wes nearly chokes on his coffee, but he quickly recovers and wipes his mouth with a paper napkin.

"Are you all right?"

"You sure you want to do this? You're not obligated to take this job. Or any job, for that matter. You're under no obligation to me. Do you hear me, Courtney? Because that's the very last thing I'd want. You're not to sacrifice yourself to some sort of servitude to pay me back."

I try to laugh it off, but his serious manner stops me. "It is the right thing to do."

"I mean it, Courtney."

I smile at him. "As do I. And I am happy to accept your offer."

I realize that Sharon is watching us, and it occurs to me that she might, like Mrs. Jennings of *Sense and Sensibility*, put her own construction on the word "offer." Which instantly makes me blush. Again.

There is a bit of an awkward silence in Wes's car on the way back to my apartment. I keep hearing myself say *I am happy to accept your offer* and blushing to the roots of my hair like a raw schoolgirl. As for his silence, I cannot imagine why he should feel awkward, unless perhaps he wonders whether he advocated too warmly on behalf of the position.

"Here's Sam's number," he says, handing me a card when we reach my house. "You should call him tonight and firm things up. He may want you to start as early as tomorrow, if you can swing it. Oh, and before I forget." He smiles. "Call me if you need directions. I know you never pay attention when you're not behind the wheel. Good news is, it's only a five-minute drive."

And that is when I realize I am expected to drive my car.

For a moment I cannot find my tongue.

"I . . . I prefer to walk."

"You. Walk." Wes stifles a laugh.

"I don't see why that's funny."

"You'd take your car down the block if no one were watching you."

I smile sweetly at him. "But walking is beneficial exercise, is it not?"

Wes attempts to keep his countenance. "Indeed, madam."

"Well, then. It's all settled."

"How hard *did* you hit your head, Courtney?"

He reaches over and brushes a stray strand of hair from my eyes, and the very tips of his fingers graze my forehead.

I am so stunned by his touch, by the sweetness of his gaze, that I must catch my breath.

Is this the gentle affection of a friend, or is there something more in his eyes?

I laugh to cover my confusion. "You happen to be the second person to ask me that question today."

He has parked the car in front of my house but isn't making any move to open his door; in fact, he hasn't even turned off the car.

Should I ask him inside, or would it be too . . . Oh, blast it to—"Would you like to come in?"

He smiles at me, and it feels as if a warm space has opened inside my heart. "I wish I could. But I've got a deadline. Going home to work. Probably an all-nighter." He sighs heavily.

Deadline. Whatever that might be, it certainly sounds disagreeable. "Well, then." I put my hand on the door handle, wishing he would touch my hair again. Or my hand. Or . . .

"What are you up to tonight?" he says.

"I think I'll read and watch my movie."

He laughs. "*My* movie. Of course. Only one movie exists in your world."

I almost cannot form words. "You mean there are more?" I realize how stupid that sounds; of course there are more; I saw one with Paula and Anna.

"Believe it or not. A whole drawerful of them, in your case."

A whole drawerful of movies. I start to laugh. What are men to books and movies? Perhaps I shall never leave the house. Except to my place of business, that is.

Twenty-two

$\mathcal{I}$t is eleven in the morning, and I am at my station behind the counter at Home, which is the name of the café. Sam, the big, burly bear of a man who owns the café, whom I met briefly this morning, put me quite at my ease, and Sharon is now schooling me in the finer points of making coffee, no simple task at this establishment. The coffee machine, she proudly informs me, is one of only a couple of hundred in the country, which sounds to me like a great number of machines until she tells me it represents less than 1 percent of cafés.

"Of course, it's a ten-thousand-dollar machine," she says. "Put it this way: What would you say is the most luxurious ride?"

"Ride?"

"You know, wheels."

"Let me see . . . a barouche-landau?"

"Don't know that one, but to me, cars are like major appliances on wheels. . . . I know, a Maserati. This is the Maserati of coffee machines."

She hands me the cup she has just brewed. "But don't take my word for it. See for yourself."

My first sip is so exquisite that I can hardly put it into words. Light and delicate and at the same time bracing. A hint of chocolate. And the scent; is it cherries or blackberries or something else?

Sharon beams her pleasure. "I know. Definitely not your mother's coffee."

I laugh. And as I make my very first espresso, carefully supervised by Sharon, whom I like more and more, I am very well pleased with myself. For there is something positively gratifying about earning my own money with my own two hands. Even if they are my two borrowed hands. And now I know I can afford to pay for the groceries I bought this morning with my credit card. Amazing how I merely handed over the card, and the purchases were mine.

Clearly, Sharon too takes great pride in her work, this young woman about to embark upon a study of the law. She has no airs about her newly elevated situation, no disgust for her business. It appears that I have landed in a world guided by work and merit, rather than blood or rank. And I must say I like it very well indeed.

At the end of the day, after Sharon schools me in closing up the café and I bid her good-bye, I carefully reverse the directions that Wes was so kind as to give me. And as I make my way down the bustling streets lighting up in the dusk of summer, I wonder if perhaps I am lacking in sensibility, for I find that I am not pining for my privileged position as a gentleman's daughter, for the richly furnished rooms and the hovering servants that were as much a part of home as the air I breathed. Of course it would be lovely to awaken and have breakfast prepared for me and not have to think about washing the clothes, but in truth, I lived in a state of the most confining dignity. No one ever asked me what I wished to do above choosing a dish at table or deciding between embroidery and reading for an evening's amusement. Everything else was set out for me—filial duty, feminine accomplishments, marriage, children—as inflexibly as the blue gown on the bed that I was to wear for dinner, and woe betide me if I dared refuse. And I did refuse. Not the accomplishments and the blue gown, but the marriage and children. Until I almost succumbed. Almost.

What I do long for are my friends. I long for my father and for Mary and for Barnes. I long for the greenery and freshness of the country; the air here is hot and close and tinged with soot, like a London winter. And while the brush-headed trees are wondrous, there is a decided lack of lawns and plants.

I even think of my mother in wistful moments, but I know I am wishing for the mother I longed for, the mother I fashioned in my mind, rather than for the mother she was. Still, she was my mother, and there is an empty place in my life where she should be.

I do think of Edgeworth, though those moments are fleeting, and with every passing day the pain dims in memory. Mostly, he visits my thoughts as I drift off to sleep. That is when his face and form appear in my mind's eye most clearly; that is when it is almost sweet to think of him. It is when I see him as I loved him best, my shining man, my great reader of poetry and plays, my champion of all that was good and clever in my world.

But last night, as I floated between the sleeping and waking worlds, his countenance became that of Wes, and it comforted me to know that *he* was here, that I could look upon his face again. I wonder if I am so inconstant that I can go from wanting to be Edgeworth's wife to finding myself drawn to Wes, a man I have known but a week. And when Frank flits across my mind, it is even more disquieting. Much as I have no wish to see him, I fear to test my resolve in his presence. For I do not trust myself to keep those disturbing memories of him at bay. Which is why I have not returned the two messages from him that were waiting for me last night.

But I have not leisure to revolve such points in my mind, as I am coming up on a cluster of young men on the pavement, and they are all staring at me in a most disconcerting manner. One of them whispers to the other, and they laugh. All of them are wearing low-slung breeches which are far too big for them, some with billowing white short-sleeved shirts without collars, others bare-chested. By now I have become a bit more accustomed to a seemingly endless variety of outlandish dress. However, what puts me on my guard are their mocking, appraising eyes.

Now one of them whistles, and the others laugh.

I cross the street as quickly as I can without breaking into a run, mustering as much dignity as I can and willing myself not to look in their direction.

"Ow baby," a voice calls out.

I nearly trip over some trash in the street.

Laughter.

I continue walking, my heart pounding in my chest. Just as I turn the corner, I sneak a look at the clutch of young men; not one of them has followed me.

It is then that I let out a breath.

I suppose they are just young men, boys more like, showing off. Still, I cannot help but think that had I been in my own village, in my own time, no farmer's son or cottager's boy would have dared do more than tug a forelock or doff a cap in my direction.

Could my lone presence in the street have been a silent invitation to their impertinence? Perhaps it is unwise for me to be walking alone at dusk in this city. Perhaps I should have heeded Frank's words. Perhaps there are limitations after all upon a lady's freedom. Or perhaps it is simply a matter of prudence.

How could I be so stupid? I quicken my steps, glancing around me in the darkening street for anyone who might be construed as a threat. By the time I put my key in the lock of my apartment door, I am slick with sweat and panting from my exertions. I practically fall through the door, locking it behind me, peeling off garments and turning on the air conditioner—bless you, Wes—as I make my way to the shower and step under a heavenly spray of cold, clean water.

How lovely to be fresh and cool and safe in my very own apartment. I shall spend the rest of the evening finishing *Mansfield Park* (never has a story kept me in more suspense) and then starting *Northanger Abbey*, now that I've finished viewing *my* movie, which was lovely indeed. The visual splendor of it gave me a little taste of home—aside, that is, from the oddity of Miss Elizabeth Bennet's daytime display of bosom (even odder that no one around her seemed to take note of it) and Mr. Darcy's lack of gloves while dancing. But I suppose I can forgive such lapses of fashion in a film which was created in a world where tiny strips of fabric are considered adequate for sea-bathing and where no one wears gloves at all.

As if in response to my thoughts about the film, the music from it issues from my phone. It's

Wes! I endeavor to calm myself before answering. How lovely to hear his voice.

"So, you okay at the café?" he asks. "Not too bad, I hope?"

"Actually, I'm quite content. It's lovely."

"Really?"

"Upon my honor."

I can hear the relief in his voice. "Then at least I won't have to worry about you while I'm out of town. I have to take off for a couple of days. Work thing."

"Oh." Somehow the thought of Wes not here, even for a couple of days, leaves me with a hollow feeling in my stomach.

What a silly creature I am.

"I don't have to worry about you, do I?" he says.

Best not to mention my little adventure walking home tonight.

"But you can always reach me on my cell," he says. "Or email."

"Of course." I force some cheer into my voice. "I wish you a safe and pleasant journey."

"I don't know how pleasant it'll be; I'll be lucky if I work less than sixteen hours out of twenty-four. But thanks."

And then, we say our good-byes, and no sooner do I end the call than there is another, no name, just a number on the phone, and when I answer it, a familiar voice says, "Finally. I thought I was going to have to show up at your door."

It's Frank.

"I keep thinking about that night at The Fortune Bar," he says. "When we kissed. And how good you tasted."

His words are like a caress, and there is a fluttering in my stomach.

"You have no idea how much I wanted to kiss you again the other night," he says. "But then you ran away."

My heart is quickening. Why does this man have such an effect on me?

"Courtney? Are you there?"

"Yes, I—I'm here."

"I miss you."

"What is it you want from me, Frank?"

"You know what I want. And I think you want it, too."

"I don't know what you mean."

"Courtney, I want to be with you."

Why does a part of me thrill to hear those words?

"And?"

"Let me come over," he says, "and show you how much I mean it."

He is just as he was the other night. All he wants is to get into my bed.

"What makes you think I hold myself so cheap?"

"Is it Wes? Is that why you're holding out on me?"

And in that moment, it is clear that his pursuit of me has everything to do with his rivalry with Wes and nothing to do with his affections for me.

And with that clarity, I am free.

"Because if it is, you should know that Mr. Perfect's got some business on the side."

"What does that mean?"

"Why don't you ask him? Unless you're afraid to find out."

"I do not suffer such a tone from my own father, let alone from a person who is of no connection to me."

"Since when do you talk to your father? And what do you mean by no connection? That's cold, Courtney."

"Good-bye, Frank."

"You're not serious. You were into that kiss."

He's insufferable. "Do not call me again."

And I end the call.

If there is work for me to do in Courtney's life, then it is clear that banishing Frank from it once and for all is the greatest service I could do her. Nevertheless, it takes some time before I can calm myself enough to lie down and read, let alone shake the unsettling feeling that the meaning of Frank's cryptic statement about Wes might be something I would rather not know.

Twenty-three

"Y{ou're not serious, Courtney," says Paula's voice from the phone tucked between my shoulder and ear.

I am bustling about the apartment the following morning, getting ready for my second day of work at the café.

"I don't understand," I say, searching through the clothes in my closet for something appropriate to wear, preferably something which might withstand coffee spills.

"Making coffee? Talk about a dead-end job."

Dead end. Must look that one up. But the sound of it doesn't promise well.

Paula raves on. I press "speaker," another ingenious invention, and place the phone on the bed while I fasten my trousers.

"And this is Wes's idea," she huffs. "Figures. His family's got so much money, he doesn't have to worry about how much he makes. But how are you going to live on it?"

Wes? From a wealthy family? And to think I took him for a servant when first we met.

"Courtney? Are you listening to me?"

"I'll manage, Paula. It will hold me over till I find something more suitable."

"Come on, Courtney. I cannot imagine you serving coffee without spilling it in someone's lap." Paula giggles. "On purpose, that is. You're just not the servile type."

"I cannot imagine anyone less servile than Sharon," I say, but I can feel myself on the verge of saying something else which I will likely regret.

"Who's Sharon?"

"The young woman who is training me. Forgive me, Paula, but I must get ready."

Of all the impertinent . . . oh, blast it all, why should Paula's opinions be of any consequence to me? And did not Deepa, who called me shortly before Paula did, congratulate me on my new job? She had nothing but kind words and encouragement to offer. Nevertheless, I stamp about the apartment as I put the last of my ensemble together, then remember my promise to Vladimir and will myself to form more ladylike steps.

It takes a brisk walk in the blessedly cooler air of the morning to cool the heat of my anger. I am not quite ready to try my hand at driving the car again; for now, I shall depend on Sharon's kindness for a ride home at night and hope that I am as safe in the daytime streets as I believe I am. I keep a watchful eye on my surroundings, but I cannot stop thinking about Paula's words.

Of course I simply had to Google "dead-end job" on the computer before I left the house. In truth, I care not whether a job provides me with advancement; what a notion. I, who before arriving in this world could choose only between the job of marriage or maiden aunt, the latter of which would be a disappointment indeed to my family but not nearly as degrading as being forced to go out as a governess, should I have been so unfortunate as to be born into a genteel yet necessitous family.

No, I do not mind at all having a job that affords no advancement.

But servile? That is a disagreeable word indeed, and one I cannot easily banish from my thoughts. Paula was rather high-handed, to be sure, but she is my friend. And she is a woman, and thus has a woman's feelings. Did she, in truth, do anything more than echo my own doubts? Was I wrong, after all, to have accepted the job?

No, it cannot be wrong. It was Wes's idea that I take the job. Wes, who is goodness itself, despite what I found in Courtney's journal, despite what Paula and Anna have said, despite Frank's insinuations—

Deepa, who is my friend, likes him very well indeed, does she not?

No, if Wes has recommended this job, it cannot be wrong. Wes, who desired me to work for him but, out of delicacy for my feelings, found me another position. Wes, who has been nothing but generous and kind and solicitous of my comfort in all things. Wes, who according to Deepa has feelings for me that are—I can feel the blush starting at my neck. Oh how I long to ask him about the past, not only about his role in Frank's deception, but also to learn if he knows the extent of Courtney's—of my —former intimacy with Frank. But I dare not; it is too awkward by half to contemplate such a thing.

Oh, dear. I cannot enter my place of work with such a disordered mind. I shall think of something else. And indeed there is much to occupy the mind and eye in these streets teeming with cars exuding smoke, and snatches of music from open windows, and people of various hues and outlandish dress, and shops selling I don't know what. And thus by the time I arrive at Home— how I love the name of the café—I am truly composed in spirit as well as countenance.

Perhaps I am a little like Catherine Morland of *Northanger Abbey*, a green girl from the country having her first adventure in the great city of Bath. Perhaps I do not yet know what is expected of me in every situation in this land, but I will not let Paula persuade me to do what I know would be wrong. And as Fanny Price said so eloquently in *Mansfield Park*, *We have all a better guide in ourselves, if we would attend to it, than any other person can be.*

Besides, I promised Wes that I would accept the position, and I promised to give proper notice at such time when I am ready to leave it. I shall not go back on my promises. Besides, I do not wish to leave my position. For now, it suits me very well indeed.

$\mathcal{T}$he café is bustling, and Sharon reminds me that it is time for my break. I can hardly believe that four hours have passed, and much more pleasantly than I would have imagined.

Just as I am about to carry my cup of coffee to a brightly covered, red-and-yellow cushioned chair near the window, I sense that I am being stared at. I look up and see a petite young woman who has just entered the café frozen, as if in mid-stride, and staring at me. At first I cannot believe that I am the object of her gaze. Yet when I glance behind me, I see that Sharon is at the other end of the counter, and there is no one else in the vicinity. I look at the lady questioningly, and she seems to recollect herself, resuming her stride towards the counter.

I am strangely unsettled, not only by her staring, but by something eerily familiar about her face, and thus I move as quickly as I can out of her path. I settle into the chair by the window and busy myself to avoid looking in her direction. But I cannot help myself, so great is my curiosity to look at her again.

And then I remember where I saw her before: She is the same woman who was staring at me in Awakening as I stood in the gallery, speaking with Wes and Deepa, though she was farther away than she is now. I study her features as she orders her coffee. She is quite pretty, in a style of beauty which is all her own. Her face is heart-shaped. Her large eyes tilt upward at the outside corners. She has a tiny nose, dimpled cheeks, and a wide, girlish mouth.

And then she looks up at me, full in the face, and resumes her staring from across the café. If she and I are acquainted, which we must be or why would she look at me so, then why does she not greet me in a proper manner? It is most unsettling. I occupy myself by watching Sharon, who glides over to the table next to mine, tray in hand, and collects empty cups and plates.

When Sharon returns to the counter, I decide to give my full attention to my coffee and a newspaper which is lying on the table. And sure enough, something much more interesting than the staring young woman captures my attention: a story about the first African American president of the United States. That such a thing should ever be possible, and that I should be alive to see it, something I'll vow not even William Wilberforce or Thomas Clarkson ever dreamt of.

"Think she fancies you, too?" says a distinctive voice and accent behind me. I turn; it is Deepa.

I rise and kiss her on both cheeks. "What a delightful surprise."

She smiles. "I had to stop by and see your new work digs, but the first thing I noticed was her." She inclines her head slightly towards the mysterious woman, who is leaning against the counter, waiting for her drink and gazing at me steadily.

"I've seen her in the club," says Deepa. "But I don't know her name. Guess her mother never told her it was rude to stare." She raises her voice slightly at the word "stare," and the woman seems to recollect herself, for she breaks her gaze and looks down at the floor.

I shrug, and Deepa says, "So how's it going here, other than being an object of fascination?"

And so I tell her about my work and the temporary shutoff of electricity and its restoration and my phone calls with Wes and Frank, and she is so full of fellow-feeling and so effusive in her praise of my set-down of Frank and I am so engrossed in our conversation that I forget all about the strange woman, who is, in fact, gone from the café when I reluctantly tear myself away from Deepa, bid her good-bye, and resume my duties behind the counter.

Sharon decides that I am now capable of doing everything on my own, and she will watch and assist if necessary. And so the hours pass as I make drinks, exchange pleasantries with guests, serve cakes and muffins, and dispense bottles of surprisingly delicious mineral water, another improvement over my world, where mineral water generally tastes like the inside of an iron pot or the contents of a drainage ditch.

By the end of our shift, I am glowing with even more pride than I did on my first day, for not once did Sharon have to step in and rescue me

288

from a barrage of orders, and not once did I have problems with the cash register, though I feared I would surely not be able to handle that end of the job on my own, I who had never even heard of a computer before I arrived in this world. I cannot help but be reminded of the same facility I have somehow acquired with my own computer and phone; it is as if these hands remember what this mind does not. I suppose it is the same part of intelligence at work as the part which lately has begun to summon heretofore unknown words to my lips.

So, yes, I am proud indeed that I have been of some use today, that I have employment which will enable me to maintain myself and, eventually, repay my debts. And, yes, I am proud to have made many people smile today by serving them coffee and cakes.

This job is by no means the highest of situations, to be sure, but I am anything but servile. In fact, I am to tolerate no disrespect, for Sharon instructed me not to serve the rare person who might be abusive. As for classing my situation with that of a servant, the very notion is an insult to the never-ending drudgery which is the lot of the servant who must live with his master's family, earns but a fraction of my pay, often labors more than sixteen hours per day, and exists behind an impenetrable barrier of class. A barrier I crossed, to my enduring regret, when I kissed James in a moment of grief and madness after I discovered Edgeworth's inconstancy. Had anyone seen us, James would have lost his place as footman in our home, and I would have been ruined.

Could my mother see me in this place, she would surely faint away on the spot. The thought of which, I own, makes me smile. But then again, I never did live up to her expectations of what a daughter should be. Mama always said I was an elf child switched with her real daughter at birth, and perhaps she was right. Perhaps, in Courtney, she will get the "real" daughter she always wanted.

Will get? It occurs to me that I am thinking of what has to be the dead and distant past as something that is happening even now, for I simply cannot comprehend the idea that everyone I know is dead, though I shed tears for them when first I arrived here. But now, when I think of myself living Courtney's life, then I know that she must be living mine. And if my mind, my sense of who I am, survived two hundred years into the future, then her mind must have survived two hundred years into the past. I know that none of this is rational, but it must be so. If I am here in her life, then she must be there in mine. And it must be happening even now. But how can that be? Is not time a straight line, with the past dead and the future not yet born?

Oh, dear; these thoughts are giving me the headache, or perhaps I truly am going mad. Is not my situation—going to sleep as one person and awakening as another—the very definition of madness? Yet I do not feel mad. I feel very much alive. More so than I remember feeling in quite some time. In two centuries, as a matter of fact. I smile to myself until I realize that Sharon is regarding me quizzically and is, in fact, waiting for me at the door of the café, having offered to drive me home, an offer which I was happy to accept. I am not eager to repeat my misadventures of last night.

Within minutes, I am once again unlocking the door of my apartment. As I pour myself a glass of iced tea, looking forward to an evening finishing *Northanger Abbey* and beginning *Persuasion*, it occurs to me that I should check my email first; I have heard more than once from my new friends that I have become a most dilatory correspondent. Not that they used such language.

And perhaps there is a message from Wes.

I run my eye over the list of messages. One from Paula offering a half-joking, half-self-justifying sort of apology for her words this morning. One from Anna hoping I'm okay and saying how busy she is this week, but of course if I need anything . . . Several of course from senders I do not recognize and have no idea as to how I am to answer their messages; it is like awakening in the middle of a conversation with absolute strangers who somehow believe you understand them perfectly.

No messages from Wes. Of course there aren't.

He is out of town, much engaged in business, and surely has no time for such things.

Ah, but there is a message from Sharon. "Sharon would like to be your friend," it says, instructing me to click on a particular line if I wish to confirm her request.

Of course I would be delighted to be Sharon's friend!

Interesting that she has requested my friendship in writing; is that how it is done here? But surely, Deepa declared herself to be my friend without writing to me for permission. Perhaps in this world there are different customs for when someone befriends you at work, and when . . .

. . . when someone befriends you in the ladies' restroom of a bar?

I have to laugh at the absurdity of it all. Apparently, it may be some time before I understand the rules.

No matter. I am honored that Sharon is befriending me. I click on the line to immediately confirm her request. This little gesture brings me to a place on the computer I've not visited before.

You, it says. Info. Photos. Pages. I click on Info, and up comes a photograph of my borrowed face, and my borrowed name, Courtney Stone.

Birth date, place of birth, university, favorite books, favorite movies. The lists of favorite books and movies begin with the titles of Jane Austen's works. No surprise there.

Interested in meeting: Men.

Oh, dear. Perhaps no one else can see this.

Profile is set to public view.

I feel my face crimson, despite sitting here alone in the apartment.

What I am doing right now: Fantasizing about running over my ex-fiancé with my car. Or a steamroller.

At this a snort of laughter escapes me, which grows after I skip over to the online dictionary and read the definition of "steamroller." Why of course, all the world must know that not only do I desire to meet men, but also that I desire them to die at my hands. Now why wouldn't any unmarried woman post such information publicly?

Oh, dear. I want to be horrified, but it is just too absurd. And after all, did I not have such thoughts about Edgeworth after I discovered his betrayal? Had I known of such things as steamrollers and cars, I've no doubt they would have played a part in my own fantasies.

My eyes return to the screen. *Birth date.* A quick calculation tells me that I am . . . my heavens—I am thirty-two years old. Thirty-two! That is two years older than I was one week ago.

Two years older? I should, in truth, be one hundred and ninety-six years older. When seen in such a light, thirty-two doesn't sound old at all.

Yet . . . Thirty-two. And not married.

But I have no cause to repine.

For I may be thirty-two years old, but I earn my own bread, live in my own apartment, and command my own time. I even keep my own carriage —I mean, car. Which I shall certainly learn to drive.

Not bad. Not bad at all.

And look at all of these friends I have—I cast my eye over their pictures—could I truly have 292 friends? Among the pictures is Wes's smiling face. I click on his picture, and now his profile is on the screen.

Profession: web developer.
About Me: When not glued to a computer screen building websites am glued to my plasma watching movies, occasionally digressing to cook, take my bike up Mt. Wilson, and contemplate what it all means.

Building websites. Definitely something to do with computers, as Deepa said. And he cooks. A rich man who cooks. For his own amusement, it seems. How very unusual. And charming.

Aspiration: good intentions that lead up instead of down.

I love the sound of that.

Favorite Quotes:
Love is not love which alters when it alteration finds.—William Shakespeare
To love oneself is the beginning of a life-long romance.—Oscar Wilde
Life is full of misery, loneliness, and suffering—and it's all over much too soon.
—Woody Allen

I laugh. Thoughtful, witty, and likes Shakespeare.

And then I cast my eye over his array of friends, and I start at the sight of—yes, it is she—the lady who was staring at me in the café, who was in *Awakening*. Morgan LeDonne is her name.

Who is this person?

I click over to her profile, and there is not much about her other than comments by friends about matters that mean nothing to me. And then I click on *Photos,* and there, at the very top of the page, is a picture of her with Wes and another man and a woman, all seated at a table holding up glasses and smiling. Much as I stare at the picture, I cannot tell if their attitude is that of a couple in a relationship or that of two friends.

Did not Wes see her staring up at us that night in *Awakening*? Why did he not greet her in any way?

It is impossible not to long to ask him about her. But how to do so is the question.

Twenty-four

I am fussing over my unruly hair in the mirror the next morning and wishing Barnes were here to put it in some kind of order—oh how I miss her, and how spoilt I was not to appreciate her constant assistance—when I drop a lovely little sparkling hairpin behind the bookcase. Squatting down beside the bookcase and stretching my arm into the tiny space behind it, my fingers just touch the edge of the hairpin when I feel something else that appears to be a book so large it would dwarf the biggest folios in my father's library.

I retrieve both the pin and the enormous book, which is covered in dust. After wiping it down in the kitchen, I open it to find that it is a book of pencil sketches and drawings. By someone clearly accomplished in drawing. And this is Courtney's book, of course.

I turn the pages in the book, admiring the studies of hands and landscapes and figures, and I catch my breath at the sight of a drawing of a lady in the dress of my time, a lady whose figure and face are unmistakably mine. Not Courtney's. Mine.

The flesh rises on my arms. How could this be?

The next several pages are various views of the same subject, and the likeness is as striking as it was in the first drawing.

How could Courtney know my face and form,

know them so well that she drew these likenesses?

It is impossible. She was here, and I was there, and never the two did meet.

Until, that is, I awoke here, in the future, with her face, in her life.

And these drawings were made before I arrived. Therefore, they must be the work of her imagination. There is no other possibility.

But I am no work of imagination. I am real.

Of course I am real. I have thoughts and feelings and memories and a whole life history that is real.

Yet no one here knows who I really am.

No one but me. And the fortune-teller. And she is no work of imagination.

This thought floods me with relief.

As I study the drawings, I wonder: Will Courtney find something in my house that will give her as much of a shock as these drawings have given me?

Finally, I must tear myself away from the drawings. If I do not attend to my hair and leave the house, I shall be late for my shift. I do, however, take the sketchbook with me, eager to peruse it again when I have my break.

By the time I've walked to the café and made my first set of lattes and cappuccinos, I am less unsettled by the thought of those sketches than I was.

As the day progresses, I manage not to think about them constantly. I am even equal to looking at them on my break without having a single thought about whether or not I exist. And before I know it, the clock tells me that there are but two hours left to my shift.

I am wiping my hands on a towel and about to put away some clean cups when Sharon approaches and reaches out her arms to me. "Courtney, it's been so much fun working with you."

I am so stunned that for a moment I cannot even speak.

"Don't look so shocked." She smiles. "You knew I was only going to train you for a few days."

"Yes, but I had no idea this was your last day." I clutch the edge of the counter, feeling almost dizzy.

"Now you look scared. Don't worry; Sam will open up every day. And he's got Keith to help out during rush times. You're covered and beyond covered. And you'll like Keith. Who'll be here in two hours, by the way. All you have to do is hang in there for two hours on your own."

I try to smile, but despite my efforts, my eyes are blurry with unshed tears. Sharon moves to embrace me, and I hug her back. A tear slides down my cheek. She releases me and dabs at my face with the towel I was using.

"You're gonna be fine. I promise. Keep in touch, okay?" she says, her large brown eyes kind.

I nod, afraid that if I say anything, I will shed more tears. I cannot believe how attached I've become to Sharon in such a short time. Or maybe I am merely frightened at the thought of working here alone. Even for two hours. With Sharon here, I felt protected somehow.

I muster a smile. And wave good-bye as she slips out of the door.

Fortunately, for the next hour or so, there are so few demands on my time that I find my confidence returning, and I even have leisure to pull out the book of sketches again, which I lay upon the counter and peruse.

Now that I am past the shock of seeing my own likeness, I can once again admire the skill of the artist. It brings to mind how much I loved to draw when I was a child, especially on those rare occasions when my father would allow me into his atelier, my pencils and paper on one of his worktables, and I sitting there endeavoring to be as quiet and as good as possible. I would try to draw, inhaling the intoxicating scent of paints, but mostly I would watch my father paint. Not so much what he put on his canvases, but the way his face would become transported with the joy and intensity of what he was creating. But he did not like to be watched, and soon I was sent back to the drawing room, where my mother would comment upon my odd choice of subjects in my drawings—what sort of child preferred to draw maids and gardeners at work rather than ladies and gentlemen or flowers and bowls of fruit?

The best times to draw were in my bedchamber, at night, by candlelight, while the rest of the house slept and I lay tucked cozily in my bed, the fire banked for the night, the bed hangings enclosing me in what I liked to imagine was my own private world. That is when my mind was calmest, when I was free from the prying eyes of my mother.

The drawings of servants I learnt to hide in the back of my portfolio of sketches, behind several sheets of blank paper. And then, one day, I had just reentered the drawing room when I saw my mother looking through the sketches in my portfolio. She had found the ones I'd hidden.

And then she looked up from the drawings, which were spread on the table, her face a white mask of rage, her voice as cold as the coldest winter.

"I never ever want to see anything like this again, do you hear me, Jane? If you cannot draw like a proper young lady"—and with that she fed one of my drawings into the fire, and glared at me triumphantly at the sound of my gasp—"then you shan't draw at all."

I watched, mute and helpless, as she put page after page into the fire.

"Now get out of my sight," she said, and sat down to her embroidery.

It was then I saw my sister, Clara, sitting on the sofa at the far end of the room, pretending to be reading a book but with a self-satisfied little smile on her face.

I knew then that I would never be one of them, never wish to be one of them. They, like my brother, were wrapped up in their own little worlds of self-consequence and vanity. My father was the only one who truly cared for me, but he sought refuge from them as well, spending the greater part of his day painting in his atelier or riding out to see to the business of the estate. How I wished to spend my days with him. But I was stuck inside the house, forced to learn how to be a "proper young lady," as my mother always put it, and failing at it indeed.

Someday, I vowed, I would be free of this stifling world. And I almost was, for I saw the prospect of marriage to Edgeworth as the escape I'd always dreamt of. With him I would not have to settle for one of the stupid, insufferable men my mother had thrown in my way. With him I would finally have an equal in mind and manners.

And then it all fell to pieces. Yet here I am, free in a way I would never have imagined.

I turn the pages of the sketchbook until I come to a blank sheet. And, using a pencil I find in the depths of my bag, I begin to draw. It has been years since I had a pencil in my hands, my desire to draw destroyed by my mother's ridiculing and burning my drawings. I had almost forgot how much I loved it. Until I found this book.

I find myself drawing a face. A woman's face. I draw her upturned eyes, her features with their strange blend of girlish beauty and womanly intensity. I do not know why, but I am drawing the face of the woman who yesterday stared at me so fiercely that she nearly put me out of countenance and, in so doing, impressed her own quite strongly upon my memory.

I cannot judge whether or not my rendering is a faithful likeness; nevertheless, it is almost a relief to be drawing again, no matter what the subject. A release somehow. It is strange to watch these hands which are not my hands, these plumper, stronger, broader hands, hold the pencil. And hold it they do, with more facility, I must say, than my own ever did. Perhaps I might have been more accomplished at the art had I not given it up at such a young age. Ah, well. I am grateful that it seems Miss Courtney Stone did not.

I am so lost in drawing that when the tinkling of the bell announces the entrance of a customer, the sound is only at the periphery of my consciousness. It is only when he is standing at the counter that I look up and realize that it is Wes who has entered. His eyes are shining from behind his glasses; his curls are damp, as if he has just washed his hair. His white shirt is crisp and pressed, his collar open.

My heart leaps in my chest. I pray my elation isn't too transparent. I quickly close the sketchbook.

"Sam told me you'd officially emerged from the training phase," he says, "so I thought I'd come in and say hey. And take you out to celebrate. If you're not busy, that is."

"I did not expect to see you before tomorrow."

"I worked most of the night so I could fly back today."

Leaning in closer, he cranes his neck towards the sketchbook, and the familiar citron scent of his skin is intoxicating.

"So are you free for dinner?"

My mouth is dry, and my palms are damp. "Dinner would be nice," I finally murmur. Oh, dear. "Nice." A word as hackneyed out of all meaning in this world as it was in mine.

"I've never seen you draw before." He reaches out his hand towards the book. "May I?"

I am handing Wes the sketchbook when the café door jingles open again, and a tall, well-muscled young man in short trousers and a sleeveless shirt strides over to the counter, a broad grin on his tanned face.

"Dude," he says to Wes, offering his clenched fist, which Wes touches with his own in a curious sort of greeting ritual. "My site traffic's through the roof since you tweaked my keywords." He turns his bright white smile on me. "Courtney, right? I'm Keith." He brushes a sun-bleached lock of hair from his forehead. "If you want to take off a few minutes early"—he looks towards

Wes meaningfully—"that's cool with me."

Ah. This must be the Keith of whom Sharon spoke before she took her leave.

"Nice to meet you, Keith," I say, having learnt that "pleased to make your acquaintance" inevitably results in a raised eyebrow. "And that's very kind of you," I add.

I am indeed anxious to spend time with Wes. I do, however, wish to splash some water on my face and attend to my hair first. I must look a perfect fright after spending hours making coffees and steaming milk. "Could you give me a few minutes?" I say to him.

"Take your time." He pats the sketchbook. "This will keep me occupied."

I close myself inside the café's little bathroom and regard my reflection in the mirror. This face which is not my face is becoming ever more familiar to me, and I ever more comfortable with it. For having a different face makes it easier for me to say and do things that I never could have done with my own.

Like dabbing my lips with a stick of shiny pink color which I dig out of my bag. Now that I've got over the guilt of doing yet another thing I was forbidden to do at home, I've learnt to appreciate Courtney's veritable arsenal of cosmetics. My mother indulged daily in the rouge pot yet swore to her friends that the roses in her cheeks were nature's gift. Here, however, cosmetics are universally advertised and even flaunted. I cannot count how many times I have observed women of all ages taking out little mirrors and applying lip color or powder to their faces at the table in public, or even while driving their cars.

I splash cool water on my skin, which I dry gently with a paper towel. These cheeks are rosy, unlike the paleness of my former complexion. All that remains is to run a brush through my hair.

Oh yes, and perhaps a little spray of perfume. I cough and open the tiny window. A last look in the mirror. I do hope I have not overdone the scent. I wish to smell and look fresh rather than artificially decorated.

I walk back towards Wes, who is seated at a little table by the window, the sketchbook open before him. He looks up as I approach and beams. "Court. These are gorgeous," he says, paging through the drawings. "I never knew you did this."

I merely smile and duck my head, for I did not draw the picture he is admiring. What a skilled impostor I have become.

Wes gasps. Somehow he has knocked over his green glass bottle of mineral water, soaking the bottom half of the book, which is now open to my drawing of the woman. Wes bolts from his chair to dodge the water, which is dripping from the table.

"It is nothing," I say, rushing over to the counter to retrieve paper napkins with which I begin mopping up the spill. "It is only water and will soon dry."

I dab at the drawing with the paper napkins, looking into the eyes of the woman in the drawing.

"Courtney, I am so sorry," says Wes.

Courtney, I am so sorry. Those words, those same words he spoke to me when I was standing in a shop on Vermont. It is another memory, and it is not my memory at all, yet it is. And I can see her, too, the woman from the drawing, standing in that shop. I had never laid eyes on her before, yet she was staring at me, just as she stared at me in the café and in the club. She was staring at me because Wes had been holding her hand and dropped it when he saw that I was in the shop. He had left her behind and walked towards me, as if she did not exist.

"Courtney," he said, "I am so sorry."

"Forget it," I said, walking away from him as fast as possible towards the back door of the shop. How dare he speak to me? He had had his chance to speak, when he knew that Frank was with another woman. Wes, my closest friend, had betrayed me. And from the looks of the lady whose hand he had been holding, I was not the only one he had wronged.

"Courtney?" Wes's voice brings me back to the café.

I am still holding a wad of paper napkins over the soaked lower half of the drawing. But the

306

face of the woman is untouched, and her eyes regard me with as much unfriendly scrutiny as the original did in the café yesterday.

And I know, in that moment, that I was lying to myself about Wes. I wanted to believe there was some misunderstanding, some reason for him to have kept Frank's inconstancy a secret.

But I was wrong.

Oh, how could I have been so stupid? Why did I not listen to Anna and Paula? Why did I think for a moment that I would be drawn to anyone but the most duplicitous, deceiving men in the world? Not only had he agreed to lie to me—to Courtney —about Frank, he had slighted that woman in my presence, that woman whose hand he was holding, who was in the picture with him, that woman who must be his—fiancée? Girlfriend? Oh, how I hate that absurd word! No doubt she bears me a great deal of ill will from the way she looked at me yesterday in the café. And that night in the club. No wonder she was staring up at us. He must have gone to her as soon as Deepa took me home that night.

"Courtney?"

My heart is hammering in my ears; I have to get out of here. And almost before I know what I am doing, I have slung my bag across my shoulder and bolted from the café, running as fast as I can towards home.

"Courtney!"

He is behind me, shouting for me to stop, but I won't listen; I have to get away from him. "Courtney, please!"

And to think I was forming an attachment to this man. The shops and buildings are but a blur as I run, the sound of my breathing hard in my ears. But I barely see my surroundings. All I can see is Wes, his eyes, how he looked at me in that shop, how his gray-blue eyes were wet with what looked like unshed tears, and how I fled from him that day, fled from that pained look in his eyes, willing myself to think of something else, anything else, as I drove myself home, as I searched through my kitchen for something to eat, something to distract me. But all I could think about were his eyes, the pain in them, and the feel of his hand on my shoulder, and the citron scent of his skin—and suddenly I was so dizzy that I found myself gripping the edge of the kitchen table to steady myself.

For it wasn't Frank I loved. It was Wes.

I see it now, so clearly, though she could not. I see what she drowned in vodka and grief, what she buried inside the pages of *Pride and Prejudice*.

And I am back there, in that memory, in the apartment, the morning after seeing Wes in that store, and I am sick with too much drink, and my head pounds as I stagger out of the apartment. And there is a blur of lopsided images, driving in the car, the sun hurting my eyes, dragging myself into work, then swimming in an enormous public bath—a pool. And I am swimming in the cold clear water, arms slicing the shimmering surface, legs kicking. And I am standing at the edge of the pool, shivering with fatigue, and I am diving into the water. And then I am lying on the floor at the side of the pool, the worried faces of the other swimmers standing over me, the drip-drip-drip of the older, skinny one as the ribbon of her tightly fitting cap deposits drop after drop onto my right cheek in a steady, rhythmic pace. How hypnotic is the sound, like a metronome lulling me to sleep, and I close my eyes, surrendering to the drip-drip-drip. Which is when I hear his voice, as if for the very first time. It is Wes's voice telling me I hit my head on the bottom of the pool when I dived in, that I'll be fine, that I should open my eyes. How strange it is to have Wes talking to me while I lie here at the pool, his hand reaching down to me. Except that I am no longer at the pool. "You're in the emergency room," he says, holding my hand. "And you're gonna be just fine."

"Courtney?" Wes's voice brings me back to the present moment. I am no longer running; I am leaning against the wall in front of my house, and I am breathing hard from my exertions.

"What's going on? Why did you run away from me?" He is holding the book of drawings, folded open to the picture of the woman.

I look down at the book. And then I meet Wes's eyes.

309

"I remember now. I wanted to believe you had good reason for not telling me about Frank. For even being willing to lie for him. But now I know there is no excuse for what you did."

He closes his eyes for a moment and lets out a sigh that is almost like a shudder. "I never meant to hurt you, Courtney."

I point to the drawing. "But what about her, Wes? What did you do to her? Did you lie to her the way you lied to me?"

"I told her I couldn't get involved. She said I wasn't the type of guy she'd ever fall in love with. She said I was too nice. She said she just wanted to have a good time."

I can see the lady's face, the hurt in her eyes when Wes dropped her hand and walked away from her in the shop.

"She didn't look as if she were having a good time that day. Or yesterday when she was in the café."

Something like fear flickers across his features. "Morgan was there?"

"I could not place her at first, except for having seen her at Awakening. But then I remembered that day."

"Courtney, can we please go inside and talk about this?"

"No, I have nothing to say."

"I have a lot to say to you."

Those words echo in my head: *I have a lot to*

say to you. It is exactly what he said to me that day in the shop, when he was with Morgan, and I was walking away from him, as I am now.

"I have no wish to hear how you used that young lady ill."

He is actually walking up the stairs after me.

"Courtney, for once would you please listen to me?"

I stop and turn to look at him. "That poor girl. Does no one of your sex understand constancy?"

And then the full meaning of my words puts me in such a state that I can feel the blush rising to the roots of my hair.

"That's not fair. How was I supposed to know she would want—" He looks down at his shoes, as if unable to continue.

The look on her face in the club, in the café. All the time Wes spent with me when he wasn't working, how he even slept on my sofa. "And so you abandoned her. This is beyond anything."

"If you really want to know, she was so angry at me after we ran into you in that store that she said she didn't want to see me anymore."

"What choice did she have, after the way you slighted her?"

Was Wes no better than *Sense and Sensibility*'s Willoughby, who humiliated poor Marianne in public?

"You should do the right thing by the lady— by Morgan," I say.

"What am I supposed to do?"

"Don't you understand? It's like Captain Wentworth."

He looks completely baffled.

"From *Persuasion*, Wes. By Jane Austen? If I am to judge by what I saw in that poor girl's eyes, then they are not so very different at all. You see, in *Persuasion* Captain Wentworth has to marry Louisa Musgrove. After all the attention he has paid her, her family expects them to marry. And so he is bound to her by honor if she wants him, lest all the world think he has rejected her because he—or someone else—has ruined her. And even if you did not"—and here I feel myself blushing furiously—"ruin her, others might believe you did. Which would ruin her marriage prospects with anyone else."

Wes looks at me, openmouthed, as if unable to speak. He shakes his head. "You really believe that a man would think a woman ruined because he, or someone else, slept with her? That is the most antiquated thing I've ever heard."

So he is just as bad as Willoughby. Or Edgeworth. Or Frank. "If I'm wrong, then why are women writing conduct books—excuse me, self-help books—in which they lament the common practice of men seducing and abandoning them? If that isn't proof of how little has changed since my day—"

"*Your* day?"

"Does that really matter?"

"It does to me. Because you're not from another time, Courtney, no matter how hard you hit your head or how often you read those books of yours. No man expects his wife to be untouched. Maybe our grandparents might have, but even that I doubt. Birth control changed everything."

"Doesn't look to me like much has changed."

"Oh, so I suppose we can just ignore the entire women's movement."

"Movement? Towards what—a lack of respect for oneself?"

"I've never heard you talk like this, Courtney. I thought you were a feminist."

"If that means I am a defender of my sex against blackguards like you, then yes, I suppose I am a feminist."

"Courtney . . ." He reaches for my hand. "This is crazy. Can't we just go inside and talk about this?"

I pull my hand from his grasp. "I wish to be alone." I turn and run up the last few steps to the door of my apartment. He follows me, and my hands are shaking so hard I cannot even put the key in the lock.

"You know why I told Morgan I couldn't get involved with her?"

I turn to meet his intense gaze. He reaches out his hand to touch my face, but I back up out of his reach. "No. I won't believe anything you have to say."

He chokes out the words. "It was because of you."

"I won't listen. It's all lies." Oh, this blasted lock. I have to get away from him. "Step out of my way, if you please."

"I don't care how many men a woman has slept with. But what no man wants to see is his woman stoop to the likes of someone like Frank. Or have such low self-esteem that she would consider a life with him. To think that she can't have better than that. Because she can."

"You have no right—"

"Courtney, when I met Morgan, you weren't even speaking to me. You wouldn't see me. You wouldn't return my calls."

"All I know is that men desire what they cannot have. But once they possess it, the object of desire loses its value."

"You don't know what you're talking about."

"Will you step aside, please, or have you forgot yourself entirely?"

"Courtney, I—" He presses himself against the side of the staircase, enabling me to pass and descend the stairs, which I do, two at a time.

I head towards the street.

"Let me walk you back to the café so you can get your car," he shouts.

My car.

And with that I am sprinting towards the brown car that is mine, putting the key in the lock, slamming the door shut and closing him out, turning the key and guiding the vehicle smoothly and effortlessly into the street, to the traffic light, and then right, and then gliding soundlessly down the lit-up street, in tandem with dozens of other cars. I am driving all on my own and it is easy and effortless and these hands and feet know exactly what to do. And a sense of calm and peace floods me, and I make my way down a street that is at once familiar and new. I cannot think, I cannot question, I cannot stop, I simply drive.

Twenty-five

I find myself on a winding, hilly road that is strangely familiar. I know this road somehow, just as I know the flatter city roads below. On this particular stretch of road, I can feel some of the tension in my shoulders releasing as I ascend the gentle rises. I am soaring above my troubles, leaving them behind. And then I am steering the car off the road, to a little paved spot at the edge of the cliff, overlooking the city. My body, my senses, remember this place as a place of refuge. And I know that I have been here many times before. I emerge from the car and sit on the hood, in the stillness of the night, looking out upon the glittering city below, its vastness arrayed in millions of fairy lights, twinkling with promise and secrets.

But that promise is not for me. And those secrets I shall never grasp.

For I do not belong here. I do not belong in a world where there are no rules yet too many of them to comprehend. I do not belong in a place where the person whose society was dearer to me than anything is not who I thought he was.

He chose to protect Frank rather than protect me. He bedded and abandoned a young woman. And he has a very low opinion of me.

No man, he said, *wants to see a woman stoop to someone like Frank.*

It is in all ways humiliating. Of course he believes me as ruined as I feared he would. And to think I had begun to believe him attached to me.

There is much work to be done here is what the fortune-teller said. *Look at the state of this life you have inherited.*

If truly I was brought here to put this life into a better state, then I have failed indeed. For I am as crossed in love here as I was in my own time.

How shall I face him again?

And then I know where it is that I most wish to go. And I pray that there is one who might help me to get there.

Within twenty minutes I am in front of Awakening.

I park the car—I am astonishingly proficient at maneuvering this machine, provided I do not think about what I am doing—and as I disembark and plunge into the jostling, jocular crowd of young men and women, I cannot help but compare my initial reaction to their outrageous hair, jewelry, and mode of dress with my detached observance now. I give my name to the hulking man at the door, who wears a tight black shirt and bright violet streaks in his cropped blond hair, and his frowning concentration on the list before him becomes a polite smile.

"I'll let Deepa know you're here," he says, and waves me in.

I wade through the press of people towards the bar; I'm parched, and I need something to drink. The loud music is a blur, but suddenly the words capture my attention:

> . . . *they were as strangers; worse than strangers,*
> *a perpetual estrangement.*
> *Once so much to each other; now nothing!*
> *A perpetual estrangement . . .*

I know these words—but of course I do; I only just read them last night. They are from *Persuasion*.

I am marveling over the fact that a singer is singing words from a novel I am reading, when a tap on my shoulder causes me to turn round, and there is Deepa.

"Darling." She kisses me on both cheeks and shouts into my ear, above the music, "I think those words would be lost on just about everyone but a true Janeite."

Janeite. What a lovely word.

I am so happy to see her—my dear Janeite friend—that I put my arms around her and hug her. She returns my embrace, then pulls back to regard me carefully.

"What is it? You look like hell."

And then I feel the tears rising unbidden to my eyes, and all I can do is shake my head.

"Come." She grabs my hand and steers me through the crowd, past the band, down a passageway to the ladies' room. Once inside, the sounds from outside are somewhat muffled.

"A little cool water on your face might make you feel better," she says.

I regard this face which has become my face in the mirror, and it does indeed look frightful. My hair is completely unruly after my run through the hot streets and then driving with the windows open. My face is shiny and blotchy from the heat. The back of my shirt is damp with perspiration, and I imagine it also smells as if it needs to be washed.

"I have an extra T-shirt in my bag," says Deepa. "Always carry one when I'm working in case I spill a drink on myself. Or someone else does it for me. Which is not an infrequent occurrence." She smiles. "I'll get it for you, if you like. And one of my special drinks. How does that sound?"

I can only nod, my eyes brimming over.

"It's all right," she says. "You have a good cry and let it all out, okay? And then you can tell me all about it if you like."

She slips out into the club, and I set about the business of washing my face, neck, and under my arms. It's not as convenient as the lovely shower at home, but it's still better than the pitcher and basin I had at Mansfield House.

By the time Deepa returns with a spotless white T-shirt, a little white towel, and a tall glass of a pink liquid, I am feeling and looking a thousand times better than I did a few minutes ago. I thank her and dry myself with the towel, and exchange my soiled shirt for the fresh white one, which fits perfectly and looks very well indeed. I take a sip of the sweet raspberry/lemon drink, which I believe also has vodka in it, tug a comb through my hair, and dig through my bag for makeup, which I start applying. I am actually beginning to look presentable.

Deepa regards me in the mirror as she leans against the wall. "Do you want to talk about it?"

I sigh. "I wouldn't know where to begin."

"Fair enough. But perhaps there's someone else you might like to talk to?"

My heart leaps in my chest. "Is she here?"

Deepa shrugs. "No idea, darling. But there's only one way to find out."

She looks at me questioningly, I nod my readiness, and she leads me by the hand, past the band, and through a door, down a passageway, and then through another door. And there we are, in that same dimly lit corridor, and my heart pounds with anticipation.

"I'm here, if you want me later," says Deepa, and with a quick kiss on the cheek, she turns to leave me on my own, but I reach for her hand, pull her to me in an embrace.

"Thank you for everything, Deepa. Your friendship has meant the world to me."

She looks at me and arches an eyebrow. "*Has* meant? I'm not sure I like the sound of that."

"It does mean the world to me." And I look down for a moment, unable to withstand her questioning gaze.

She appraises me with her large brown eyes and smiles wryly. "Say good-bye before you leave."

And then she disappears behind the door, leaving me trembling. For my future depends on the lady, on her being here, and I am by no means assured that I will find her behind that door at the end of the corridor.

And if I do? Everything rests on her ability—or willingness—to help me.

I reach the door at the end of the corridor; there is no sound from within, no light issuing from the tiny opening at the bottom. I put my head against the smooth black surface and strain to hear, but my ears can distinguish nothing from within; all I hear is the muffled music from the club.

I rap on the door; no answer. I lean my cheek against the surface of the door and endeavor to calm my breathing. I knock again.

I put my hand on the doorknob and turn it; the door opens easily. It is all darkness in the room; I can make out nothing.

"Hello? Is anyone here?"

I turn around but can see no opened door; all is blackness in the room. I put my hands before me to feel my way around, but there is nothing to bump into, nothing at all except blackness and emptiness.

"Hello?"

My hands touch a curtain of rough canvas; I fumble till I find an opening, slip through it to the other side, and suddenly all is a white, blinding glare.

I can make out nothing but this bright white light. "Hello? What is this about? Are you here?"

Then the scene slowly resolves itself into fuzzy white shapes moving about, and I begin to smell familiar scents of earth and horses and unwashed clothes, of perfume and ale and gingerbread. And the fuzzy white shapes become sharper until they are people and horses and tents and peddlers' stalls and gentlemen and ladies and farmers and workingmen and children, all strolling and sauntering and skipping about happily. And I am no longer in that strange world I have been inhabiting, or in that body, or in that future time.

I am myself again, at a fair. *The* fair where I first met the fortune-teller—dear heavens—I am back!

Twenty-six

I feel Mary's arm linked through mine, and I turn to her and she smiles at me. And at the edge of everything around us, there is a sort of shimmering quality, as if everything I see is a reflection in a pool. And Mary speaks, and it is as if I am in a dream, for I know every word that her voice, that deep, throaty, well-loved voice, will say before she utters it.

"Shall we try our luck, Jane?" says she. "Oh how delightful to have our fortunes told!"

We are walking towards the brown tent of the fortune-teller, the same tent where I sat that day which seems so long ago. It is all happening again, all happening as it did before.

"Shall I go inside with you?" she says. "Or shall I wait for you here?"

And I say to her now, just as I said then, "Would you mind at all if I went in alone?"

She laughs and taps me playfully with her fan. "Of course not, silly girl."

I part the flaps of the tent and enter, and the sweet scent of roses fills my nostrils, the same scent as before. And she is there, as she was before, an elderly woman in a simple yet elegantly cut black gown, a fringed shawl over her shoulders, greeting me with a bow and a wave of her hand to the chair which sits before her table.

"What may I do for you today?" says she.

I want to answer, but not in the way I did before, for I do not wish to relive what has already occurred. And though I am back here, in my own time, which is what I realized I wanted most fervently as I sat on my car atop that hill, I do not wish to retrace my steps with every word and breath. I wish to go forward. I open my mouth to say so, but the words will not come out.

I wish to be here, in my own time, in my own country, I say inside my mind to the lady, her wise face impassive. *But I do not wish to repeat what happened before.*

And I hear her voice inside my mind, answering me: *Ah, but this is the price of your wish.*

Could I not awaken after my fall, in my own bed in Somerset?

Courtney Stone has done that for you. All you could do is go back to your own time and repeat what you have already lived through.

But knowing what I now know, I would not wish for a different life. I would not ride Belle that day. I would do things differently.

But don't you see, if you never took the ride, then you would never have had the fall, and so all that you have seen and done and learned in the future world and all whom you have met and known and all to whom you have become attached would fade away like this. . . .

And I am walking through the fair with Mary as before, her arm linked in mine, and it is as if the curtains of my mind are closing, and behind them, fading from view, till they are nothing but blackness and dust and void, are Deepa and Paula and Anna and Frank and the streets of the wondrous city and the tall palm trees and airplanes and movies and all that I have seen and known and Wes, yes, even Wes. All are fading till they are but thin shadows and dust and nothingness and still Mary is by my side, chattering away in her deep, throaty voice, and my own voice inside is crying out *No! No! I want to remember!* But even that fades into the hum and murmur of the fair-going crowd and the lilting tones of the flute and the sound of children laughing until it is only a nagging worry at the back of my mind, like something I know I should remember but have forgotten to do, and even that fades to nothingness. . . .

Which means there can be nothing known differently, nothing remembered. . . .

And once again I am back inside the tent, looking into the kind eyes of the fortune-teller.

But I don't belong in that strange future world, I say to her in my mind.

"Now answer me. Even if I did possess such powers as to bring you back to what you call your own time and to do things differently," she says, and now she is speaking aloud, and the world of the fair has vanished and I am in complete darkness again, "would you leave before you finish what you have started?"

"I do not understand."

"Shall I explain it to you?"

"May I see you, please?"

"Where would you like to see me?"

"In the little room in Deepa's club. Please. I wish to talk to you and not be bound by the past."

And all at once, I am in the room in the club with her again, and she is no longer the elderly fortune-teller from the fair but rather the young woman in the fine muslin gown, brown curls framing her lovely face and her golden-brown eyes regarding me kindly. She is again sitting before her little table, offering me a cup of tea.

"It will do you good, Miss Mansfield," she says, and a fire burns cheerfully behind her within a marble chimneypiece, and the fact that it is high summer is of no consequence.

"Are we truly back in the club?"

"Does that really matter, my dear? A fire is most comforting, I find."

"What did you mean by my finishing what I have started?"

"Consider," she says, "all the good you have done in Courtney's life. For one, she would probably not have left her situation as David's assistant, as you have done. For another, it is quite possible that she might have chosen to be so charmed by Frank's apology and admittance of guilt that she could be packing her things even now to move in with him."

"But what of my life?" I ask.

"Oh, you left that a perfect mess as well—judging all and sundry as you are wont to do, acting out of self-righteous certainty when you really know nothing at all, riding though you were warned against it, causing untold amounts of grief through your self-destructive actions. And feeding your own delusions about forbearance and fidelity and trust, I might add. Poor Courtney. She does have her work cut out for her."

At first I cannot even speak, and finally I sputter, "You mean Edgeworth, don't you. I was the wronged party in this business, not him!"

"Is that so." She regards me calmly, coolly.

"So you would have Courtney in command of my life. How long do you suppose it will take before she is drawn in by Edgeworth's charm and address? Especially if she has arrived in my world with as little memory of my life as I have of hers."

"Would that be such a crime?"

"He does not deserve her good opinion!"

"What right have you to say what he deserves and what he does not?"

"How could he be any less guilty than he

looked that day on his estate when I spied him with his own servant?"

"Perhaps the answer will be revealed someday. But for now the past is of little consequence. In the meantime, you might do well to remember the words of your favorite heroine: *It is particularly incumbent on those who never change their opinion, to be secure of judging properly at first.* Even if a man who looks like a thief is, indeed, a thief, that is not the whole story. Only by stepping into his shoes can you begin to comprehend what made him a thief, and what else he is besides a thief, for we are not only just one thing, we are many. You of all people should know that."

And she starts to laugh, a high, clear, musical laugh.

"Now, now," she says. "Do not look so downcast. And do have some of your tea. It will do you good, I am sure of it."

I want to refuse. I want to be stubborn, as if giving in would be beneath my dignity. But I cannot resist the kindness in her countenance. And so I sip at my tea, and, sure enough, I do feel calmed. I would like to be angry, but somehow it requires too much effort.

"So, my dear," says the lady, putting down her teacup. "We both know that it is not Mr. Edgeworth who is behind your sudden wish to revisit the past."

I want to say something in my defense, but my face burns with shame.

"Best to get it out all at once," she says kindly.

"The truth is, I am ruined," I say. "And no respectable man will ever pay his addresses to me."

"Are you so sure of that?"

"I am no longer sure of anything."

"Now that is the wisest thing I have heard you say yet." She smiles.

Despite my best efforts, I smile back at her, but the thought of what I must tell her next is sobering indeed. "At first I was able to say that this is what Courtney did, not I, but I can no longer do so. . . . You see, I—"

I cannot even get out the words.

"It's all right, my dear."

"I have had these—feelings—in my body. These —memories somehow. And I am mortified by them."

She knows; I can tell she does. Yet there is no judgment, no revulsion, in her countenance. "Let's get the worst part over and done with, shall we? Like having a tooth drawn. Best not to hesitate." She smiles again, radiating kindness.

"The worst part. Well, that these feelings, or memories, or whatever they are, were of Frank, a man for whom I have no respect. And when I had these memories, it felt as if I were not mistress of myself. Such feelings are bad enough, but what is worse is that there is someone else. Someone whom I greatly esteem—or at least I did esteem him until I discovered his . . . intimate connection with another woman. A woman whom he then deserted. And that is not his only offense. He had lied to protect Frank, whom he knew was with another woman while engaged to me. I thought Wes must have had his reasons but—oh dear, I do not know what to think. I thought I knew him. I thought I knew myself. I know that things are supposed to be different in this time, in this place, than they were in my own world. But I do not know that they are different at all."

She leans across the little table and pats my hand. "There, there, my dear. That was very brave of you. And to reward your courage I shall tell you something that will help you greatly: These, shall we say, impulses of attraction to Frank are merely cellular memories."

I ponder her words for a moment. "You mean like Cowper's words in *The Task*, 'It opens all the cells Where Mem'ry slept'? "

She smiles, delighted. "Very good, my dear. But there is much more to the human body than the cells of which Cowper wrote. For he, and those of his time, had no conception of how truly tiny and numerous those cells are, and not only in the brain, but in the entire body. For your body is made up of trillions of tiny cells. Science has made many discoveries since your time, and the body is indeed a miraculous machine.

"So you see, in addition to the memories stored in your brain, which you experience like the revisiting of scenes of your life—or in this case, of Courtney's life—there are also the less easily identifiable cellular memories. The cells of the body retain memories of the experiences the body has had—and not just the aches and pains and tastes and smells, but the joys and sorrows, the desires and longings. Which is why one day you might awaken feeling cheerful, while another day you may awaken feeling depressed. Your body remembers that a year ago today or ten years ago today, you felt cheerful or depressed. And it feels that way again.

"The key is to be aware of the fact that cellular memory exists and to know that you have the choice to let those memories retreat into the past or allow them to rule your present. Once you understand what they are, you can choose to focus on the present moment and see what it offers you."

I try to absorb it all, but I'm not sure. "So you mean I have a choice?"

"Of course you do, my dear. That is the blessing of free will. Just because you may feel a fleeting desire in your body does not mean that your mind must follow it."

I think again about Wes's words. "He said that the lady—Morgan is her name—told him she just wanted to have a good time."

She looks at me carefully. "So did Courtney. And so did you, I might add."

I feel myself blushing yet again as I think of those memories I had of Frank and of the desire I had for Edgeworth. "But I loved Edgeworth. And Courtney loved Frank."

"And that makes you better than Morgan? Do not be so quick to judge. You, like she, still wanted pleasure, and why would you not? After all, pleasure is the opposite of pain. And humans will do anything to keep the pain at bay."

I think of James, our footman, and how I kissed him that one night when I was mad with grief over Edgeworth. And I know that the lady is right. I had no thought for what my recklessness might cost James. Or myself. I only wanted to keep my pain at bay.

The lady sips her tea and regards me kindly. "Today's women are no less desirous of love, and marrying for love, than they were in your time. But they, like so many women before them, simply fear it is an unattainable goal. And thus they settle for what fleeting pleasures they can find, creating an endless cycle of pleasure, despair, pleasure, despair, ad infinitum. Human nature is the same today as it was in your time. The only difference between today's world and your world is that people have more choices now than they did then. Do drink your tea, my dear."

I raise the cup to my lips, and as I gaze at the fire burning merrily behind the lady, I cannot deny that in the brief time I have been here, I have had more choices in a single day than I had in my entire life as a gentleman's daughter. Choices of everything from what I might wear and how I might spend my day to how I could earn my living. But yet the thing which I now know I want the most seems the farthest from my reach.

I take a deep breath. "You said before that I had not finished what I started. But what else can I do? I thought Wes was a good man, and indeed, I cannot deny that I formed an attachment to him."

She smiles. "No. You cannot."

"But what is there to be done? On the one hand, he said he told Morgan that he could not get involved, and he claims this was all for me. But is he not bound in honor to her? And even if he were not, what he said to me clearly undoes any feelings he might have had."

"Is that so." She pours more tea into my cup. "Drink, my dear."

I take a tiny sip.

"Why don't you tell me what he said. Exactly."

"He said that he didn't care how many men a woman had slept with. But that no man wants to see a woman stoop to someone like Frank. You see? In his eyes I am worse than ruined!"

"Are you sure that is exactly what he said?"

"Of course I am."

"Drink your tea, my dear."

I do. And it is as if my mind has slowed.

She cocks her head to the side, smiling kindly

at me. "You're sure those were his exact words."

"Well, I—" Somehow being right is not all that important anymore. "He said"—and I close my eyes to picture him speaking—*"I don't care how many men a woman has slept with. But what no man wants to see is his woman stoop to the likes of someone like Frank."*

She arches an eyebrow. "Whose woman?"

I gasp. "His woman."

"And?"

And I summon his words as if he is speaking them himself: *"Or have such low self-esteem that she would consider a life with him. To think that she can't have better than that. Because she can."*

"Very good. And what is the most important part of what he said?"

"Low self-esteem? I gather from my reading that the word has taken on a somewhat different shade of meaning in this time."

"Yes, it is more than simply having a favorable opinion of oneself. It is about respect for one's true dignity, not simply for the face we present to the world. And surely it is true that a lady who would choose a life with Frank, or someone like Frank, must not esteem herself very highly. And for Wes, it was painful to watch. So yes, this is an important part of what he said, but not the most important."

And all at once I understand. "It pained him that she thought she could not have someone better than Frank. *Because she can.*"

"And who, my dear, is this mysterious 'she'?"

I smile with the most glorious happiness. "I am."

"You see? There is still much to be done."

Yes, there is. Because I *can* have better. For myself. And for Courtney. After all, am I not the steward of her life? Her future happiness—and mine—is in my hands. Except—

"What of the lady? Morgan. Is she to be forgot?"

"The lady, as a creature of this time, has far more choices than she would have had in your time. And with choice comes responsibility. Wes told her what the limitations of their alliance would be, and yet she chose to pursue it. That she suffers now deserves all of our compassion, but it does not require the sacrifice of Wes's liberty. He has not acted dishonorably."

A thrill of relief rushes through me at the thought of Wes unshackled and free, as Anne thought of Captain Wentworth when she learnt he was not to marry Louisa Musgrove after all.

Yet there is still one unanswered, and unavoidable, question.

"What am I to make of his lying to protect Frank, whom he knew was with another woman?"

"You must ask him that yourself," says she. "Welcome to the age of communication, my dear. One needn't wait till one is engaged to engage in the difficult subjects."

And if he acquits himself? What then? Will I, in turn, be whole in his eyes? Her eyes are gentleness itself, and she answers my thought as if I have spoken it aloud. "When you unite with your true love, it will be as if he is your first, and you his. In the eyes of love, there is no past."

And my eyes fill with tears of joy. All forgiven. All washed away.

"Go forth," says she, "and choose the present."

Twenty-seven

The lady rises and offers her hand. "I do hope we meet again, Miss Stone."

Miss Stone!

She smiles slyly and holds my hand between both of hers. "That is your name, is it not?"

I laugh. "Yes, I suppose it is."

Her eyes twinkle. "A rose by any other name, and all that. Now go forth and do that life proud, because it is the only life you can manage. We cannot be trying to manage two lives at once, can we? So don't you worry about what you left behind. Well, off with you, then."

She pats my hand, and I bow. "I am most grateful to you."

"Yes, yes, now let's see what you do with it."

She gestures towards the door, which has opened somehow on its own. I turn back to her, and she is gone, and so is the cheerful little parlor, and the table, and the chairs, and the fire—the room is once again the dark little store-closet it became after our last meeting.

I shiver, but not with cold, as I reenter the corridor outside the room and close the door behind me.

Let's see what you do with it, she said. What she gave me is a great gift, and what I do with that gift is my choice. *With choice comes responsibility,* she said. *Go forth, and choose the present.*

What was it Anna talked of the very first day I arrived here? *Each of us has the power to create heaven or hell, right here, right now.* The present. Right now.

I rush out of the passageway and into the club again, making my way through the press of people and the wall of music, and I spy Deepa leaning against the bar.

"Deepa!" I grab her and enfold her in my arms.

"Let a girl take a breath," she laughs when I finally release her. She regards me and smiles her delight. "You look like a different woman."

I laugh. "That is it—I *am* a different woman! And it's the best thing that ever happened to me! Must run—thank you, Deepa!"

And I dash through the club and out of the door and to my car. Pull the phone from my bag. Call Wes.

The phone is ringing. Oh, dear, what shall I say? I have never done anything like this in my life. It's going to be all right. Just remember what the lady said about the age of communication.

The phone stops in mid-ring. "Courtney?" says

Wes's voice into my ear. "Courtney? Are you there?"

"Yes, I—Wes, I would very much like to talk to you and would it be convenient if I—"

"Thank God," he says. "I can be there in five minutes."

"No, I'll come to you." And instantly my mind traces the route to his house, until I see the house itself, though I have never been there before. Cellular memory.

"Tonight?" he says.

"Now, if that is okay with you." What a forward little baggage I am. Proposing I drive myself, unescorted, at night, to the home of a single man.

"Of course."

"Excellent. I'll be there soon." Well, well. Different world, different rules. Besides, I wish to have the freedom to drive off whenever I wish, rather than repeat that trapped feeling I had earlier when I could not even escape into my own home. And I shall be stronger if I am not in my own apartment, where the working lights and all those other lovely conveniences restored shall be a reminder of my obligation to Wes's kindness.

Enough thinking. I must drive.

My inner map does me proud, so long as I direct my attention only to driving and not to the conversation before me, and within five minutes, I am parking across the street from the very same house I saw in my mind's eye, a low rectangular box of a house partially obscured by tall shrubs.

As I approach the door, I take a deep breath and knock. It opens instantly, as if he has been waiting on the threshold for my arrival. His face is flushed, his expression grave.

"I'm so happy you're here," he says, and smiles almost shyly, gesturing for me to enter.

The large, open space is at once new and familiar. I know I have never been here, but there is something comforting in its familiarity, and indeed there are fleeting little pictures in my mind of sitting at the long table, having a meal with Wes and several friends, and of lying down afterwards on the low, cream-colored sofa.

"Something to drink?" he asks.

"Yes, please."

I gaze out upon a softly lit garden beyond a wall of windows. There are tall wildflowers, shrubs, and little stone benches bordering a winding gravel path.

"Here." He hands me a tall iced glass. "Why don't you sit down?" He motions to the sofa, and a book lying on a low table before it catches my eye—*Northanger Abbey*.

I pick up the book. "You have read this?"

He smiles. "Don't look so surprised. I even liked it."

I cannot help but wonder . . . "Wes, did I—did I ask you to read this book?"

He looks puzzled. "No. My niece, Emma, did." He smiles again. "I believe her words were, 'Solid coming-of-age story with a clever satire of gothic novels and a feminist subtext.' Emma's thirteen."

"I can hardly imagine being so self-possessed at such an age."

But before I get too distracted by the precocity of Wes's relations, I must attend to the business that brought me here. I sip my drink for courage, but it gives me none, despite its being heavily laced with vodka. If only I had some of the fortune-teller's tea.

I look out on the garden again; it feels like an age since I walked amongst green growing things. "Wes, might we go outside?"

He hastens to the wall of windows, slides one of them open, and motions for me to go through it.

I step outside, and the sound of the gravel beneath my shoes instantly summons a memory. I am pacing this very same path, the gravel crunching beneath my shoes, and I am fretting over the fact that Frank is supposed to be here and is not, and neither is Wes, and I am unable to reach either of them and I just know that something is amiss and—

"Courtney?"

Wes's voice brings me back to the present. *Choose the present,* the lady said. A most unusual credo for a fortune-teller, now that I think on it. And most wise.

"Wes, I must ask—" Oh dear, there is no polite way of posing such a question. "Wes, you lied to me about Frank when you knew he was with another woman, and I would very much like to know why."

There. I've said it. Easier than I could have imagined, though my heart is racing so fast I can hardly breathe.

He draws in a long, shuddering breath, meets my eyes, and looks down at the ground before raising his eyes to me again.

"I knew he was there. He called me forty-five minutes after he was supposed to have shown up here, and I heard a woman's voice in the background answering the phone for the cake place. I knew he was up to something, but I had no proof. When I confronted him, he swore there was nothing going on. Said he was on his way out of there and would explain it all later. Don't make a mess where there is none, is what he said to me. And so he asked me to tell you his meeting was running late if you called and, God forgive me, that's what I agreed to do."

"But why not tell me what you suspected?"

"I had no proof. And frankly, I didn't trust my own motivations for telling you."

Wes looks down for a moment and then meets my gaze. "I didn't want the woman I loved—the woman I *love*—to marry this guy. But who was I to decide what would make her happy?"

The woman I love. That is all I can hear. *The woman I love.* He loves me. He loves *me.*

"Agreeing to be his alibi was the worst mistake I ever made, Courtney. I don't blame you if you can't forgive me."

There are tears in his eyes, and one of them breaks free and runs down his cheek.

I reach up to his face to wipe his tear, and he moves my fingers to his lips and kisses them.

"I think we've both made mistakes," I say, and for a moment I am afraid to meet his gaze. But I do. "Can you forgive *me?*"

He raises my chin with his hand and looks into my eyes. "There's nothing to forgive," he breathes. "Nothing at all. I love you, Courtney. I've always loved you."

He puts his arms around me and I can hardly breathe. I reach my arms up around his neck and he leans down and touches my lips with his own, and it is the softest gentlest sweetest kiss I could ever imagine. And then the kiss becomes more urgent, and he wraps his arms around me even tighter and I am dizzy with his kiss, with his scent, with the sound of his breathing and the little moans that escape me, and I have never wanted anyone as much as I want Wes right now. I am shuddering with desire, and when finally the kiss ends, he is trembling, too, and I rest against his chest, listening to the thudding of his heart, and I know that this is more than mere desire, that I

341

love this man more than I have ever imagined I could love anyone.

Which is why I must be completely honest with him.

I summon my courage for what I have to say.

"I have a confession to make."

And I take a deep, deep breath, for I have been warned by Deepa that some things should not be shared with just anyone. But Wes is not just anyone, and I want no dissembling, no dishonesty, no pretense in my connection with him of all people.

"Whatever you want to tell me," he says, giving me little kisses all over my forehead and cheeks and moving down lower to my neck. My breathing quickens and I am getting so distracted that if I do not pull away—very gently—I shall not be able to go on.

"Wes, if you truly want to be with me, then you must allow that I am not who you think I am."

"I don't understand."

"Please allow me to say what I have to say, or I will lose the courage to do so. I will agree that Courtney is my name and that somehow I have come to be in her life, and in this body. But I cannot be with you and carry this around inside me. I cannot pretend that I am someone I am not. I cannot continually try to hide from you that I do not remember almost everything that Courtney did and lived and felt and thought because I did not live her life. I shall, I know I must, pretend, with the rest of the world. But not with you. Please. Not with you."

"Courtney, this is crazy. How am I supposed to understand you?"

"You think me crazy."

"Of course not. But how am I supposed to believe that you're not who you are? You're standing right here in front of me."

"Am I not different from the Courtney you knew before?"

"You had a bad concussion, and your memory—"

"Wes, you know as well as I that this has nothing to do with a concussion. And while a few memories have appeared, I may never know the rest. Is not who we are the sum total of what we have experienced, what we remember?"

"No, because I would rather not ever remember another minute of what I suffered watching you with Frank, and then knowing you were in the world and refusing to see me or speak to me."

I cannot help but smile. "Yet you know as well as I that I am not the person you think I am."

"Then how about this: I don't care who you are." He puts his arms around me and moves his face so close to mine that I can smell the inimitable scent of his skin and feel the warmth of his breath against my forehead. "All I care about is that you're here, in my arms, right here and right now."

I breathe in the scent of him, hold him close

against me, then look up into his eyes. "You truly don't care that I do not remember you past that first day I woke up here, save for that memory of you in the hospital and in the shop and when I came here looking for Frank? And little fleeting pictures of happier times in this house? You don't care that you—someone I am supposed to know so well—are a wholly new person to me?"

"You're kidding, right?" he says, touching his lips to my forehead and then bending his head lower so that his lips hover just above mine. "Who wouldn't want to be wholly new with the woman he loves more than anything in the world?"

His lips meet mine, and now I can receive his kiss without restraint or fear. I am free. Completely and utterly free. Of the past. Of Jane. Of Courtney. The past does not exist. Nor does Jane. Or Courtney. There is only this woman—whoever she is—kissing this man in this one divine moment.

He moves his lips to my ear and whispers, "I want to spend the rest of my life with you, Courtney."

I gasp.

"Did I scare you?" he says.

"Are you proposing marriage to me?"

His gray-blue eyes are vulnerable. "I'm going too fast, aren't I."

"No—I mean, yes—I mean, I don't know."

"You don't know how you feel about me."

"No! I do."

"And . . . ?" His eyes are hopeful.

"I love you. Of course I do."

He takes me in his arms again. "That wasn't so hard to say, was it?" And he kisses me, long and deeply.

"No," I breathe. "Not at all." I listen to the rhythm of his heart. "It is just that I—"

I cannot put into words what my feelings are. I came here wanting more than anything to feel his love, to know that it was not just a fancy but true and steady and real. But am I ready to give up all the independence I have earned? And have yet to earn?

"What is it?" he says. "What ever it is, you can tell me."

He gazes at me for a long moment.

"Indeed I do love you. More than I can say. It is just that I do not know if I am quite ready for —I think I need—"

"Time," he says simply. "You need time." And it is but a statement of fact, not an accusation, not an expression of disappointment.

I hug him gratefully. "That is it exactly, Wes. I need time to get my bearings a bit more in this strange new world. I need time to acquaint myself a little better with this new person I am becoming. And I need—I would like, in truth— time to see if I might earn more of a competence."

I feel myself blushing. It is strange to say such

a thing at all, and most particularly to a man who has just made me an offer of marriage.

He looks perplexed. "A competence?"

"You cannot always be rescuing me from my embarrassments, you know."

He still looks as if he does not comprehend.

"I speak of money matters, Wes."

I must, I shall, apply myself to learning the vernacular.

"I don't want you to worry about money anymore, Courtney."

"You are a kind and generous man. But I wish to know what it is like to be truly independent. I need to know what it is like."

He nods. "I understand. Completely. And I support you. For as long as it takes."

He enfolds me in his arms, and I nestle against his chest.

He kisses the top of my head. "I'm not going anywhere, Courtney."

Twenty-eight

As I lean over my sketchbook, which lies upon the counter in the café, it occurs to me that although I am no closer to earning a competence than I was two weeks ago when Wes spoke to me of marriage, my drawing has certainly improved. Perhaps it is the natural result of both cellular memory and my daily practice. In fact, the drawing to which I am putting the finishing touch is something I may even frame. The gentleman subject is dressed in the clothes of my time, as are all of my subjects, and he is alighting from a carriage. I like to think that he is filled with wonder at his first glimpse of his destination but that he dare not reveal his wonder lest he be judged less worldly than other young men. I doubt that to an observer other than myself such feelings would be visible on his countenance, but I fancy I can see them all the same.

This has become a motif of sorts in my drawings. My subjects are always entering rooms or stepping out of doors or alighting from carriages, all on the threshold of an exciting and novel experience.

Which is how my life feels every morning when I awaken, and throughout the day as well, for I am not only living as a wholly different person in a wholly different time and civilization, with all its attendant wonders, I am also experiencing, for the first time, a taste of true independence.

Thanks to the hoped-for severance money from David, I have repaid Wes in full and still have a little money left in the bank. I've not yet divined a way to make my income from the café stretch to the point where I may leave those funds untouched and available only for extreme circumstances, but I continue to draw up plans of economy and to think up ways to augment my income.

My latest effort at retrenching was to do without cable TV service—a measure inspired by one memorable night which I spent rooted to the sofa, watching a woman with enormous white teeth peddle fake amethyst necklaces while I battled the impulse to call the number on the screen and purchase one with my credit card, after which I spent several more hours immersed in a potpourri of news programs in which horrific reports of bloody wars were interrupted by advertisements for deodorant and dating services. It was as if I were divested of my free will, and when finally I tore myself from the screen, bleary-eyed and bewildered, I vowed never again to subject myself to such disagreeable fare, especially when I discovered how expensive it was. Besides, I can get everything worth watching on DVD, and more important, I already own a fine collection of movies from Jane Austen's novels. Some of which are silly indeed, with all their immodest attire and "public displays of affection" (or PDAs, a term I have recently acquired; oh how diverting twenty-first-century American English is), but pleasing nonetheless. And they give me a little taste of home, or what I wish to remember of home, for in those films, there is little of dirt or poverty and none at all of such things as assizes and public hangings. But who would wish to watch them if such things were on offer?

Which is why my drawing has become such a

solace as I make my way round a wondrous and bewildering new world. I find drawing a way of revisiting what is beautiful about my past with fond detachment rather than with longing. Indeed, how could I long for my past when I have Wes's company, which is ever more dear to me? In fact, I shall have the pleasure of seeing him again tonight. How relieved I am that his reasons for having lied about Frank came not from blind allegiance to a rigid code of honor that would render him unable to betray his friend's confidence or to speak an ill word of him to me as the betrothed of that friend. After all, how many ill-fated marriages might have been prevented if only the polite world would speak freely of what they knew?

No, I have nothing to reproach Wes for; he has done nothing worse than what my own weaknesses have been. For yes, I must own that if I am to be the steward of Courtney's life, then I must bear the responsibility for all of her deeds, past and present. Yet there is no need to give the past any power over me. I feel, as Wes said it so perfectly, wholly new.

Wes has been most patient as I get my bearings in my new life. His proposal, as he put it, has no expiration date. I have only to say the word, and the subject shall be reopened. In the meantime, he assures me of his love most fervently, yet with true gentlemanly restraint, never pushing beyond the most passionate of kisses. He has also assured me that such forbearance is a trial, but he has left any move towards something more entirely in my power.

Something more . . . I own that forbearance is a trial for me as well. And I know that when at last I unite with him, it will indeed be as if he is my first, and I his. I long to give myself to him completely, yet it is almost unimaginable to think that anything could be more heavenly than kissing him; when I am in his arms, I lose the very sense of where my body ends and his begins. It is complete and utter surrender. Just the stroke of his hand on the back of my neck is almost enough to make me . . .

Indeed such thoughts are entirely too distracting for the workplace. I had much better attend to the petite woman who is peering at the posted menu of drinks on the wall behind me.

"May I help you?" I push the sketchbook aside, at which the lady makes a sharp intake of breath.

"That drawing!" she says, abandoning the menu and staring at the picture. She says not a word for a full five minutes, during which time I wait and wonder what could have fascinated her so. I cannot help but note that this is the second occasion on which one of my drawings has had an extraordinary effect upon a person in this café. Fortunately, they do not, in general, create such effusions, for I bring the book with me daily, having been encouraged to do so by Sam, who noticed me drawing during my break one day and said what a "cool" thing it was to have a barista who was also an artist. I hardly think of myself as an artist, but I must say I warmed to his praise. Sam, who is already the model of a kind and liberal employer, said I should take every opportunity to draw when business is slow, and I do.

Finally, the blond lady raises her eyes from the drawing and addresses me. "Did you draw this picture?"

"I did."

"But this is uncanny. I happen to be in pre-production on a film set in Regency England, and can you believe that I was just today researching this particular type of men's boots?" She points at the boots the gentleman in my drawing is wearing. "And that little detail above the tassels"—she points to a circular design that would have been stamped into the leather—"how could you have known about such an obscure little signature flourish made by only one bootmaker in London?"

I suppose I had better not tell her that my brother had such a pair of boots from that very bootmaker. "I guess I—I drew what I saw."

"What you saw? Where could you have possibly seen these boots?"

I clear my throat; I could interpret her manner to be merely impertinent, though from the look in her eyes, I can see that she is excited and thus likely to forget herself. And so I muster a smile. "I saw them in my mind's eye, of course."

The woman regards me solemnly, peering over her glasses. "I've been researching the minutiae of Regency dress and décor for a very long time. That I should have happened to read about that very type of boot today and then walk into this café, where I have never been before, and see this drawing and meet you is—well, serendipitous to say the least. May I ask where you read about or saw a picture of these boots?"

How to answer such a question? "I cannot say that I recall where I came across that particular type of boot. But I can say that I have made a life-long study of the style and manners of the period."

At least the latter part is no lie.

The woman looks at the drawing again and begins to lift a corner of the page. "May I?" she asks eagerly, and I nod, whereupon she pages through the sketchbook, examining all of the drawings that are my time. "These are extraordinary," she murmurs. "Such authentic detail in every one. Well then," she says, closing the book and smiling at me broadly. "This is too good an opportunity to pass up. I could use someone like you on my team. Would you be interested in talking to me and my coproducer about coming on board as a researcher? Or a consultant?"

A film. To think that I might take part in creating one of those wonders that have given me so much delight since I arrived in this place. This offer could be the opportunity I have been hoping for—how could I have imagined such a thing could happen?

"I can see by that smile that you're not averse to the idea," she says, and that is when I realize I am grinning broadly.

But Sam—and the café. I cannot deny that I have grown attached to my place here at the café. But it cannot be my future; I know that. But I would have to give him two weeks' notice and—

"Of course I wouldn't expect you to start tomorrow," she says, as if reading my mind. "But does the idea interest you at all?"

"It does."

"Excellent," says the lady. "I'm Imogen, and this is my card. Do you have a card, or could you just write down your info on the back of this one?"

We exchange information, she promises to call me tomorrow, and for the rest of my shift and during my drive home, I float on a cloud of happiness. To think that my knowledge of my own time could translate into a wonderful new situation. On a movie, no less.

I am so buoyant when I return home that I find myself cleaning and tidying and even digging into the back of my clothes closet, from which I pull out the white gown I wore that very first day I arrived here, the white dress which was to be my wedding gown. The white dress which made my friends think I was insane, and small wonder that they did think such a thing.

What am I doing with this dress still in my closet? For when I do finally say yes to my beloved Wes, I shall wear something entirely fashioned for him and not for another man.

I unearth a couple of flattened boxes from the closet, one of which, when assembled, fits the gown perfectly. For now, I shall leave it outside the door, next to the laundry room. I know it's silly, but I simply cannot have it in the house for another moment.

I am so happy, between the packing and disposal of the wedding gown and the job offer, that I decide to have a tiny little glass of vodka before I change clothes, for Anna and Paula and Wes and Deepa will be here in little more than an hour, and we are going to have dinner together.

This is the first time that Anna and Paula have made plans with Wes and me, and I realize I am a little anxious about it. Both of them were initially shocked when I told them about Wes and me. Paula took it harder than Anna, who quickly saw how happy I am—but Paula seems to have come round a bit. It is still a little awkward between us, however. As for Deepa, she has been nothing but delighted and has already met us once for a drink. She and Wes are fast becoming friends, and I'm grateful that she will be here tonight to balance out the group.

Paula, Anna, and Deepa arrive within minutes of one another; Wes is the last to arrive, stammering apologies for his lateness and looking red-faced and altogether uncomfortable before Anna and Paula, who greet him politely but without much warmth. Deepa, however, rises from her seat on the sofa and kisses him on both cheeks, which seems to put him at ease, and which is perhaps what inspires Anna to rise herself and kiss him on the cheek as well.

And then Paula grumbles, "Not quite ready for that yet," and we all laugh, Paula included.

And that is when I tell them all about Imogen and the job offer and they are all just as delighted as I am. Deepa mixes drinks, and everyone toasts to my success. Wes assures me that Sam will be nothing but pleased for me. Anna starts speculating on the amount of my salary and tells me I should wait for an offer so that I don't negotiate against myself. "And if they try and lowball you," she says, "remind them that hiring you is like hiring someone who's truly lived during that time period."

How right she is. By the time our dinners arrive, delivered to the door and paid for by Wes, who insists on treating us all in celebration of my news, I am filled with confidence. I truly do have something unique and valuable to offer, though there is no need for Imogen or her colleagues ever to know just how unique are the origins of my expertise.

Just as I am about to taste the chicken mole on my plate, the sound of a gunshot pierces the night.

Anna gasps and drops her fork with a clatter. "Oh my God."

I pat her hand. "It is only a gun, Anna."

She looks at me, aghast. "Are you kidding me?"

"Well, it certainly sounds like a gun."

Her face is as white as a sheet. "I haven't heard one of those in a while."

"Well, I suppose there is little worth hunting in town."

Deepa bursts out laughing.

Paula lets out a snort of merriment but covers her mouth to suppress her mirth in the face of Anna's glare. "Oh come on, Anna," she says finally. "You used to live in this neighborhood. This is L.A., for God's sake. Firepower is part of our auditory landscape."

Deepa laughs even harder, and Anna gives her a look. "Sorry," says Deepa.

"I fail to see what is so amusing," I say, "for there really would be little need to take out a gun here, let alone shoot."

Anna still looks a bit shocked. "Courtney," she says, "you've been talking about moving out of this place since I've known you. Don't you think it's time for a change?"

"I happen to like it here, though I own I would prefer more greenery. And the bars on the windows are rather ugly. Though I do not notice them as much as I did when—as much as I used to do."

"Gotta love a fearless woman," says Paula cheerfully, and raises her glass. "To Courtney. They broke the mold when they made you, darling."

I, a fearless woman? I am not quite sure I have earned such praise, but I like it nonetheless.

Paula comes over to me and gives me a hug, and it feels as if an old friend has come round after a long thaw, which is, in fact, the case. I hold her tightly, and she squeezes me back.

And then she raises her glass again. "And to Wes," says she, and I look over at Wes, who was pouring himself a drink and is now as immobile with surprise as I. "Because I've never seen Courtney this happy before."

"To Wes and Courtney," says Deepa.

"To Wes and Courtney," say Anna and Paula.

We drink, and as I look round the room at the faces of the man I love and these three lovely women, my caring, devoted friends, I am filled with gratitude at my good fortune.

*L*ater, when the ladies have departed and Wes, who has lingered to stay and help me clean up, finishes drying the last of the dishes—how I love the willingness of the modern man to engage in domestic drudgery—he takes me in his arms and kisses the top of my head.

"So. It looks like you'll be earning that competence after all."

I smile contentedly. "I believe I shall."

"Remember what you said before about preferring more greenery?"

"Yes?"

"Well, I was thinking. Why don't you enjoy the greenery on my estate?" He smiles at me mischievously. "In fact, why don't you make it *your* estate?"

I gaze up at him, and there is so much tenderness and love in his eyes that I can hardly speak.

"I offer myself to you again," he says, "with a heart even more your own than when you almost broke it, eleven weeks ago."

He is proposing to me again, speaking words from *Persuasion*!

"Yeah," he says, as if answering my thought. "I liked that one even better than *Northanger Abbey*."

"Oh, Wes."

"I know I said it would be up to you to reopen the subject of marriage, but you can't blame a guy for trying, can you?"

"No." I smile. "I cannot."

And then he kneels down on one knee and removes a tiny velvet box from his pocket.

He opens the box and shows me a sparkling, perfect ring. A blue sapphire surrounded by diamonds.

"Then will you marry me, Courtney? Will you be my wife? Will you make me"—he smiles—"the happiest of men?"

My eyes fill with tears. And I touch his beautiful, angelic face. Could I ever have imagined that such happiness existed?

"Yes, I will, Wes. I'll marry you."

And he slips the ring on my finger. "It was my grandmother's," he says. "Do you like it?"

"I love it."

He beams his delight and rises, then dips his head to touch my lips with his own. And we kiss, our breaths quickening, our bodies melting into one another.

And I know, in that moment, that Anna was right. We all have the power to create heaven on earth, right here, right now.

Twenty-nine

It is the morning after our wedding, and I am in that place between sleep and wakefulness, nestled against Wes, who sleeps like an angel, and thanking God for the happiness I have found in Courtney's life. I pray that she, too, will find happiness in mine.

Will I one day awaken back in my old life, and will Courtney return to hers? I suppose I shall never know. And so I shall treasure every moment, every morning, every day, and every night, for each of them might be my last.

Time is fleeting, and few of us are fortunate enough to notice that there is always another chance at happiness. I have found mine with Wes. I hope that Courtney finds hers.

I find myself thinking of that most beautiful moment in *Persuasion* in which Anne reads the letter that Captain Wentworth left for her. *Unjust I may have been, weak and resentful I have been, but never inconstant. You alone have brought me to Bath. For you alone, I think and plan.*

And then I see myself, in my mind's eye, dancing with Edgeworth in Bath. It is as clear and vivid as the most brilliant memory, though I have never danced with him there. And he is watching me as the man next to him turns me. I am conscious of displaying the movement of my body as Edgeworth watches. And I observe him with equal intensity as he turns the lady diagonally across from him; she, too, smiles into his eyes.

And then the scene shifts, and I see myself, years later, in a town house in London. And I am with Edgeworth, and it is our town house. I have never seen this house before, yet I know it is my house. Our house, for I am married to Edgeworth. And he is reading out to me those words from *Persuasion*: *"Unjust I may have been, weak and resentful I have been, but never inconstant."* And I know that those words have special meaning for us, and that somehow I am living out that life—that Courtney is living out that life—and living it with Edgeworth, as his wife, and happily.

There is no separation any longer between Courtney and me. My life is hers, and hers is mine.

My heart swells with happiness, for myself, for Jane, for Edgeworth, for Wes. And somehow I know that as Courtney lives out her life as me, or, I should say, as who I was, she must necessarily have those memories of her former life in a future time fade in order to be quite comfortable in the past, while I may have perfect recall of the past without its impeding the pleasures of the present.

As for what is in store for me, I have not the smallest notion, and I glory in that state of not knowing. There is no better place to be. For the past does not exist. There is only the present. Only the eternal beautiful ever-unfolding now.

Acknowledgments

 $\mathcal{M}$ y boundless gratitude to my beloved teacher and beautiful BFF, Aurelia Haslboeck, whose presence in my life is proof that we live in a magical world, and without whose extraordinary kindness and generosity this book would not exist. Thank you, Aurelia, for reading and critiquing draft after draft, sharing your peerless knowledge of storytelling, always inspiring me to give my best, and, most of all, for the infinite comfort of knowing that you are there for me every step of the way.

I am filled with love and gratitude for my magnificent husband, Thomas Rigler—my rock, my champion, my real-life Austen hero. Thank you, Thomas, for your love, your compassion, your constant support, advice, and encourage-ment. If there were an award for the most patient life partner ever, you would win hands down. Your shining presence in my world is a daily blessing and a constant inspiration. And thank you for producing the most gorgeous website ever.

I am deeply grateful to my extraordinary agent Marly Rusoff, she of the ready laugh and angelic voice, for her kindness, strength, and candor. My heartfelt thanks to Marly's fellow agent Michael Radulescu for making the international editions of my books a reality and for his diligence and humor; to their lovely associate Julie Mosow; to the always delightful Paula Breen; and to everyone at Marly Rusoff and Associates.

I am tremendously grateful to an extraordinary team at Dutton and Plume for shepherding, launching, and championing this book and its predecessor. Some of these people are still around; others have moved onward and upward, within and without the Penguin Group. To all of them I am deeply grateful. First is my gifted editor Erika Imranyi, for her superb story notes and edits, which provided the balance of big picture and details that helped me get this book into its final form. My enduring gratitude to Susan Petersen Kennedy, Brian Tart, Christine Ball, Stacy Noble, Amanda Walker, Carrie Swetonic, Tala Oszkay, and the entire team at Dutton. I am grateful to Kathryn Court, Cherise Fisher, Marie Coolman, Mary Pomponio, Cristi Hall, and the entire team at Plume who launched the paperback of *Confessions*; and of course to the original Dutton team who launched the *Confessions* hardcover: Trena Keating, Lisa Johnson, Amanda Tobier, Rachel Ekstrom, Lily Kosner, and Sarah Muszynski. I would also like to thank John Lawton, Patrick Nolan, and the rest of the extraordinary sales team at Dutton and Plume.

I am deeply grateful to Anita Artukovich, an early reader of this book whose enthusiasm buoyed me up just when I needed it. Many thanks to Brit gals Beth Shube and Jessica Sully, the latter for vetting the Britishisms in the manuscript and the former for being the voice of the candidate in my Jane '08 parody ads; Roman Jakobi for my author photos; Deborah Zeitman for hilarious input on the title; Dr. Irl Extein and Lisa McGee for allowing me to interview them for my research; Lisa Daily for providing my protagonist with dating advice from her book *Stop Getting Dumped!*; Tom Edgar for programming my website; and Scott Benoit for designing it.

My love and gratitude to my mother, Sara Levine, and my sisters, Cary Puma and Felice Levine Simons, for their love, support, and understanding. I am also deeply grateful for the blessings of my family of friends who encourage and inspire me and even show up at my readings.

My heartfelt thanks to my readers, whose questions, insights, emails, letters, and participation on my website forum are precious gifts. I love hearing from you.

My abiding gratitude to the devoted legions of booksellers and librarians who promote the love of the word and give us a place to recharge and be inspired. If it weren't for the bookmobiles and library buses of my childhood, I would not be writing today.

Heartfelt thanks to my fellow storytellers who

attend my writing workshops and inspire me with their creativity, diligence, and wisdom.

For information on everyday life in Jane Austen's world, I am indebted to the works of many fine scholars and enthusiasts of the period, of which there are too many to include a full list here. Among these authors are Penelope Byrde, Sheryl Craig, Susannah Fullerton, Christina Hardyment, Maggie Lane, Deirdre LeFaye, Kirstin Olsen, Josephine Ross, Venetia Murray, David Selwyn, Maggie Sullivan, E. S. Turner, and many more. And of course no one writing an Austen-inspired book should ever be without the indispensible *Persuasions*, the journal of the Jane Austen Society of North America, of which I am a life member.

And finally, my enduring gratitude to Jane Austen, who did not suffer fools gladly but couldn't resist writing about them anyway.

About the Author

L aurie Viera Rigler's first novel, *Confessions of a Jane Austen Addict*, was a national best- seller.

When not indulging herself in rereadings of Jane Austen's six novels, Laurie teaches writing workshops, including classes in Vroman's, Southern California's oldest and largest independent bookstore. Laurie lives in Los Angeles and holds a lifetime membership in the Jane Austen Society of North America.

Awaken to your Austen addiction at www.jane austenaddict.com.

Center Point Publishing

600 Brooks Road ● PO Box 1
Thorndike ME 04986-0001 USA

(207) 568-3717

US & Canada:
1 800 929-9108
www.centerpointlargeprint.com